BONDED

BOOK 1 IN THE BONDED BILLIONAIRE SHAPESHIFTER SERIES

DAWN GREENFIELD IRELAND

ARTiSTiC
ORiGiNS

Nonfiction	
The Puppy Baby Book	Mastering Your Money (2022)
Puppy Adoption and Beyond	Writers Preparation Handbook
Mastering Your Money (2008)	What's Breaking Your Budget
Online Classes	
Writers Preparation Handbook	How to Format Word Docs Like A Pro
Cozy Mysteries	**Sci-Fi-Fantasy**
The Alcott Family Adventures	**The Thol Series**
Hot Chocolate	Prophecy of Thol
Bitter Chocolate	Gifts From Thol
Spicy Chocolate	Love of Thol
Nutty Chocolate	King of Thol
Katz' Cat Series	Earth Calling Thol
Katz' Cat	**Sci-Fi Romance Adventure**
Bill Hill's Pills	Forced Dreams
The Detectives	**Dystopian**
The Pact	The Last Dog
	Texmexzona
Books by my Alter Ego ~ DG Ireland	
Bonded Shapeshifter Billionaire Series	
Bonded	
Tothars	
Tilted	
Unforeseen	
Connected	
Need A Notebook?	
See my 54 themed notebooks on my website www.degreenfield.com/notebooks	
Screenplays formatted as books	
Plan B (Dark Comedy)	Where's Ralphie? (Family Comedy)
The God Child (Action Adventure)	Standing Dead (Drama/Tragedy)
The Far Corner (Sci-Fi/Psychological/Creatures)	
Screenplays as TV Episodes	
Hot Chocolate ~ Episode 1	Prophecy of Thol ~ Episode 1
Bonded ~ Episode 1	
See my screenplays and awards on my website: degreenfield.com Filmfreeway, ISA Network	

Bonded by DG Ireland Published by Artistic Origins

Copyright © 2018 Dawn Greenfield Ireland

Cover design by Marcha Fox / Kalliope Rising Press

Interior layout by Yours Truly (me). Corrections: January 2024; November 2025; April 2026

Woman's image: https://pixabay.com/en/users/ melancholiaphotography-2312503/

Eagle in flight image (Vasile_Pralea): https://pixabay.com/en/birds-navy-eagle-eagle-217590/

Panther licking paw image: https://goo.gl/images/kt6La

Panther head icon by Kemesh Mahajan from Noun Project

Eagle icon by Renault from Noun Project

ISBN 9781940385167 (eBook)

ISBN 9781940385174 (paperback)

Dawn Greenfield Ireland

Artistic Origins

http://www.degreenfield.com/

Publisher's Note: This is a work of fiction. Names, characters, places, and incidents are a product of the author's imagination. Locales and public names are sometimes used for atmospheric purposes. Any resemblance to actual people, living or dead, or to businesses, companies, events, institutions, or locales is completely coincidental.

Please visit my website: http://www.degreenfield.com/

Sign up for my newsletter and get the latest news before the public.

ACKNOWLEDGMENTS

Many thanks to the Noun Project for their fabulous collection of icons, specifically Kemesh Mahajan for the Panther head icon, and Renault for the Eagle icon.

I wish I could thank the photographer (by name) for the picture of the panther licking his paw. I searched the Internet and could not find a name. So, whoever you are—Thank You so much for this gorgeous picture.

Special thanks to Joseph Lawrence Thompson for his legal advice and for keeping me out of trouble.

A great cover says it all. Once again, Marcha Fox of the Kalliope Rising Press delivered the goods. The photograph of the woman on the cover is by Olga of Melan Cholia Photography. I fell in love with that picture when I saw it—I knew it depicted my character, Ari.

To my beta readers who poked and prodded me with suggestions, you're the best.

And, finally, Jeff Gonyea, my proofreader with eyes like magnifying glasses—you've done it again... kept me out of trouble! Thanks, cuz!

Readers: if you find any bloopers, let me know at dawn@degreenfield.com. I'll give you a free eBook for your efforts!

Inuit poem, collected by the explorer,
Knud Rasmussen:

*'In the very earliest time, When both people and animals lived
on earth, A person could become an animal if he
wanted to, And an animal could become a human
being All spoke the same language.'*

Creativity is a drug I cannot live without.
Cecil B. DeMille
US movie producer (1881 - 1959)

AGE RESTRICTION

CHAPTER ONE

ROMAN DAVENPORT STOOD naked in the grass outside his secluded house on the edge of the forest. Not a cabin by any stretch of the imagination. His four-thousand square foot house, with floor to ceiling windows in the sunroom on the ground floor and in the upstairs bedrooms, would be the envy of his friends—if he had any.

A deep porch with round columns was at the front of the house. Off to the side stood a five-car garage with two empty slots. He didn't have to worry about anyone gawking—he owned the two-thousand acres surrounding the house.

At six-foot two and weighing in at two-hundred-twenty pounds, his sinewy body sported powerful strength. Roman had the body of a god. A six-pack ab, muscled thighs and arms —his body had a natural musculature that men begged their trainers to deliver.

Thick black hair fell to his shoulders, sweeping across his tattoos. One arm sported the head of a black panther just below his shoulders. A tattoo of a black panther was on his back.

At forty, he had everything. A company that made him

millions, women falling at his feet loving his unnaturally bright green eyes, and every comfort available to the modern millionaire.

What was missing were true friendships and love.

As he gazed into the forest, forlorn, he raked his hair.

I can't continue alone; he thought.

He had a great relationship with his employees. The community respected him. But he was drowning in loneliness.

Roman drew in a deep breath, savoring the earthy aromas of the trees, the ground, and everything around him. He listened to the birds and the scurrying of squirrels. He glanced at the ground.

I can't go another twenty years like this. My heart is empty.

Where are my people? My kind?

Deep pain etched his face from his thoughts. Roman shook it off, looking around.

It is what it is, but I'm sick of this shit.

Roman stretched out and leaped forward. He transformed into his panther. He shook himself.

The big cat, much larger than an actual panther in the wild or at a zoo, sprinted into the forest at full speed.

He didn't get enough opportunities to shift with all the obligations nipping at his heels. So, when he took time off from the city to come to the house in the woods, he let his animal loose. Sometimes he didn't shift back for the entire weekend.

Wealth had its advantages.

He could travel the world whenever he wanted, which he did.

Roman sought information about his condition. Since the first time he shifted at twenty, he had never come across any other shifter.

He spent a lot of time and money seeking ancient tribal

elders in hidden villages away from the prying eyes of civilization.

Roman searched across the globe hoping to find his own kind, or legends he might study and trace.

He aged so very slowly; he wondered if he were immortal. He chided himself for even thinking it.

I'd find a way to end my life. No one should have to suffer this loneliness decade after decade.

Roman stopped at the stream that ran through his property. His human hair was as black as his cat's, and they shared bright green eyes. He padded into the water, lapping as he walked. The panther raised his head and took in a deep breath, scenting the air. He left the water and approached the gigantic old oak tree where he liked to perch.

A noise broke the peace. It sounded as if something large fell through the trees, breaking branches on the downward spiral.

Roman looked to the sky.

No planes, gliders, or anything else that would have lost parts.

Maybe a meteor?

The panther ran through the forest toward the sound. A thud and an anguished screech ended whatever had come down from the top of the trees or the sky.

Roman approached the small clearing and stopped in his tracks. There on the ground was a naked man, not quite human.

Shifter! Oh, my God! Please don't be dead!

The better part of the man was half-shifted from a rather large bird, with an arrow in his partially shifted wing.

After recovering from his shock of discovering another shifter, Roman ran to the man and shifted back to his human form. He surmised that he would be able to remove the arrow.

The shifter was covered in lacerations from the fall through the trees.

He approached closer and kneeled. "Can you hear me? I'm going to help you."

The man slowly opened his eyes. They were a tawny color and filled with pain.

His head, part of his torso, arms and legs were covered with white, golden and brown feathers.

Roman could only wonder how painful it must be to be wounded and not be able to shift back to his human form.

The panther shifter sent a soothing pulse of healing energy to the birdman. He saw him visibly relax a bit.

The man stared at Roman. He noticed his lack of clothing. "Shifter?" His pain-filled eyes held hope.

Roman nodded.

The man smiled through his pain and lifted his good hand. "Brother."

Roman swallowed a lump and took the offered hand. "Brother. I'm going to remove the arrow—but this isn't going to be pleasant for you. I'll try to compensate by sending you relief."

"Do what you have to do," the birdman said. His voice was hoarse with pain.

Roman knew the shifter would heal once he removed the arrow. Roman grabbed the shaft with one hand and steadied the feathered arm on the ground with the other. He focused on sending more soothing thoughts.

He yanked.

A screech—a half-human, half-bird sound Roman would never forget.

The arrow came out clean. The birdman passed out. Roman picked him up, slung him over his shoulder, grabbed the arrow, and adjusted the load. He ran through the forest to the house. Roman raced into the house and up the stairs to a bedroom. He placed the birdman gently on the bed.

He assessed the arm, went into the bathroom and returned with supplies. Roman cleansed the wound and let nature take its course. The healing would be slow until the birdman shifted.

Roman straightened out the feathered arm as much as possible. He left the room, dressed, grabbed the arrow, and ran outside. Roman lifted his face and inhaled. He detected the scent of the hunters. He took off at a run.

THE TWO HUNTERS were at the edge of a clearing.

"I know I hit that bird," the hunter in the dark green shirt said.

"Where the heck did it fall?" the hunter with the long hair asked. "Did we go past it?"

Roman observed the hunters. *Goddamn trespassers!* He fumed silent curses.

The green-shirt guy carried a Krohns Recurve Bow and a quiver of arrows.

The long-haired hunter carried a rifle.

Roman whistled and announced his approach. "You're on posted private property." Roman stepped into the clearing, holding the arrow.

"We didn't see any signs," The green-shirt guy said.

His attitude was cocky and would benefit from an attitude adjustment. His eyes took in Roman's size and the fact that he was unarmed.

"Where did you enter the forest?" Roman asked.

"Gunter Hill Road," The long hair guy said.

"Two miles down from the highway on Gunter Hill Road,

there are large signs on both sides of the road. They say private property. You're telling me you didn't see them?" Roman asked.

"Look, buddy, I didn't see any signs. Right now, I'm only interested in finding the bird I shot," the green-shirt guy said. He spotted the arrow. "You found my bird?"

Roman shot a look of pure disdain at the hunter. "Yeah, you damaged his wing. I'll take care of him. In the meantime, get your eyes checked and get off my property—now. If I see you on my property again, I'll take action."

"Oh, I'm scared. What are you going to do?" The green-shirted guy asked.

Fucking piece of shit, Roman thought.

"You have a choice. You can either leave peacefully or end up under the ground. Your choice," Roman said.

"Come on, let's leave," the long-haired guy said.

"I'm not going anywhere until I get my bird," the green-shirted guy stated.

Roman stepped forward. "You take one more step onto my property and I've got a problem."

"Think you're faster than a bullet?" The green-shirted guy asked. He pulled a handgun out of his vest and pointed it at Roman.

"I don't want to hurt you," Roman said.

The green-shirted guy laughed. His finger flicked off the safety.

The long-haired guy watched as the unbelievable happened. He heard a deep growl that only a wild animal made.

Roman leaped through the air with the grace of a black belt martial artist. He kicked the gun out of the hunter's hand.

It spun in the air.

Roman snatched it out of a spin and bashed the guy alongside the head with it, then tossed the gun to the ground.

He kicked and pounded the guy, then he allowed his panther claws to come forth and he ripped them down the guy's chest. The shirt offered no protection from those claws.

The green-shirt guy screamed and fell to the ground as blood soaked through what was left of his shirt.

The attack was over before the green-shirted or long-haired guy could figure out what had happened.

"Get off my property. If I ever see you here again, you won't leave. Understand?"

The long-haired guy helped the green-shirt guy up. He reached for the gun, but Roman stomped his foot on top of the gun, making his meaning known. That gun wasn't going anywhere.

The two hunters ran back where they came from. Roman picked up the gun and headed back to the house.

GAGE STRYKER SAT against the pillows at the headboard of the bed, pain rolling off him. Tattoos adorned his chest and arms. He sported the head of an eagle on each of his upper arms. Other tattoos adorned his chest. He rolled off the bed and staggered to the bathroom.

An eagle in flight took up his entire back.

When he returned to the bed, he collapsed against the pillows.

Roman entered the room. He placed the arrow on the bedside table and then sat in a chair.

"Little souvenir for you," Roman said.

They stared at each other as they assessed one another—neither had ever come across a shifter before. Both were blocking their thoughts from the other.

Brown, white, and gold feathers met sandy blond hair on

Gage's head. He still hadn't been able to shift, which delayed the healing process.

Gage was about the same age as Roman. Women would declare him as hot, sexy, and muscular as his rescuer.

He was just as lonely.

"Where are you from?" Roman asked.

"Boston," Gage said. "I just moved to Reading. Relocated my electronics business. Had to get away from New England. Needed this," he spread his good arm out. "The forest. Skies. A place to shift. Thought it would be safe. You?"

"I grew up in Reading and Wyomissing," Roman said. "Looks like we have more in common besides our unique abilities. I inherited my father's electronics business. We specialize in security systems and do a lot of work for the government."

"Huh." Gage nodded. "We design circuits and components for IBM and DEC, and for other companies. Plus, we create electronic components for radios and receivers."

"Did you come across any other shifters in Boston?" Roman asked. "What about your parents—were they shifters?"

Gage shook his head. "I figured I was a freak of nature, so I'm happy—relieved—I'm not alone anymore. I never saw my parents shift or heard them talk about shifters. I'm an only child, so it's not like I can watch nieces or nephews for telltale signs."

"Same here. I don't know where this shifting came from unless there was someone in my family that no one talked about," Roman said. "There's got to be others out there."

THAT WAS 50 YEARS AGO.

Roman and Gage still had not found any other shifters, which perplexed them. They combined forces over those years. Both were astute in the way of business, with similar ethics and morals, along with the ability to read people. They created an empire they were proud of. Both were excessively wealthy—in the billionaire category—and were excellent roommates.

Roman and Gage both still looked no older than mid-forties. Neither had lasting relationships with women. They were always searching for *the one* and never finding her.

Then Ari Davis crossed their path.

ROMAN AND GAGE sat in the limo, working on their phones. Business never stopped. They could communicate with staff from around the globe at the click of a button on their cellphones.

Suddenly, Roman sat up straight and inhaled deeply. His eyes went wild. He turned to Gage. "Did you smell that?"

"Stop the car!" Gage yelled at the driver.

The limo eased to the curb. The driver was used to his employer's strange behavior.

Roman and Gage clambered out onto the sidewalk. They drew deep breaths.

"Do you get a whiff of that?" Gage asked.

Roman's face was bathed in euphoria as the sun shone down on him. "Where is she?"

Gage twirled his fingers in a silent *roll down the window* to the driver. "We're going on foot for a while."

The limo pulled away from the curb as the men drew in the scents of the area. They stood in front of an apartment complex.

Roman led the way. "Let's look around."

They entered the apartment complex parking lot.

Gage's keen eagle eyesight scanned over everything in the vicinity, searching.

Roman sucked in a deep breath. His cat could scent prey, or anything else he wanted, and he tracked the scent of this woman purposely.

Roman tapped Gage's arm. "This way."

They walked to the right, and Roman stopped before an empty parking space. He stared up at the second floor to the door directly in front of them.

"That's where she lives. We just missed her."

Gage turned around and faced the road in front of the complex. "Can you tell where she took off to? Is she close by?"

"Come on." Roman led them two streets away to a restaurant. He stopped by a late-model Honda Civic. "This is her car. Do you recognize the scent?"

Gage sucked in a breath and stumbled as if he were drunk.

"Christ, don't act like a fool!" Roman elbowed Gage in the ribs.

"How come we both detected her? Shouldn't she be yours or mine?" Gage drilled his eyes into Roman.

"How the hell should I know? It's not like we have an instruction manual."

Roman walked to the front door of the establishment. "We'll figure it out. Just so you know, I'm not going to fight over her. She's human, and you're the only other shifter. Understand?"

Gage grunted. "Come on, open the fucking door already!"

CHAPTER TWO

ARI WAITED for her sons at the restaurant, at the bar. She checked her phone for texts and messages. A bit of impatience showed as she drummed her fingers on the shiny wood of the bar.

Where in the world are my boys?

She glanced at the door, eyeing people entering for lunch. Her boys needed lessons in time management and being punctual. They should understand that it was rude to keep someone waiting. Even if she didn't have to be somewhere else after lunch, they shouldn't treat her like this.

Gage and Roman came through the door. They looked around. Gage searched with his keen eagle eyes. Roman's superior scenting detected the exact location of the woman. Something drew them to her like flowers stretching toward the sun. The two of them made a beeline for the bar and stood off to the side, taking her in.

That's her! Roman sent.

I know, you idiot! Gage sent.

Roman elbowed Gage as he squinted a dirty look at the insult.

God! She's beautiful! Roman sent.

I've got a hard-on just looking at her, Gage sent.

Keep it under control for Christ's sake! Roman sent.

At seventy, which was deceptive because she looked fifty, with thick, wavy, waist-long pure white hair, Ari was striking. She wore no hint of makeup on her unlined face, except for a pale pink lip gloss. Her body was soft from leading a sedentary life, but she was slender and curvy at five-foot-four.

Roman and Gage made up their minds and approached her.

"Hi," Gage said. He leaned on the bar. His face stretched into a smile.

Don't grin like a hyena. She'll think you're a weird stalker, Roman said in mind-talk.

Gage shot his elbow back into Roman's gut.

Roman maneuvered beside Gage, vying for a better position, closer to Ari.

Stop blocking me! Roman sent.

Ari stared at the two smiling, hot, sexy men who were grinning at her.

What's up with these two? Do they miss their grandmother?

Roman coughed into his hand to stop from laughing out loud as he read her thoughts.

"Hi," she said. She studied them, drawn to their attractiveness.

Ari felt herself getting wet—a surprise in and of itself since she hadn't had sex in over twenty years. She thought her feelings in *that department* were shut down and sealed off from the world.

"Can we buy you a drink?" Roman asked.

"Why?" Ari asked. Her eyebrows rose at that question.

What the hell do these jokers want?

"Because you're a beautiful woman waiting in a bar for friends," Gage said.

"We're here, and they aren't." Roman presented his gleaming white teeth in a disarming smile.

"How do you know I'm waiting for anyone? Perhaps I'm here by myself," Ari said a little defensive. "Or maybe I'm looking for a sugar daddy or a sugar mommy. Why is it that people assume older women in a bar are not there on their own?"

"Touché," Gage said.

Touché? Did you just say Touché? What decade were you ... Roman said.

Okay! Just shut up, will you? It's not like I can stuff it back in my mouth!

Roman reached out and tucked a strand of hair behind her ear. He breathed in deeply. He smelled her sex and scented she was dripping wet. His eyes temporarily went out of focus from longing. He pulled himself together.

"You have gorgeous hair," he said. "I'm not sure if I can keep my hands out of your hair."

Ari pulled back and studied Roman. "How long have you had this hair fetish?"

"Since right now," Roman said. "There's something about it. Perhaps it's the color or texture. It's not gray. It's a stunning white. Your hair feels like silk."

"Your eyes are like the night sky," Gage said. "I don't think I've ever seen that shade of blue before."

"Where are your girlfriends?" Ari asked.

"No girlfriends. Not for a long time," Gage said.

"Oh, come on. Two good-looking hunks like you? If you snapped your fingers, women would be all over you," Ari said. Her perfectly shaped lips stretched into a wide smile.

Roman smirked. "So, you think we're hunks? That sounds promising."

Gage elbowed Roman.

Christ, Roman! You'll scare her off!

"We don't want them. Most are gold diggers and only want to get their names in the society column," Gage confessed.

"Oh, so you two are *wealthy* hunks then." A huge grin spread across her face. She chuckled as she shook her head in disbelief.

"That would be us," Gage said. "Where's your husband, boyfriend, or man?"

Ari held up her left hand. "Do you see a ring?" They stared at her hands.

Roman smiled. "Maybe we can solve that problem."

Ari became indignant. "Who said it was a problem?"

Jason and Kevin, Ari's sons, entered the restaurant and approached their mom. They eyed Roman and Gage.

"Hi, Mom," Jason said. He became all protective. "Are these guys bothering you?"

Ari stared at her admirers. "No, honey, they were just keeping me company while I waited for you two slackers."

She looked at Kevin, her quiet son. "Are you okay, Kev?"

"Yeah," he said. He kissed her on the cheek. "Just having a *day*."

Gage stuck his hand out to Jason. "I'm Gage, and this is Roman. This is one of our favorite restaurants."

The men all shook hands. Gage stared at Ari, his hand outstretched to her.

"Ari," she said after a long moment. She accepted his hand.

Arianna's her real name, Roman said.

Gage grasped her hand, clasping it firmly. An electrical current shot through each of them.

Ari jerked her hand away. *What the heck was that?*

Thoughts flooded her head.

Roman elbowed Gage to get out of his way. He picked up Ari's hand and kissed her fingertips, receiving a little shock on his lips.

Ari stared from her hand to the men.

Just static electricity... just static, she convinced herself.

They all chatted for a few minutes. Ari's sons fell into easy conversation with Roman and Gage.

"Would you want additional company for lunch?" Roman asked. He glanced from Ari to her sons.

"Sure, why not," Jason said. He looked at his mom. "That okay, Mom?"

Ari stared at Roman and Gage.

Oh, no! How do I get out of this without freaking out my kids?

She's going to bail! Gage sent.

Shut up! She's not going to drag her sons out the door! Roman sent.

Gage sent a pulse of calm to Ari.

What the fuck are you doing? You can't influence her decision! Roman ranted.

I just wanted her to know we're not a threat, Gage returned.

After a moment, she nodded. "Sure."

Roman exhaled a breath he hadn't realized he was holding. They approached the hostess stand.

"Can we have Lucy's section?" Gage asked. The hostess escorted them to a table.

Roman pulled out a chair for Ari. He took the chair to her left, and Gage claimed the chair to her right, forcing her sons to sit opposite them. The waitress approached the table.

"Hi Mr. Davenport. Hi Mr. Stryker," she said.

"Hey Lucy. This is on me," Gage said. He looked across at Jason and Kevin to confirm that he was buying lunch.

"Sure, I can always use a free lunch," Jason said. He elbowed his brother.

Kevin grunted with a smile.

Ari pressed her back against her chair and turned to Gage, then Roman. "That's generous of you. Thank you. My boys can use all the help they can get."

"Mom..." Kevin moaned. "Jeez, let me have a little dignity!"

"Facts, Kev. Just stating the facts of the matter, and it's nothing to be ashamed of," Ari said. "People sometimes struggle until they find their true place in life."

"I grew up to take over my father's electronics business. If I had been left to my own decision-making about my future, I would not have had a clue," Roman said.

"It took me ten years to figure out what I was really good at," Gage said. "Yours will come."

"Electronics?" Kevin asked.

"Everything you can think of, but we specialize in security systems and details," Roman said.

"That sounds interesting," Jason said.

They ordered food and drinks and chatted throughout the meal.

Ari was not unaware that each of her legs was warmed with one of Roman and Gage's legs up against hers. She realized it was rather odd, and she wondered why she wasn't offended. All she focused on was how comforting the contact was.

When Roman shifted in his chair, their legs separated. Ari had a current of abandonment rush through her until Roman moved his leg back against hers.

She wants the contact Roman sent to Gage.

I got that Gage sent to Roman.

She's so beautiful! Her sons like us, Roman sent.

Ari sipped her wine, deep in contemplation. Crazy things flowed through her imagination.

Am I having some type of mental breakdown?

Have I been single so long that I'm fantasizing these two men are into me? Lord have mercy, how embarrassing!

Roman grinned.

She's thinking about possibilities, Roman sent.

Yeah, but she thinks she's having a breakdown, Gage sent.

Just considering the age differences made her blush. Jason and Kevin appeared comfortable with Roman and Gage. Their conversations flowed naturally, and even her quiet son seemed to enjoy their company.

On Ari's side of the table, though, a current seemed to be charged between the three of them.

I want to kiss her, Roman sent. *I can't stop fantasizing about kissing her.*

I want to touch her, Gage sent.

Ari surmised there was only a few years difference between all the men at the table.

Not since becoming sexually active as a teenager had she ever experienced the sensations racing through her body.

Not through two failed marriages.

Not through sexual partners she could count on one hand.

No one had ever made her feel so in tune with every cell in her body. The longer they sat beside her, the wetter she became.

Oh my God! I can't believe how these guys are affecting me!

Inwardly, Roman and Gage could hardly suppress their glee.

AFTER LUNCH, her boys left to go back to work. Ari walked out of the restaurant between Gage and Roman. They stopped on the sidewalk in a little cluster.

Roman took out his phone and sent a text.

"Come with us?" Gage asked softly. He looked deep into her eyes. His smoldered with lust.

Ari stood before them. Her head swam with crazy thoughts. She saw they were both aroused. She fought her desire. It seemed unrealistic, and she couldn't understand where these feelings were coming from. They were strong emotions, unlike anything she had ever experienced.

She didn't recall any man who had turned her on as much as these two without even touching her.

"Please," Roman said—it sounded on the verge of begging.

He ran a finger down her cheek.

She looked at them, slightly flushed, lips parted. Dripping with want.

"You understand that those were my sons? I'm over seventy years old."

Roman put his arm around her waist. "Age is not relevant, Ari."

A limo pulled up in front of them. Gage opened the door.

Roman entered first and reached out his hand to Ari.

Please, please! He sent to Gage.

Ari stared at Roman in the limo. Her eyes swept over Gage on the sidewalk.

"I can't!" She stammered as she took two steps back.

She turned and hurried away to her car, trying not to run in an all-out panic of emotions.

Ari dropped her keys beside her car. She grabbed them and pushed the button to unlock the car with shaking fingers. She slipped inside and locked the doors and gripped the wheel.

Oh, my God! What was that all about? I haven't had a relationship in over TWO DECADES. I've got to get home. Oh, God! Get me home!

Ari started the car, backed out of the parking space and got on the road.

She glanced in the rearview mirror and saw Roman get out of the limo and join Gage on the sidewalk as they watched her drive away.

She was soaked from the stress and the pull for sex. *Oh, my God! Let me get home without wrecking the car!*

Ari didn't understand what was going on with her, but she could barely focus to drive. Her attraction to Gage and Roman was so overpowering that she shook with longing.

"LET HER GO," Roman said. He rested a hand on Gage's arm. "We scared her, and she scared herself with her reaction to us."

"We can't just let her walk away!" Gage ran his hand through his sandy blond hair. He walked in a circle on the sidewalk, mystified over his reaction to Ari. "I've never suffered like this for any other woman—or any other human being—ever!"

Roman watched as the car vanished from sight. "Me neither. It hurts as if she's pulling on me. I need her so badly."

Gage turned to the waiting limo. "Come on, let's go home. I'm going to get drunk."

ARI PACED IN HER APARTMENT. Isabel, a Maine Coon cat, and Bodie, a black cat with green eyes and medium-length hair, eyed her. They tracked her movements as she walked from the kitchen to the living room and back and forth.

She sat on the sofa, then jumped up. A million thoughts ran

through her head. Once again, she considered she was having some type of breakdown.

"What the hell just happened? What was that?" She ranted.

Ari examined the whole scenario from the restaurant.

Her reactions to the two men were unreasonable and so out of character for her.

What would her sons say if they heard what was going through her mind—that she wanted to go with Roman and Gage *so badly*?

She ached between her legs. Just the thought of them made her juices flow.

Ari flung herself on the sofa, determined to take a nap. It was all she could do to calm her mind and let sleep take her to a peaceful place.

WHEN ARI WOKE, it was dark in the apartment. She fumbled for the table lamp and turned the switch. The room lit up, and she got up. The cats were snuggled in their corners, snoozing.

Ari walked to the kitchen, opened a cabinet, and stared at the contents.

Two bottles of red wine, a half-bottle of white, some lime vodka and bourbon.

Her hand veered from the white wine to the vodka. She filled a rocks glass with ice, poured vodka and added lime tonic. She swirled the contents and gulped down a mouthful.

"What the hell is wrong with me? Who are these guys? WHY—why do I want them so badly? I WANT THEM! BOTH OF THEM! What is that all about?"

The cats woke and gave her questioning looks during her ranting.

She drained her glass and slammed it down on the kitchen counter.

GAGE'S EAGLE gripped the iron railing on Ari's balcony. He heard and saw enough. He took off into the night sky and flew home, landing on the balcony, shifting and sliding open the sliding glass door and walking naked into the living room.

"Well?" Roman asked. His eyes looked pained.

Gage reported what he saw and heard at Ari's apartment.

"She's confused," Roman said. "We need to let her work through this. We don't want to strong-arm her and make her run away."

"But we need her!" Gage yelled. "How long are we going to wait?"

"As long as it takes!" Roman railed back at Gage.

They each headed down separate hallways to their rooms.

Doors slammed.

FOUR DAYS IN A ROW, Gage returned to the penthouse in a foul mood.

"She's not there. I tried communicating with her cats, but they're useless," he said.

"She must have gone out of town," Roman said. "We need to find her sons."

Roman picked up the phone and made a call. "Sherm, I need you to find someone for me. Actually, two guys. Kevin and

Jason Davis. Their mother is Ari Davis. They all live here in the city."

He listened as Sherm's fingers clacked across the keyboard on the other end of the phone.

Roman rushed into the kitchen and grabbed a small pad and a pen. He scribbled information.

"Thanks, Sherm," he said. "It's personal. Maybe later." He tore off the sheet of paper and waved it at Gage. Cellphone numbers, work locations, home addresses.

Roman sent a text to each of them inviting them for drinks after work.

Jason replied first with, *Who is this?*

Roman reminded him of their lunch with their mother.

Oh, I remember you. Sure. Where?

They set the time and place. Roman asked Jason to pass it along to his brother. He didn't mention their mother since he and Gage didn't know if they had had conversations with her about their *special invitation* after lunch that day.

PIANO MUSIC GREETED Kevin and Jason as they entered the wine bar. They glanced around and found Roman and Gage at the bar. They all shook hands.

"Let's grab a booth," Roman suggested. He called to the bartender. "Put their orders on my tab."

The bartender gave a thumbs up, finished with his customer and walked to their end of the bar. "What can I get you?"

"Whatever beer you have on tap," Jason said.

"Yeah, me too," Kevin said.

The bartender served the beer, and the four men walked to an empty booth.

"How's your week going?" Gage asked them.

"You know... nowhere. Bottom of the pit jobs, not enough money. Mom feeds us a couple of times a week, but I feel guilty that I'm forty and can barely support myself," Jason said.

"At least your mom feeds you," Roman said. "How's she doing?"

"Probably great right about now. She's lying on a beach in Cozumel while we babysit the cats," Kevin said.

"Yeah, she seemed stressed out about something, but wouldn't tell us what was going on," Jason said.

At least she didn't tell them, Gage sent.

That was kind of obvious since they didn't cuss us out in the text, Roman sent.

Gage sent a visual of him pecking Roman on the head.

Roman retaliated by sending a visual of his claws raking the eagle.

A waitress approached the table.

"Can we get a round of steaks?" Gage asked. He looked to Ari's sons. "How do you like your rib-eyes?"

"Medium rare for us," Kevin said. "Thanks, Gage. My cooking would kill someone."

"Baked potatoes and veggies?" the waitress asked.

"Bring it on," Gage said. He turned to Kevin and Jason. "Make sure you check her mail so no one knows she's not home."

"I've been bringing in her mail and newspaper every day," Jason said. "I've got to pick her up at the airport tomorrow."

"Do you get docked at work?" Roman asked. "We can pick her up."

ARI WALKED with the crowd to the baggage claim area. She found her airline and flight number on the information monitors and waited for the bags to appear on the carousel conveyor belt. Several years ago, she quit lugging her bags onboard. It was just too difficult to stuff them into the overhead compartment. The baggage claim process gave her enough time to stop in the restroom and freshen up before meeting the son who volunteered to drive her home.

Ari looked around for Jason. Her stomach did a flip as she saw Roman and Gage heading her way.

"What are you doing here? Where's Jason?" She tried to control her shock, so it didn't make it to her face.

"The four of us met for dinner and drinks last night. He didn't want to miss work, so we volunteered to fetch you," Roman said. "Is that okay?"

Ari stared at the two in front of her with warring emotions crossing her face. "You're here."

OMG! Should I get back on the plane?

The buzzer sounded the arrival of the luggage.

Ari turned to the conveyor system and watched for her bag.

Five minutes with these guys and my panties are soaked!

Gage grinned like a fool. He covered his mouth with his hand.

What possessed me to wear a sundress? I'm going to drip all over the floor! I should have worn slacks!

Roman dropped a glance to the floor and searched. He didn't see any telltale sign.

Both Gage and Roman inhaled her scent as they stood on either side of her.

Roman pulled his hand through his hair, trying to distract himself from her sex. He felt frantic, as if he were sliding off a ledge. He wanted her so badly.

Gage arranged his jacket so his hard-on would not be conspicuous.

Water, water everywhere, and not a drop to drink. Water, water everywhere, and all the boards did shrink...

What are you babbling on about? Roman asked.

The Rime of the Ancient Mariner. I'm trying to lose my hard-on, Gage sent.

He met Roman's gaze that was full of despair. He shrugged.

"There's my bag," Ari pointed to a medium-sized gray roller.

Roman pulled it off the conveyor, set it on the floor, and extended the handle. "Just one bag?"

"I travel light," Ari said.

They walked out of the baggage claim door as the limo pulled up and stopped.

ROMAN CARRIED the luggage to the second-floor apartment. He couldn't keep his eyes off Ari's tanned legs and the sway of her dress across her ass as she climbed the stairs. He was in pain for wanting her.

She unlocked her door, and they all went inside.

Gage kept a hand in his pants pocket all the while babbling Coleridge's poem silently.

Roman caught a wave of pain from Gage. He was sure Gage was securing his cock in place so it wouldn't be so obvious. They didn't want to scare Ari into thinking they were rapists.

Isabel hissed. All her fur stood on end and her tail bushed out as she stared at the men, wide-eyed. She rolled out a growl.

Bodie rubbed against Roman in ecstasy.

"I don't know why Isabel reacted the way she did. She's usually the friendlier of the two," Ari said.

Probably because I called her stupid since she couldn't give me information, Gage sent to Roman.

Gage sat on the floor, determined to win Isabel over. He patted his lap and then reached out to her.

Isabel, I'm sorry. You're not stupid. You're beautiful, a warrior kitty.

She wasn't having any part of him. She sauntered off to the living room, jumped on the sofa and glared at him from a safe distance.

Gage stood. "She'll come around."

Yeah, if she ever forgives you! Roman sent. "Do you need anything?" Roman asked.

"Not really," Ari said. "A nap, perhaps. Travel exhausts me."

"Why don't you let us take you to dinner after your nap?" Roman asked. "You're not going to want to cook."

Ari watched them closely. She assumed her rock-hard nipples were visible through the thin dress. She pressed her legs together to contain the cum soaking her panties.

"Dinner would be nice. I typically don't see the boys until I unpack. We go to lunch the day after."

"Get some rest. We'll be back at seven," Gage said.

CHAPTER THREE

ROMAN AND GAGE agonized over the ride from Ari's to the restaurant.

"I hope you like the restaurant we picked. It's one of our favorites," Gage said.

Why can't we sit closer so we can touch with our legs at least? Gage bitched.

Do you want her to jump out of the goddamn limo? Roman sent.

Gage's eagle screeched inside Roman's head. Roman's eyes twitched from the racket.

When the limo pulled up at Tango's Seafood, Gage and Roman exited both back doors at the same time. Gage helped Ari out of the sleek car. They entered the restaurant.

"Ah, Mr. Davenport, Mr. Stryker," the maître d´ said. "We have your special table ready."

"Thanks," Roman said.

He slipped the maître d´ a twenty. One of the staff showed them to their table.

Roman and Gage had discussed seating arrangements

before picking up Ari. They agreed they could not make a spectacle of themselves by wanting to sit on the same side of the table as her so they could be touching.

This new chapter in their lives was confusing. They would just have to be satisfied with being near her.

They sat at a table for six to be across from Ari and have space between them.

She figured it was a little odd but refrained from saying anything.

"So, tell us about your trip," Gage said. "You're nice and tanned."

"Did you do anything special while you were in Cozumel?" Roman asked.

Ari considered what she was going to reveal.

"I visited some old churches—they have some beautiful old churches—but that's about all. I drank a lot. Danced. Walked the beach."

Roman rearranged his face at her *dance* comment.

Did she sleep with men when she got drunk? Did we push her there?

Gage kicked him under the table.

It's her fucking life. She can do as she pleases.

"It sounds like you had a good time." Gage tried to make his smile appear natural.

Their waitress took their drink orders and left them with the menus.

"Is seafood okay? It just occurred to me you may have eaten a lot of seafood in Mexico," Roman said.

"I can never get enough seafood," Ari said.

Roman decided on the grilled shrimp stuffed with mozzarella and provolone. It was wrapped in bacon and drizzled with lemon garlic butter, and a side of angel hair pasta.

Ari chose shrimp tossed with linguini, roasted portobellos, spinach, garlic, lemon and heavy cream.

Gage wavered between two dishes but chose fresh fish and shellfish tossed with linguini, toasted garlic, fresh basil and a spicy marinara.

Their wine arrived, and they placed their food orders. "So, what have you been up to while I've been tanning and dancing?" Ari asked.

"Don't forget the drinking," Roman said with a grin.

"Yeah... I did a lot of that," she said.

"Unfortunately, we only bored ourselves with work," Gage said. "Our highlight was meeting up with your sons."

"That was nice of you," Ari said.

Their food arrived and saved them from awkward silences and more banal conversation.

At the end of the meal, Gage pulled money out of his wallet, and they left.

The limo pulled up, and they got in.

"Would you like to see where we live?" Roman asked. Tension was rolling off him.

Ari bit her bottom lip. Her eyes searched theirs as she chewed on her lower lip. She nodded her head ever so slightly.

"Home," Gage told the driver. He closed the darkened dividing window.

Roman placed his hand on the back of her head and gently drew her to his lips. He kissed her tenderly, stroking her lips with his tongue until she opened to him. She grasped his arm with one hand.

Gage turned her to face him. He was not as reserved. His lips crushed down on hers as he practically consumed her mouth.

Ari gasped for air between his kisses and his tongue all over her lips and inside her mouth.

Roman cupped her breasts.

Her nipples peaked, straining for his touch.

Roman's fingers brushed against one nipple, pinching it gently. He lowered his mouth and pulled the nipple with his teeth, along with the material of her dress.

Ari's hand grabbed Roman's thigh from the sensation. Her fingers dug into his leg as she gasped through her passion.

Oh, God! More! I need more! Ari screamed in her head.

Gage groaned as her words registered in his mind. He pressed his palm into her mound.

She panted, drowning in heat, ready to explode.

The fragrance of her dripping sex filled the back of the vehicle where they huddled in a pile of arousal.

The limo came to a stop.

Roman tucked Ari's hair into place and looked her over. "I'm sorry. I've rumpled you." He brushed his hand down the front of her dress, trying to remove wrinkles and the wet marks he had created.

He and Gage straightened their clothes.

Gage opened the door. They were in a high-rise in the better part of downtown. All three got out of the car. Ari was a little shaky as they led her to the door.

The doorman opened the door.

"Thanks, Alex," Roman handed the doorman a twenty.

"Thank you, Mr. Roman," the doorman said. "Mr. Gage. Ma'am."

Alex tipped his hat to Ari.

They walked to the elevator, and Roman inserted a cardkey into a slot. Inside the elevator, he pressed the P for the penthouse.

"You live in a penthouse?" Ari's eyes widened.

"We own the building," Roman said.

"You own a high-rise?" Ari asked in amazement.

They rode the elevator to the top floor in silence.

Ari questioned her sanity. *What was I thinking? I need to stop right now and go home. Maybe move!*

Roman lifted his eyebrows.

Gage shook his head slightly. *It will be okay, you'll see*, he told Roman.

The door opened to an enormous apartment with a view of the city, along with the mountains and forest in the distance.

Ari was drawn to the windows and looked out over the other buildings. "Breathtaking! I've never seen the city from anything other than the ground or a plane. You're so fortunate to experience this every day."

Gage slid her purse off her shoulder and placed it on the coffee table.

Roman put his arm around her back. "We love the view."

Gage pointed to one of the sofas. "Coffee or a drink, right here. Every day. Every night. I love staring at the forest and the mountains. Sometimes I wish I were a bird."

Roman mentally rolled his eyes. *How original.*

Gage and Roman turned her from the window. Their hands and lips were all over her, and she sucked in a breath of pleasure. They undressed her and discarded their own clothes.

The three of them stood naked, sandwiched together, touching and kissing.

Hearts pounding.

Her juices dripping.

Their cocks aching.

Roman scooped her up and carried her to a bedroom where an enormous, custom-sized bed stood. He placed her on the bed, and they joined her.

Their mouths devoured her with kisses, their tongues leaving trails of passionate desire on her fevered skin.

Gage was in front of her, Roman in back. Gage ran his tongue over Ari's taut nipple and then devoured it with his mouth.

Roman's fingers circled her clit as his lips pressed whisper kisses down her neck.

One of Gage's fingers slipped inside her.

Ari was a dripping mess of volcanic passion. She screamed as an orgasm exploded inside her—the first of its kind.

"Oh! Roman! Gage!" she barely whispered through the pulsating pleasure.

Her orgasms had typically been like tiny mosquito bites. She'd never had a pounding explosion like this. It lasted for several moments. She thought she was going to die from the experience. Her heart pounded in her chest.

"Oh, Ari!" Roman moaned.

Gage lifted and turned her so her back was facing Roman.

"Darling, I can't wait any longer. I have to be inside you," Gage gasped out.

One of his arms wrapped around her middle while he used his other hand to guide his cock inside her.

Ari moaned as he inched into her tight, slick core. Her juices flowed like a river, and she clung to his broad, muscular shoulders.

"That's so good," Ari mumbled mindlessly.

As Gage pumped into her, Roman's thumb rubbed her sweet little nub.

Ari's hand circled Roman's cock. She stroked him and rubbed her thumb over the slit, spreading his pre-cum.

She screamed out in agonized pleasure as she came again. Her walls clenched down on Gage, making him come way too soon for his pleasure.

As they all panted from their release, Roman tugged her off the bed.

"Let's shower. Then it's my turn," he said.

They led her to the bathroom, where a huge shower stall with clear glass walls awaited.

Gage turned the water on.

Water sprayed from several shower heads. They entered the shower and soaped each other.

Gage dropped to his knees and put his mouth on her nub.

"No! Please don't! I don't know if I can take anymore."

Ari's eyes rolled up. Her mouth was open. She panted from the sheer want of them.

"Shh," Roman said. "We all need this."

Gage's tongue dipped inside her. His fingers gripped her ass, holding her in place while he sucked her juices.

Roman kissed her and caressed her breasts. He gently tweaked her nipples.

Gage stood. He shut the water off and reached for a towel. He wrapped her in a large towel while Roman got another towel for her long hair.

She looked half-drunk with lust. She kissed Gage, then Roman. Her towel dropped to the floor. Her hands grasped hold of each of their enormous erections.

All three groaned while she stroked them. They laughed at their reactions.

"You're so big," she said as she looked at one shaft and then the other.

"I didn't hurt you, did I?" Gage's forehead creased with worry as he examined her face for telltale signs.

"No, you were gentle, and I appreciate that. I assumed I was all dried up inside, but you two proved me wrong."

Roman took her hand and led her to the bed. He crawled on top of her. He devoured her mouth and then crawled down her body, stopping at her hard nipples. Roman sucked one nipple while gently pinching the other. He continued his descent down her body and sank his face between her legs.

Ari arched up, her heels digging into the bedding, wanting him to stay right where he was. Little gasps of pleasure escaped her parted lips, her head thrown back.

Roman couldn't wait any longer. The need to be inside her was so great he could hardly focus as he pulled his face away from her dripping land of promise. He positioned his shaft at her entrance. When he slid inside, they both gasped.

She was like a running faucet, so wet.

Ari bent her legs, her feet planted on either side of him. She matched his strokes, then her heels dug into the bedding, and then slid. She grasped his back, fingers digging into his flesh.

"I can't wrap my legs around you. My bones are almost frozen from lack of use in this position," she explained between kisses.

"It's okay. That'll change," Gage said as he climbed into bed beside them.

Ari clenched as an orgasm slammed her. She screamed Roman's name, and her legs tightened to his sides. Her head flung back onto the mattress as her mind and body processed the ecstasy.

When it ended and they separated, Gage pressed a hand towel between her legs.

The three of them lay against each other and dozed off.

ARI AWOKE TWO HOURS LATER, alone. She felt an immediate sensation of abandonment, as if she had experienced the greatest loss in her life.

Someone had placed a robe on the edge of the bed. She got

up and slipped into it. Then her head started churning nonstop chatter.

What just happened? I can't believe I had sex with two gorgeous men practically the same age as my sons! I must be having a senior crisis! A breakdown! Or something.

She sat on the edge of the bed fretting about her threesome.

As if they sensed her awake, they both appeared in the doorway.

She's having second thoughts! Gage sent, panic wafting off him.

Knock it off! Roman sent, with a hint of anger. "Did you sleep well?" Roman asked.

"Yes, it was the most solid sleep I've had in years," Ari said. She stood to face them.

Gage strode into the bathroom and returned with a brush. He stepped behind her and brushed her long hair.

"I love your hair. It's luscious. So healthy."

Roman kissed her gently. "Would you like a cup of tea?"

"That would be nice," she said. Her nerves ratcheted up a notch.

Be cool, Roman sent to Gage.

Gage scowled at Roman as he finished brushing her hair.

They all went into the kitchen.

Roman prepared tea.

Gage sliced cheese and apples and added crackers to a plate.

They sat and sipped tea and nibbled.

"Ari, just so you know, neither of us has ever had a threesome before. We don't want you to assume this is something we do every day," Roman said.

Ari blushed in embarrassment. She met their eyes. "I've never had an experience like this before, and I'm not sure how I should react. It's like I skipped college sex 101 forty years ago.

It's confusing. You two are different, and I'm drawn to you—I'm not sure that even describes the feeling. It's almost like I'm bound to the two of you. Not more to one than the other, but equally."

"It's the same for us, Ari. Believe it or not, we were miles away when we sensed you that day we met at the restaurant," Gage said.

She balked.

Oh, great, just dive right in, Roman sent, furious.

No point in beating around the bush, Gage snapped back.

"What do you mean, you *sensed* me?" She grabbed a slice of apple.

Sure, hope you know what the hell you're doing! I swear, if you jeopardize this, I'll beat the shit out of you! Roman sent, along with an image of his enormous teeth and claws ready to attack Gage.

"I realize this will sound a little crazy, but we're not completely human," Gage said.

Ari stared at him, then shifted her eyes to Roman, waiting for an explanation that made sense.

Oh, no! Do they think they're aliens? Please don't have one of them say they're Captain Kirk!

"We're shifters." Gage said.

Great. Just great. We totally fucked our only chance. Roman snarled silently.

Calm the fuck down. We don't know that Gage sent back.

Ari belted out a laugh. When she saw they were serious, the apple dropped to the table.

"Shifters? Like in romance novels? Bears, wolves...?"

"Yeah, but those are just romance stories writers made up. We haven't found any other shifters in the past fifty years since we discovered each other," Roman said.

"Roman and I are older than you by over twenty years,"

Gage said. "We're frozen at this age for some reason. Since we haven't found any other shifters to talk to, there's no one to answer our questions."

Ari stared at the table while processing what she had heard. "You're serious? Shifters—you change from men to animals?"

"Yes. Please trust us. We're serious," Gage begged. "You're the first woman we've been drawn to. The first woman we've ever shared," Roman said. "Your scent is like heroin to us. We can't get enough of you."

Oh, great. That sounds sort of like Edward and Bella in Twilight! *Are these two crazy?*

Gage and Roman frowned.

Wonderful. Just fucking wonderful. Now she thinks we're fucking lunatics! Roman ranted.

We've got to show her! Gage sent.

She was shocked speechless while she processed his words. "Why are we drawn to each other?"

Her eyes were wide with unasked questions. She wasn't even sure how to express her thoughts in words. She sucked in a breath.

Roman shrugged. "Have no idea—it has to be a shifter trait."

"That's why I ran away to Cozumel and drank myself into oblivion. I didn't understand what was happening. I ached for you so badly my entire body was practically screaming. I imagined that perhaps I was having some type of strange possession or obsession or a psychotic episode.

"It made no difference that I was in another country. My mind wouldn't let go of you."

"Whatever it is, it's the strongest I have ever been pulled to anyone—ever," Gage said. "We had a very difficult time being separated from you. It's not going to work for any of us to be apart like that."

Ari shook her head in puzzlement. "When I woke up, and you were gone, I had an awful sense of separation."

"That's what we experience," Gage said. "It's a terrible feeling."

"You may be older than me but you look like forty. I..."

"You're a beautiful, desirable woman who doesn't look a day over fifty," Roman said. "You've got good genetics going on there. How old are your sons?"

"They're thirty-eight and forty," Ari said.

Gage nodded. "Great genetics. They look at least a decade younger, possibly more. You've taken care of yourself."

"What are your animals?" Ari asked. *If I'm going to get on board this crazy train, this is an appropriate question.*

"Gage is an eagle and I'm a panther," Roman said. "And not your normal size of either animal you'd find in any zoo. We're enormous."

"Can I see you shift?" Ari asked. *This I've got to see. Wonder what excuse they'll make when it doesn't work?*

She can handle us shifting, Gage sent.

God, I hope so! Roman sent.

"Just so you know, Gage and I can communicate between our minds, but I'm not sure we can communicate with you," Roman said. "We'll have to test that."

Keeping her face neutral, Ari didn't know what to expect.

Roman morphed into a very large black panther.

Ari screamed and jumped back. "Oh My God! Oh My God—you weren't lying! Please don't hurt me!"

The panther's eyes met hers as he walked to her and rubbed against her. His size almost knocked her down—his shoulders came up to just below her chest. His tongue swiped across the top of her hand.

Ari recovered from the shock of seeing the man shift into

the giant cat. She ran her hands through his luxurious coat. "Oh, my God! You're so beautiful, Roman. You're so big!"

A loud squawk sounded.

Ari turned to where Gage had been standing a moment ago. She gasped at the gigantic eagle. Its body was twice the size of a normal eagle. She walked over to him and ran her hands over his beautiful feathers.

"Oh, Gage! I can't keep my hands off your feathers. Can I touch your head?"

He squawked.

She took that as a yes, and she ran her fingers over his head. He was magnificent.

Ari patted her heart, letting them understand how thrilled she was at what she saw.

They shifted back to their human forms. "We're not bull-shitters, Ari," Gage said.

"Do you work? Have jobs? You obviously have money, what with the limo, this place, and your upscale clothing," Ari said.

"Yes, we run several companies, but our attendance isn't mandatory unless there are executive decisions," Roman said. "Are you still in the workforce?"

She shook her head. "I retired a few years ago, but I've been searching for something that seemed to be missing my entire life."

Gage stared hard at her. "Have you found it?"

Ari swallowed. Her eyes drifted from one to the other. "I may have, but it's all confusing right now."

"You're not going to run away again, are you?" Roman asked. There was just a pinch of panic in his voice.

He tried to mask the pain that question caused. He felt his chest constricting, almost like a panic attack coming on.

Gage gripped the edge of the table, waiting for her answer.

"I don't know." She chewed her lower lip. "To be honest, I'm not sure what to do with this. It's crazy."

They sat in an awkward silence while finishing their tea.

Ari gathered her clothes and returned to the bedroom. Her brain practically shut down because so many things flooded her head. She dressed and returned to the kitchen, where the men were having a quiet but tense conversation.

Gage stood against the island and faced Roman on the other side. They stopped their discussion when Ari entered the room.

They both faced her.

Something serious had passed between them. She stopped in her tracks and grabbed the back of a chair, not knowing what was to come.

"Would you consider living here?" Gage asked.

She flinched.

"We need you," Roman said. "It's not just for the sex — which is absolutely mind-blowing. It's this bonding thing that's making us a little crazy with thoughts of not having you close."

Ari stared right through them. "That's impossible. My sons... friends... how would I ever explain such a relationship?"

They smiled like schoolboys who just found fifty bucks.

"So, you'd consider living here with us?" Roman asked.

Ari flinched again. "I had no idea of even considering it, but I have this strange need to be near you two."

"You could tell them you're our personal assistant, or housekeeper or something. That we're CEOs of several companies, which is true, and we need someone we could trust to take care of us," Roman said.

"The apartment has four suites, and we could set one up for you. We each have our own suites. You've seen Roman's. It's very comfortable," Gage said.

"What about all my possessions?" Ari asked.

Roman reached out and grasped her hand. "Come look at the extra bedrooms."

There were three hallways. The first was to Roman's suite, the bedroom where they had been earlier.

The second corridor had two doors at the opposite end. "That's where my rooms are," Gage said.

They continued to the next hallway, where four more doors stood closed, two on each end of the hallway.

Gage opened the first door on the right side of the entryway. There was a king bed, a large private bath, and a doorway to an enormous sitting room beyond.

"I believe the rooms at the other end of the hallway would be perfect for you," he said.

They walked down to the other end of the hall and saw the other suite of rooms. Large windows offered a view overlooking the city, mountains, and forest in the distance.

Ari gasped. "Yes, this one."

"Let's go look at your place," Roman suggested. "We didn't pay attention to what was there when we dropped you off from the airport."

They returned to the living room, and Ari gathered her purse.

CHAPTER FOUR

ARI UNLOCKED and opened the door. The two cats stood nearby as if expecting them.

Ari gave Roman and Gage the tour of the eleven-hundred square-foot apartment. Compact kitchen, a living room with bookcases on every available wall, a small dining room, and a bedroom. A patio with lush foliage, a table and chairs, and a fountain made up the entire space.

"We'll hire a carpenter to build bookcases in your suite. The sitting room is about the size of your entire apartment," Roman said.

He ran his hand across the back of the sofa, and Isabel arched her back and hissed. "Come on, beautiful. Give us a chance."

Isabel whacked at his hand and leapt to the top of a bookcase and glared down at him.

Damn, she holds a grudge forever!

Gage walked into the bedroom and looked around. Ari and Roman followed.

All three of them eyed the queen bed at the same time.

Then they were in it. Kissing and undressing.

THREE WEEKS LATER, Ari's kitchenware, clothes, books and office boxes were moved to the penthouse along with her desk and a couple of other pieces of furniture. Workers delivered everything else to a storage unit until Ari could decide if she wanted some of the furniture in her suite.

During those three weeks, the three of them were rarely away from each other. They satiated each other completely. Roman and Gage treated Ari as if she were the only woman alive. It took her a while to understand they were dead serious. She was their world. Their true north.

Her sons and friends were surprised that she accepted the job offer. She assured them that the only thing that had changed was her address. They'd be able to access her one-hundred percent of the time.

When her two close friends, Victoria and Margaret, both widows in their 70s, met Roman and Gage, they questioned Ari afterwards like the inquisition.

She explained she would cook for them, keep them presentable and make sure they were on time for work, board meetings and social events.

They stared at her as if she had sprouted green warts.

Kevin and Jason seemed happy that they didn't need to worry about her being alone any longer. They liked Roman and Gage and trusted their mother's decision about her new position.

Her first night of living in the penthouse wasn't exactly awkward, but she could tell the guys were giving her space to settle in. They didn't hover.

Gage ordered Chinese takeout delivered. They ate, then

Ari returned to her suite to finish unpacking clothes and personal items.

Near midnight, she dropped into her bed, exhausted.

Roman slid into her bed about an hour later. He curled into her.

Gage arrived a little later.

They slept in a tangle with no need of satisfying each other.

GAGE WAS the first to wake.

His hand roamed across Ari's hip and ass, then across her breasts. He pressed his lips to hers.

She woke to his kiss, then she noticed Roman's erection against her backside.

Gage nudged her onto her back.

Roman pulled his arm from around her. He got out of bed and went to the bathroom, then left the bedroom.

Gage's mouth was all over her. His kiss was ardent. His hands claimed her breasts.

Roman slipped back into bed. He pushed one of Gage's hands out of the way, and his lips claimed her other breast. One of his fingers rubbed her clit.

Gage slipped two fingers inside her. Ari arched from their ministrations.

Roman's mouth devoured hers. He swallowed her moans.

Ari screamed through her orgasm. She bucked when Gage's mouth captured her tight bud. She shook off Roman's kiss, needing to breathe through the pulsing spasms inside her.

Roman transferred his mouth to a nipple while his fingers tweaked and pulled the other nipple.

As they were all engaged, Ari started laughing.

Both men stopped their lovemaking and stared at her.

Oh, no! She's flipped out! Roman sent.

She laughed and shook her head. Tears came to her eyes.

"I had the sudden thought..." she laughed even harder. "What if I had a heart attack or stroke from all this? It's not like I've been having sex for the past two *decades*, and suddenly I'm your *sex goddess*."

Their concern turned into laughs as they understood the irony.

When they settled down, Roman pulled her onto his lap. She straddled him and took him inside her. They made love while Gage waited patiently.

ROMAN DRAPED his suit jacket over the back of a chair. He poured coffee while Ari sautéed chopped veggies and sliced sausage links. She beat a dozen eggs and added that to the pan.

Gage made the toast. They all settled around the kitchen table. Bodie visited on the way to his food dish, and they lavished him with attention.

Isabel rushed past the table into the large butler's pantry. The litter box was amid the washer and dryer, a pants presser, steamer, cabinets, and countertop for folding clothes.

She did her business and returned to the kitchen and eyed her food bowl. Isabel gauged the distance between the bowl and the men and deemed it safe. She dashed over to her bowl.

"She'll settle in," Gage said. "We just need to give her some space."

"She likes it here, but she's still exploring," Ari said. They finished eating and retired to the living room. Roman's phone rang. He snatched it up, viewed the caller ID, sighed, and answered.

"What's going on, Celeste?"

Gage rolled his eyes.

Ari gave a questioning glance his way.

"Okay, bring them by and I'll sign them," Roman said. He ended the call, pressed a button on his phone, and spoke to Gage.

"I need to sign the Baker papers. She'll notarize and file them by nine this morning."

Within minutes, the elevator dinged, signaling Celeste's arrival. The tall, leggy brunette, in a skin-tight tiny black skirt, four-inch red fuck-me heels and a red scooped tank, stepped into the foyer. She held a file folder and her notary stamp.

She strutted into the living room as if she belonged there.

Ari watched Celeste's approach. *Will you get a load of this little temptress?*

Uh-oh. Roman sent Gage. *This may not be such a good idea. Celeste will say or do something inappropriate.*

Get her out of here as quick as you can, Gage sent.

"Hey, Gage," Celeste said as she walked past him on her way to Roman.

Then she stopped abruptly as her eyes discovered Ari on the sofa.

Celeste's eyes moved from Ari to Roman to Gage.

"Oh, is this your mom?" Celeste asked. There was a hint of disbelief in her tone.

Ari tensed. *Their mom? Oh, jeez! This little bitch feels threatened by my presence.*

Gage smirked. "Hardly."

Roman gave Gage a stink-eye, then directed his gaze to Celeste. "This is Ari."

Celeste studied Ari. She was a classic, ageless beauty in a long white shirt, black leggings and ballet flats.

What the hell is this woman doing here at this time of the morning? Celeste was practically blowing smoke out of her ears with Ari's presence.

She fake-smiled as she held out her hand. "Hi, I'm Celeste."

Ari rose and shook Celeste's hand. *If I had an animal, it would be a lioness, and you'd be lunch.* "Hi Celeste. It's nice to meet you."

This is so not good, Roman sent.

Why the hell didn't you think this through? Gage sent.

Ari's hair swung forward, and Celeste gasped. "Oh, what beautiful hair!"

"Thanks. I'm going to braid it this morning." She sat back on the sofa, and Gage joined her.

He nudged her forward and braided her long hair. Celeste pulled her gaze away from them and turned to Roman. "I've placed arrow stickies where you are required to initial and sign."

Celeste sat on the sofa opposite Gage and Ari and opened the folder and extracted the pen clipped to the front.

Roman sat on the sofa, keeping a distance from Celeste, and picked up the pages.

Celeste handed him the pen. She couldn't stop watching Gage braid Ari's beautiful, long, white hair. *What the hell is going on here?*

Roman perused the contract line by line. He circled something.

"This isn't right. Get with Rick and verify this number."

Celeste read the paragraph. "I'm sorry. This is supposed to be the final document."

"I know this isn't the right figure," Roman said. He circled another figure. "I'll be down a little later."

Celeste gathered the pages, the folder, and the pen. Her eyes slid to Ari and then back to Roman.

"I'm so sorry to have bothered you. I'll make Rick go through each line to be sure it's correct for your signature."

Celeste hurried to the foyer, pressed the button and stepped inside the elevator.

"Well, that was interesting," Ari said. "Your mom, huh?"

"She's been chasing Roman for two years," Gage said with a sneer.

"You don't like her?" Ari asked.

"She's the type of woman we try to avoid. She can get pushy," Roman said.

Never let these two cross paths again, Roman sent.

Celeste went a little too far, Gage sent. *Going to evaluate this situation. Will not let that bitch ever treat Ari that way again.*

"Is this going to be awkward for your employees? Or your board of directors, or anything?" Ari asked.

"Nope. Don't even go there, Ari," Roman said. "There's no reason for you to be concerned about our private relationship." He pointed from himself to Ari and then to Gage. "We are on solid ground. Our employees are just that, except for Sherm, Lonnie and the private security division they take care of.

"Regular staff don't get into our private affairs. If they did, they would be terminated."

"But Celeste..."

"If she becomes a problem, she's replaceable," Roman said. "I won't tolerate anyone who crosses that line. Gage and I have a lot to lose. We may outlive our employees, but we'll move the company if it comes down to that."

Ari chewed her bottom lip.

Gage rubbed her shoulder. "Listen to Roman. Don't fret. There will never be anything coming between the three of us. And neither of us will be jealous of your time with the other.

All I can tell you is that we three are one now. I, for one, am finally thrilled."

Roman nodded in agreement.

"Do people from your company come up here all the time? It's sort of uncomfortable because there's no front door—they get off the elevator and are just *here*."

"Yeah, but they call or text ahead of time to announce they're coming; otherwise, the doors won't open," Gage said.

"Oh, that's good." Ari relaxed with that knowledge.

He showed her his phone. "We have to buzz them in."

"Which of your companies are in this building?" Ari asked. She recalled their saying that they had several companies.

"Half of our companies take up twenty floors in this building. All but one company of the remaining half are next door in leased space. We have three thousand employees," Roman said.

"What types of businesses do you run? I remember you talking about this with my sons, but that was a while ago."

Ari was curious how they could employ so many people. "Our biggest business is a global security company that Sherm is in charge of—you'll meet him later. There's an electronics development company, which includes an offsite manufacturing facility, and related service companies," Gage explained.

"What are your backgrounds?" Ari asked.

She knew this conversation should have come way before she agreed to live with them, but she shrugged it off — they were discussing it now.

"I've got an EE and a law degree, and many decades ago I studied to be a doctor," Roman said. "Gage is both an electrical and mechanical engineer, plus he's studied a few other things."

Ari raised her eyebrows. "That's a little vague. What else did you study, Gage?"

"I've puttered around with physics," Gage said. They turned to her.

"And you?" Gage asked.

"Accounting. I worked in that field for several years. Then I returned to school and studied forensic accounting and programming, which I loved. The two go together when you're snooping around looking for crooked dealings in the books. Between the three of us, we have just about everything covered," Ari said.

"You don't wear a ring," Roman began. "Are you widowed or divorced?"

"Unfortunately, I'm not widowed. Tom was a bastard through and through, and I'm glad to be rid of him," Ari said. "The boys won't have anything to do with him."

"Does he live here in Reading?" Roman asked.

"He's in Philly. The further away, the better," Ari said. "I was married before him. It was short-term, only two years. We were very young."

We'll get to the bottom of that later Roman sent. "Want to go down to the gym?" Gage asked.

"Why am I not surprised there's a gym in the building?" Ari said. "I haven't been to a gym in years, but I own some old gym clothes and workout gloves."

"I'll change. That document won't be ready for a while," Roman said. He grabbed his suit jacket and went to his bedroom to change.

THE COMPANY GYM contained all the equipment in a typical gym but was upgraded with high-end commercial performance pieces.

Gage and Roman got her signed up at the service desk.

The clerk handed her a temporary badge.

They walked over to a rack of towels and each grabbed one.

"Later, we'll go to the legal department and get you set up as an employee so you can take advantage of all the benefits. They'll get you a cardkey for the elevator, an employee badge with access to all the floors and buildings, and a permanent gym badge," Gage said.

"Don't forget direct deposit for Ari's salary," Roman said.

"You're paying me, on top of living in the penthouse rent-free and all the rest?" Ari felt shocked.

"Of course, you're getting paid. How did you expect to live?" Roman said.

"Well, my retirement fund and a small pension, and social security," Ari said.

"And now you'll have a lot more," Gage said. "We're taking care of you. You're like our—wife."

He and Roman exchanged glances and nodded, turning their focus back to her.

Ari stared back at them, speechless. She hadn't been called that in decades.

They walked over to the machines. She looked around the room.

"I'm familiar with the leg press, the row machine, and some of these upper-body machines. I'm not sure how to make adjustments for my size."

There were around forty people in the gym working out. Some men and women snuck glances at her, curious about who she was. They knew who Roman and Gage were.

Ari was aware of eyes on her.

Roman and Gage picked up stray thoughts.

Damn! She's beautiful.

Who's that gorgeous woman? Doesn't resemble either of them.

Whoa! Will you look at that fine, juicy morsel?

Roman and Gage quirked eyebrows at that thought. *She's not a steak,* Roman sent to Gage.

She whispered to Roman and Gage. "They most likely think I'm your mother or grandmother, like Celeste."

Gage roared with laughter. "Let them."

Roman slugged him in the arm.

"Ow! What'd you do that for?"

"People will be curious," Roman said. "Ari is the first woman we've ever been seen steadily with. They probably thought we were gay all this time, and now there's another equation they'll never be able to figure out."

Ari shook her head. "Oh, I'm pretty sure someone will suspect we're lovers."

Gage grinned. That didn't break his heart.

ARI TOOK A SHOWER AND DRESSED, then joined the men in the living room. "Oh, I ache all over!"

"After we set you up downstairs and give you a tour of the place, soak in the tub with some Epsom salt. It's in the cabinet," Gage said.

"That will be my next order of business," Ari said.

"You'll loosen up as you continue to work out," Roman said.

They took the elevator downstairs, and Roman headed in the opposite direction to search for Celeste while Gage explained the lay of the land on the thirtieth floor, where the legal department was located.

They walked into an office with a door sign that read 'Sandy Turner'.

Gage made the introduction. "Sandy, this is Ari Davis."

The thirty-five-year-old looked like a soccer mom with a short blond blunt cut, a crisp white blouse, and a pair of black slacks and low heels.

Sandy held out her hand. "Hi Ari, it's nice to meet you. I have your paperwork all set." *Oh, this woman is so lovely!*

They shook hands, then Sandy said to Gage. "You can come back in an hour, Gage. We should be finished by then."

Gage turned to Ari. "You okay?"

Ari nodded. "A-Okay. See you later."

Sandy closed the door after Gage left. "Let's move over to my table so we can go over this ream of paperwork."

A round table sat in front a bookcase. Ari spotted some framed photos. "Are these your kids?"

"Yeah, my little squirts. They're a handful!" Sandy said.

"They're precious. Wait until they grow up," Ari joked.

Sandy got a wistful expression on her face. "I'm not looking forward to that. I don't think I'll do the empty-nest syndrome very well."

"They're never really gone," Ari said. She patted Sandy's hand. "Think bungee cords throughout college and beyond."

Sandy laughed. "I can do bungee cords!"

I'm going to like getting to know Sandy. What a wonderful mother!

They sat at the table, and Sandy opened the thick folder.

She pulled out a small manila envelope.

"Let's start with this." She opened the envelope and pulled out the cardkey to the penthouse and a gym badge.

"The cardkey will give you access to all the buildings. Roman mentioned that besides your duties, you may work with the security division because of your background in forensic accounting," Sandy said. "This cardkey will give you access to the secured floor where some of that work is done."

"I can't wait to see their setup," Ari said.

"What type of cellphone do you have?" Sandy asked.

"An old iPhone," Ari said.

"We'll upgrade you. You'll need our private app to open the penthouse elevator doors. We have an account with Apple, and they'll transfer everything—not just your contacts. They'll get all your apps moved over, so it isn't a pain in the ass," Sandy said.

"Thank God. That's one thing I hate about the standard upgrade. The last time I had my phone upgraded, they dropped most of my contacts, and I had to enter dozens of people manually," Ari said.

They went over packet after packet of documents. When they came to her employment contract and salary, Ari had to force herself not to squeal out in surprise.

A hundred fifty-thousand dollars per year? Besides all the benefits?

She could hardly believe it and couldn't wait to talk to her lovers. What were they thinking?

Sandy presented her with car keys, auto insurance cards, medical, dental, and vision cards, and two credit cards. Her head spun when she saw the black American Express Centurion card and a white Stratus Rewards Visa card. Each credit card had a hundred-thousand-dollar limit.

Just as they finished up, Gage and Roman tapped on the closed door.

"Come in," Sandy called out.

"You ready for lunch, Ari?" Gage asked.

"Why don't we go upstairs first so I can put this paperwork away?" Ari asked.

"Good idea, you can try out your cardkey," Roman said.

"You need to take her to the Apple Store and get her new phone and devices," Sandy said.

"Oh, right, the elevator app," Gage said. "We'll drop your phone off and they can take care of that while we grab a bite to eat."

Ari shook Sandy's hand. "Thanks so much for everything, Sandy."

"My pleasure. You ever get bored up there, come on down and visit," Sandy said.

She watched them leave her office and walk down the hall.

Gage's arm wrapped around Ari's waist and Roman's across her shoulders.

Sandy hitched an eyebrow. *Definitely a free spirit, but a lady above all else.*

At the elevator, Ari inserted her cardkey. The doors opened, and they entered.

Gage pressed the P for the penthouse.

"I can't believe everything I sat through! How could you pay me so much money? And what are these car keys for? I own a vehicle."

"Ari, we're worth billions. We passed the million status years ago," Roman said. "Your salary is as small as the top of a pinhead compared to our fortune."

"That may be so, but..." she started.

"Your car is twelve years old! Now you'll be able to use any of our vehicles," Gage said.

"But it's been a great vehicle," she stammered.

"We can donate it to a women's shelter," Roman said.

The doors opened, and they stepped into the foyer. "Go put your paperwork in your room and let's go," Roman said. "I'm starving."

"You ate a huge breakfast," Ari said.

"Our animals expend a lot of energy, and those calories burn off pretty quickly," Gage said.

Ari hurried to her sitting room and dropped the packet into the desk drawer.

"Grab your laptop," Roman yelled out from the other end of the hallway.

"What do I need that for?" Ari said. She removed the power cord and slid the laptop into her case, and left the room.

CHAPTER FIVE

THEY STOPPED at the Apple Store, and Roman greeted their account representative. "Did Sandy send over an account for Ari Davis?"

The guy jumped onto a console and typed in his credentials, then surfed to their account. "Sure did. iPhone, iPad and MacBook Pro."

Woof! What a babe someone in the store thought.

Roman perused the room, a scowl on his face.

Let it go. No matter where we go, men will want to be all over Ari Gage sent.

Gage grabbed the computer case from Ari and handed it to the guy behind the counter. He turned to her. "Do you have a password to access your laptop?"

"Yes, I better write it down because it's complicated," Ari said. "It's the same password for all my devices."

The Apple guy looked at what she wrote. "That's a good, strong password. I'll use that on your new devices."

"I try to keep everything protected. If I lose one or it gets stolen, I want the thief to work for access," Ari said with a smile.

"We're going to lunch. When do you want us back?" Roman asked.

"Give me a couple of hours," the guy said.

They left the Apple Store and drove three streets away to Pomodoro's, an upscale restaurant. The maître 'd greeted them.

"Good morning, Mr. Davenport, Mr. Stryker. Will anyone else be joining your party?" he asked.

"No, just the three of us; this is Ms. Davis," Roman said.

"How nice to meet you, Ms. Davis," the maître'd said, with a little bow.

Ari tilted her head to him.

A waiter escorted them to a table.

After they sat down, Ari leaned on the table. "Do you come here often? The maître'd seemed to know you."

"We're here at least two or three times a week," Gage said. He picked up his menu and perused it.

Ari opened the menu.

"Ignore the prices. Just order what sounds good," Roman said.

Ari struggled with the new concept of living. She hadn't been poor by any stretch, but she had never been wealthy either. She took a deep breath and looked over the continental food choices.

They placed their orders. When the waiter left, Ari leaned forward.

"What's with the two credit cards with the gigantic credit limits? What exactly do you think I'm going to buy? Why would you think I needed two cards?"

Roman snatched up her hand. "Honey, it's okay. You've got them if you ever need them. If an emergency comes up, you're covered. If the boys get into a jam, they're covered."

AFTER LUNCH, they stopped at an office supply store, then returned to the Apple store and picked up Ari's new equipment.

She kept her old phone and laptop as emergency backups.

Roman and Gage brought her to the twenty-eighth floor in the high-rise. Only the employees of the security company, Roman, Gage, and now Ari, had access with their coded card keys.

They walked into a glass-enclosed office lined with several wall monitors. A desk and credenza held laptops and other pieces of equipment.

"Sherm, I want you to meet Ari Davis," Roman said.

An Asian man in his thirties stood and shook her hand. "Nice to meet you, Ari. Sherman Foo," he said. "But please, everyone calls me Sherm."

He had a deep southern drawl. They shook hands.

"You remind me of my former dentist who retired, Sherm. His Chinese name was impossible for me to pronounce, but he had a Texas drawl. It was so odd," Ari said.

Sherm laughed. "So, Roman mentioned that you have a degree in forensic accounting. You ever get a chance to use what you learned?"

Ari smirked. "Boy, did I. I helped pull the plug on those doctors who were bilking Medicare. They had accounts buried so deep I figured I'd need a bulldozer to uncover them."

Sherm's jaw dropped. He took two steps back and pointed at Ari and hooted in disbelief. "You're 'the sifter'!"

Roman and Gage exchanged shrugs.

Ari flushed. "How could you possibly know that nickname?"

"In this industry, we keep tabs on everything and everyone. You're practically a legend," Sherm said.

"I don't think I'd go that far," Ari said. She blushed crimson.

Sherm wagged a finger at her. "If the pants fit, put 'em on and zip 'em up. Everything I've heard or read about that case, those pants fit. The government retrieved a good portion of the money when they confiscated mansions, yachts, jets, and everything in between from that ring of thieves."

Ari glanced over at one of his monitors, where columns of numbers flew up the screen. "What are you running?"

Sherm nodded at the screen. "Looking for a key."

Ari nodded.

"Well, I hate to break up this budding friendship, but we should get going," Roman said. "See you later, Sherm."

Sherm and Ari shook hands.

"Call me if you need anything." Ari said.

She looked longingly at the setup.

"Will do, but I don't know if your guys will cut the chain," Sherm said.

Ari gave a little snort.

Gage wrapped his arm around her waist and guided her to the door. Roman hugged her shoulder to his.

Sherm's brows crinkled as he watched them leave.

What are these guys up to now?

He remembered the call when Roman asked to hunt down the two Davis men. He had run a low-key background check on Arianna Davis.

THE CARPENTERS HAD BUILT the most beautiful bookcases Ari had ever seen. It amazed her that they finished within the three weeks between her accepting her new living arrangements and when she moved in.

They even installed a library ladder—something she had longed for over the years.

Ari and Gage worked on different sections of the bookcases while Roman slit open another box. Ari had placed sticky notes on each section along the walls. She liked her books categorized.

Several shelves were dedicated to her career. She had books on police procedurals, detectives and investigating techniques, and everything in between. There were a slew of books on various aspects of accounting, forensic investigations, and related subject matter that filled the other shelves.

After that, books were shelved according to subject, or in the case of fiction, by author. She had an entire section devoted to esoteric subjects, including all her spiritual and astrology books.

Ari looked around the pile of unopened boxes. She wanted to find one set of books in particular to show them to her lovers. It had been a long time since she perused them, but Roman and Gage might discover something of their roots.

Ari looked around the pile of boxes waiting to be emptied and spotted a longer box. She was sure the books were of that size. They were oversized and contained handwritten pages and drawings. She was certain they were ancient.

"Roman, can you open this box? You and Gage should take a look at these books," she said.

Roman pulled the box toward him and carefully slit through the tape along the top and ends. He opened it, lifted the crumpled packing paper from the box, and stared at the old volume on top. He carefully picked up the book.

"Where did you get these?" Roman asked in a reverential tone.

Gage looked over Roman's shoulder, then dug another book out of the box. "Holy shit! Will you get a load of this?"

"I went to an estate sale with one of my friends ten or fifteen years ago," Ari said. "This Asian family was clearing out their grandfather's things. I wish I had had the foresight to grab more of the other books. I would have bought everything they were selling if I had had the credit cards you gave me. I'll bet anything Grandpa had secrets stashed in the furniture."

Roman studied the binding and the paper. "This is a hand-tooled cover, and I'm not sure about the paper and ink. How many more are there?"

"There were eight in all. I bought the entire set," Ari said.

Gage kissed her passionately. "We may find answers about our kind in these pages."

"Why don't we go to the cabin?" Roman said. "I could use a run."

"Yeah, that sounds good," Gage said.

"Where's your cabin?" Ari asked.

Roman turned to the window and pointed. "Way over there, close to the mountains."

"When did you want to go? We'll need food and supplies," Ari said.

Gage glanced around the room. "Why don't we finish up here tonight? Tomorrow we can pack up, stop at the grocery store, and grab some food. It takes two to two-and-a-half hours to get there."

They resumed unboxing books and shelving them.

AFTER SUPPER they all sat on various chairs in the living room with their faces buried in books. Mostly, all they could do was study the drawings and sketches. The writing was in neat columns of Chinese.

"How can we get these translated?" Roman asked.

"Maybe we should scan in the pages and get them translated online," Ari said. "We don't know what these books contain. For all I know, these could be the only copies. I don't think we should let the books out of our sight. Besides their age, which seems to be ancient, they could be priceless."

Gage nodded. "Yeah, Ari's right. We don't know what we have here."

They went back to perusing their individual books.

"Gage! Look at this!" Roman sat on the edge of the sofa.

Ari leaned in and looked across his arm; Gage kneeled and eyed the page.

"Shifters!" Gage all but shouted. "Look at the different types. We've got to find out if these are authentic findings, or if Grandpa was writing stories for his grandkids."

"Hadn't thought of that," Roman said.

"Me neither," Ari said. "I was drawn to them when I saw them on the table at the estate sale; had to have them. Maybe something was telling me to get them for the future."

Gage pressed a sloppy kiss on her mouth.

"This is the most excited I've ever been about a book," Roman said. "We should try to scan just this page to see if we can get it translated."

Gage stood. "I'll get the hand scanner." He took off at a jaunt toward his suite. He returned with a dual-functionality scanner.

The long, flat device was designed to have paper fed into it through a slot, or to be run across a page on a flat surface.

"Should I choose PDF or JPG?" Gage asked.

"Why don't we experiment with both?" Ari said. "Chinese characters may be tricky."

Gage pressed the power button and then keyed in a choice. The bottom of the device lit up with a bright light. He placed the scanner at the top of the page and pushed it down the page. He pressed another button and repeated the process.

"Let's go see what we've got," he said.

Roman and Ari followed Gage to his home office.

Gage flipped out a USB device and separated it from the scanner. He stuck it into his computer and brought up the directory of files and folders. He clicked on the PDF file.

The first line was a little fuzzy, but the rest of the page was as clear and unblemished as the original page in the book. Gage clicked on the JPG. It was also clean.

"Wow, what a great little device! Should we try Google Translator?" Ari asked.

Gage opened a tab on his MacBook Pro and pulled up the page. He had to search the screen to find where to upload a file instead of typing in a word or phrase.

They discovered that Grandpa definitely was not making up stories for the kiddos. The information detailed the shifters. If they could scan the complete set of books, they might learn the origin of their kind.

"Wow. This is mind-blowing," Roman said as he read the scanned text.

Man and beast share skin and souls. Jump from skin of man to skin of animal. Skin of animal to skin of man.

Little mouse unfolds to Sparkling Princess. Cave of bear-people. Men who become bears.

Yu the Great Xia Dynasty

Three Sovereigns and Five Emperors

He pointed out a word that seemed garbled. "Only a couple of glitches on this page. I'm impressed with that scanner."

"We'll have to take the books apart and feed them into a

regular scanner," Ari said. "Otherwise, hand scanning will take a long time."

"For now, we can continue to look at the pictures until we get that worked out," Gage said.

He thumped her thigh. "Why don't we get packed so we can leave early?"

Roman returned his book to the box in Ari's study. He grabbed their books from the living room and added them to the box. Roman carried the box to the foyer and set it on the floor.

He returned to Ari's room. She was pulling things out of her dresser and placing them into a weekend bag.

"Is it cooler there? I'm trying to determine what type of clothes to pack," she asked.

"Bring a pair of jeans, leggings, and shorts," Roman said. "Same thing with tops. Sleeveless, short, and long sleeves. Tennis shoes and sandals, and a light jacket or hoodie."

He pulled her into his arms and kissed her passionately until she opened her mouth to him. His hands were in her hair and then down her back. He roamed over her ass, squeezing the firm flesh. Her body was gaining definition as her workouts at the gym paid off.

"I don't know what I love more. Your hair, your ass or your clit," Roman said.

"No discrimination. I want you to love all of me," Ari said between kisses. She was blazing with desire.

She pressed her hand against his chest. "Okay, buddy. Put a cork in it. Let me finish packing. You go pack. We can play later."

He grabbed her hand and placed it on the front of his jeans. "But I've got this giant boner."

"I seriously doubt if he won't show up again in, say, an hour?" she teased.

Gage wandered into the room. He pressed into Ari's back. "You started without me."

Ari squeezed out from between them. "Listen, you bad boys, let me finish getting my gear ready for tomorrow. You can hold off for an hour, can't you?"

She playfully glared at them.

Isabel chose that moment to strut into Ari's room and jump on the bed.

Gage hesitantly reached out to her. She sniffed his fingertips and let him stroke the top of her head.

"What a good girl." He tried to run his hand down her back, but she hissed and arched at him.

Please don't be mad at me, Isabel. I'm sorry I called you stupid. I was stressed.

"Okay. I get it—too much, too soon."

"Progress," Ari said. She stroked Isabel. The cat's purr was loud.

"Now you guys run along while I pack."

ARI'S BAG sat on the floor by the door to her suite. She ran the shower in her bathroom and stepped into the glass stall. Roman and Gage joined her, both naked and ready.

They entered the stall and Ari turned her face upward to receive the spray. She reached out to each of the men and grabbed hold of their cocks and stroked them. They were thick and long, and she loved the way they filled her.

"Me first," Gage said. "You always hog her." He lifted Ari above his cock and lowered her onto his shaft.

"Do not," Roman said. He ran his palm over the cheeks of her ass, then reached around and rubbed her sensitive nub as Gage controlled the rhythm of his thrusts.

Ari was soon screaming out with her orgasm. She clamped her hand over Roman's hand between her and Gage.

"Stop, Roman!" She whined from the sensitivity.

Gage quickened his thrusts and let his load blow into her.

He held her close and buried his face into her neck. "Oh, Ari."

He released her, and she slid down his body until her feet touched the floor.

They soaped each other and rinsed. Roman wrapped her in a towel and grabbed one for her hair. He dried her off, then himself, and led her to the bed.

CHAPTER SIX

THEY PILED the grocery cart with meat and vegetables, fruit, and snack items. Ari recalled what Gage said about their animals burning through calories. There were several packages of rib eyes, roasts, and chicken. She didn't think they'd go hungry.

"What about drinks?" she asked.

"The wine cellar is stocked, as well as the bar," Roman said.

Ari raised a brow. "Okay. I guess I'll see when we get there."

Roman kissed her on the nose. "You're so cute when you're curious."

She swatted him.

Gage dumped fish, shrimp, lobster tails, scallops, and crab claws into the cart. "If I remember correctly, the freezer is low."

"Do you have ice cream?" she asked. Her eyes twinkled with mischief.

Gage disappeared toward the freezer section while Roman steered the cart in that direction.

BONDED   69

"Do they have pistachio?" Ari asked. "If not, get butter pecan."

They added several gallons to the bulging cart along with ice cream bars.

As they left the freezer section, Roman grabbed a couple of cans of whipped cream.

Gage smirked.

Ari elbowed him in the ribs. "Honestly!"

Roman pushed the cart to a checkout counter, and he and Gage unloaded everything onto the conveyor belt.

The final bill was staggering. It was more than Ari had spent in two months in her previous life, and she had spent a lot on organic food.

The guys helped the sacker. They loaded up the cart again and headed out to the large, black, custom Yukon Denali SUV. It had a full front row of three seats. Unlike other vehicles of its kind, the console ran along the dashboard instead of separating the two front bucket seats.

They placed the ice cream and other meltable items in ice chests in the back for the long drive.

Ari ran her hand over the butter-soft black leather seats. "I love this vehicle."

"It's my favorite of all our vehicles," Gage said.

They buckled up, and Gage navigated through the city and hit the highway. He ramped up to eighty mph, passing many slower vehicles.

Two and a half hours later, he turned off the highway into the forest. The two-lane paved road curved like a continuous 'S'. After several miles, Gage turned right onto what looked like a wide dirt trail with signs posting Private Road.

Ari's eyes bounced from front to the right then to the left. "I'll never find this cabin on my own."

As the words left her mouth, Gage pulled the SUV up to a

house that left Ari speechless. After she found her tongue again, she unbuckled her seatbelt.

"Cabin? Who called this a cabin?"

"Okay, house in the woods," Roman said. "Come on, let's get the food into the house."

THEY STOCKED the Wolf refrigerator and freezer.

Ari folded the paper sacks, and Roman showed her where to stash them. She loved the kitchen. It even had refrigerator drawers for the produce on the island. She liked the convenience.

Ari walked to one of the floor-to-ceiling windows and stared out into the forest. It mesmerized her with the quiet surrounding the house and the beauty of the trees. There was minimal need for landscaping when you had this wonderful view.

Roman slid his arm around her waist. Gage joined them at the window.

"Beautiful, isn't it? I fell in love with it fifty years ago when Roman carried me here after a hunter shot me down with an arrow. It always has the same effect on me when I arrive after a long time," Gage said.

"I may not want to leave," Ari said.

"Wait until you see the rest of the house," Roman said. "We had everything modernized and upgraded five years ago."

"We may have to tie you up and drag you to the SUV," Gage said.

Downstairs comprised of a large kitchen, the butler's pantry where the washer and dryer were, an immense living room, a dining room, and a small bedroom. There was a half-bath off the living room. It was the largest Ari had ever seen for just a sink and toilet.

The upstairs bedrooms were even more luxurious than in the penthouse apartment. Each bathroom had a large soaking tub and a shower stall with multiple spray nozzles along the wall and ceiling. There was also a sauna in an alcove in the hall that accommodated six.

They tromped downstairs and Roman prepared a marinade for steaks.

Gage brought in their luggage and deposited it upstairs in the first bedroom. He returned to the SUV and hauled in the box of books. He set the box on the coffee table.

Roman placed the dish with the marinating meat in the refrigerator.

"Ari, would you mind if we shifted? We might be gone for a couple of hours."

She squeezed his upper arm. "Let your animals loose."

The guys shed their clothes, and they all walked to the sliding glass doors.

Roman unlocked the door, and they stepped outside onto the flagstones.

"Stay indoors and lock the doors. We have a hidden key, so we'll let ourselves in," Roman said. "Tomorrow we'll go for a walk through the woods, but for now, stay here and get comfortable with the house."

Roman and Gage walked a few feet away. They parted company and looked at her one last time.

Then they shifted.

"Have a good time. I'm going to take a nap." She retreated to the house.

Roman turned and looked at her.

Something sounded in her head. She stopped at the sliding glass doors and turned to the animals.

"Did you say something to me? I didn't make it out. Try again," Ari said.

Roman stared intently.

I love you, Ari.

"I love you too," Ari said. "Be safe."

Gage opened his wings and leaped into the air. His twenty-five-foot wingspan lifted him off the ground.

Ari shielded her eyes as she watched him glide into the sky above the treetops. "Oh, Gage! I wish I had your wings!"

He squawked loudly.

Roman ran into the trees.

Ari stood outside for a few minutes, listening. The forest had quieted down. She assumed the forest creatures felt a predator. Ari went inside and locked the door behind her.

She gathered their discarded clothes, climbed the stairs and hung them in the closet, then unpacked their bags. Ari came downstairs, eyed the sofa, and stretched out for a nap.

A NOISE JARRED her back to consciousness. She stayed still, trying to determine what it was.

A clink-clink sounded against glass.

She lifted her head and noticed the kitchen light was on. Ari got up and sauntered into the kitchen to find Roman, still naked, tending to the steaks.

"Hey gorgeous. Did you have a good nap?"

"I did. Has Gage returned?"

"Not yet. I detected human scents in the woods. Gage is searching from the sky to see if he can discover anyone camping," Roman said. "The property is posted private, so no one should be within miles of the house."

"Should we be worried?" Ari asked.

"Don't know. Probably just someone hiking. I detected two different traces about a mile back. I walked around the house, and my cat didn't pick up any strange scents here," Roman said.

A loud screech outside announced Gage's return.

Roman walked to the sliding door and stepped outside, followed by Ari.

Gage's head turned this way and that. He wasn't shifting back, so Ari figured he saw something he didn't like and was reporting to Roman.

She heard nothing in her head. Roman walked Ari back to the house.

"Lock the door. Stay inside, out of sight. There's two men headed this way with guns. There's a loaded gun between the mattress and headboard. Do you know how to turn off the safety?"

"I'm sure I can figure it out," she said. Her stomach lurched.

"Get the gun. Always be ready for the worst," Roman said. He kissed her, shifted and ran into the forest.

Ari hurried inside, locked the door, and took to the stairs. She ran into the bedroom and felt between the mattress and the headboard. She found the gun.

It was heavy.

She found the safety button and flicked it off.

She crept over to the window, approaching it from the side. Her eyes searched through the trees.

Ari spotted a glint of something. She wondered if someone was watching the house with binoculars.

A loud screech sounded overhead, and she knew Gage was close by.

She focused her mind.

Do you see anyone? I saw something shiny—maybe some-one's watching the house with binoculars.

Ari didn't know if either of her men heard her. She tried to project her words loudly to carry out, but since this was a new experience, she wasn't sure of anything.

Two men—they are trying to keep under cover, so we can assume they want to get into the house. Shoot first, Ari. Never hesitate, Gage sent.

Be careful. You could get killed, she sent.

Ari shook with fear. She saw movement at the edge of the trees.

Strangers approached, holding handguns.

Roman let out a vicious growl that reverberated through the forest.

The hair stood up on Ari's arms.

She watched as Roman leaped on the man closest to the trees.

A gun fired.

Gage screeched from the sky.

He descended, talons outstretched. He grabbed the second man's outstretched arm.

The gun fell to the ground.

The animals subdued both men.

Ari, come outside with the gun. Get their weapons, Roman sent.

Ari ran down the stairs and unlocked the door. She launched herself outside and approached the men.

"Don't move, if you want to live."

She grabbed their guns, made sure the safeties were on, and tossed them toward the house.

Fear filled the stranger's eyes.

"What are you doing here? This is private property that's posted very clearly," Ari said.

"We were just hiking in the woods," the man in the blue shirt said.

"Yeah, I bet. You always approach a house with your weapon drawn?" Ari asked. "I'll bet you're lying, so let's try again, or my animals will have you for a snack."

Both men cringed.

Roman growled low in his throat.

Gage pecked at his guy's foot. His large, powerful beak pierced through the man's work boot.

The guy screamed in terror.

"We just saw your house the other day and didn't know anyone lived here," Blue Shirt said.

"You honestly think a house like this just sits here empty?" Ari was getting mad. "If you assumed it was empty, explain why you returned with guns."

The man in the plaid shirt squirmed an inch away from Gage.

Gage snatched the guy's ankle in his beak.

"If you want that ankle, you'd better not move, and you'd better explain," she said.

Ari, go inside; call Sherm. Tell him what's going on.

Grab our clothes and put them by the back door, Roman said.

Ari nodded. "You two stay put."

She ran to the house, stopping to pick up the guns and let herself inside. Ari launched herself up the stairs and grabbed her purse. She found her new cellphone and discovered it had all the Wi-Fi bars. Ari found Sherm's number.

The rep from the Apple store must have loaded company contact information on her phone. She was grateful.

She hit Sherm's name.

Sherm answered after two short rings. "Well, hello Ari, bored already?"

Ari blurted out the situation.

"Stay calm. We'll be there shortly," Sherm said and disconnected the call.

Next, Ari pulled together jeans, t-shirts, briefs, socks, and tennis shoes.

She raced down the stairs and quietly opened the back door and placed the clothes on a table near a huge grill.

Sherm said he'd be here shortly. Your clothes are at the back door.

Ari returned to the men outside.

Roman rubbed up against her and then stared at her. "Go hunt," she told him.

The gigantic cat growled into the blue shirt's face, then launched himself into the trees.

A few minutes later, Roman ran around the corner of the house, dressed. He approached Ari, retrieved the gun from her and waved the gun at the plaid-shirt guy.

"You, over here with your buddy," Roman said.

Gage pressed his beak down on the guy's ankle before letting go.

Plaid shirt guy screamed. He scurried over to his friend.

Gage took to the sky.

Ari heard a helicopter approaching.

"They'll land in the clearing," Gage said as he joined them, fully dressed.

He cradled his arm around Ari protectively.

The helicopter landed. The rotors shut down.

Several pairs of feet thundered in their direction.

The newcomers broke through the trees, Sherm in the lead.

Ari held a poker face as if this was an everyday occurrence. Commandos in full gear decked out to head into war—at her beck and call.

The trespassers were wide-eyed.

Sherm barked orders.

"Miller, secure these two. Garcia, take the team and find their vehicle." He turned to Roman. "Which direction did they come from?"

The commando named Miller and a team member used military zip-type handcuffs on the two stranger's hands and ankles.

Roman pointed them in the direction where they had emerged from the trees. "That way, Sherm."

Sherm nodded to his team. "Miller, you stay behind and keep an eye on these two."

"I've got their weapons inside," Ari said.

Roman slid his arm across her shoulder and kissed the side of her head. "You okay?"

"Yeah. A little shook up, but I'm fine."

"Want a beer?" Gage asked Sherm.

"Yeah, a beer sounds good. Miller, you want a brew?" Sherm asked.

"I'll never turn down a cold beer," Miller said.

Gage, Roman, Ari, and Sherm entered the house.

Sherm looked over the handguns from the coffee table.

"A Hudson H9 and a SAR 9. These guys aren't your run-of-the-mill rednecks hiking through the woods, buddies," Sherm said. "These weapons mean *purpose*."

Gage went to the kitchen and returned with two beers. He handed one to Sherm and handed the other off to Miller outside.

"Send their pictures to Lonnie."

Miller took out his cell and snapped pictures. Gage came back inside.

Ari stared at Sherm. "I hardly recognize you, Sherm." He winked at her.

CHAPTER SEVEN

THE COMMANDO'S returned to the house. The lead guy slid the glass door open and stepped inside.

"Found a pickup truck. Derek's driving it back to the shop so we can go over it."

Sherm's phone dinged an incoming message. He clicked and opened the message.

Two photos and details appeared.

Roman, Gage and Ari surrounded Sherm's phone.

Matt Pendleton, blue shirt, worked at a lumber store. He had been a Boy Scout. Divorced. Two kids. Drowning in child support.

Joe LaThompse, plaid shirt guy, was an engineer with the power company. Married. Three kids under the age of twelve.

"These yahoos both have subscriptions to gun magazines and a couple of adventurous story magazines about mercenaries and spies," Sherman said. "They're lucky they didn't accidentally kill each other."

"What are you going to do with them?" Roman asked.

"We'll take them back to the shop, shoot them up with

some truth serum and see what the hell they were thinking," Sherm said. "Not sure if they had a plan. Who knows what they intended if they broke into the house?"

"Are you going to bring the police in?" Gage asked.

"I'll see where the interrogation leads, and if interesting intel crops up. Derek will tear the truck apart. If it comes up clean, we'll let them go with a warning," Sherm said.

They headed out the sliding glass doors.

Sherm signaled to his team to grab the men and head back to the chopper.

Ari placed her hand on his arm. "Thanks so much."

"That's what these guys pay me for," Sherm said. He tipped his head toward Roman and Gage.

"You could have fooled me. I thought you were a computer geek," Ari said.

"Sherm's multifaceted," Gage said.

"Yeah, and deadly," Roman added.

Sherm grinned.

ARI, Roman and Gage returned to the house. The helicopter took off in the distance.

"I'm going to hit the shower," Roman said.

"Yeah, good idea," Gage said.

"I'm heading for the bar," Ari said.

The guys headed upstairs, and Ari took off to the kitchen. She perused the bottles, selected one and uncorked it.

Ari pulled the marinating steaks out of the refrigerator so they could come to room temperature. Then she grabbed salad fixings and two huge potatoes and a smaller one for herself.

She assumed the guys would be ravenous after their after-noon adventures.

Roman padded down the stairs, barefoot, in jeans, shirt-less with damp hair.

He wrapped his arms around her and licked her lips.

Ari opened her mouth to him and their tongues merged. They ended with a chaste kiss while he ran his hands down her sides.

Roman rested his forehead against hers.

"I don't know what I'd do if anything happened to you," he said.

"Everything's okay," she said. "Don't go getting all maudlin on me."

Gage came into the kitchen and sandwiched into Ari's back.

His hair dripped onto her.

"Gage! Get a towel and dry your hair." She giggled.

"It'll dry outside," he said.

He shook his hair and sprayed Ari and Roman.

Water dripped down Gage's bare chest and disappeared into his cutoffs.

Ari had a moment. She ran her hands over his well-formed chest down and across his six-pack abs. She caught herself before she licked him.

Gage and Roman were ready to engage. They'd never say no to her advances—ever. Wasn't going to happen.

"Sorry. Food first. Ignore me." She shook her head at her actions. She glared at them to halt their thoughts where they were.

"Focus on food!"

The guys grabbed a beer and Ari poured her wine and they headed outside.

"You've gotten into much better shape working out," Gage said. "I think you should work with Sherm on some self-defense tactics."

"Good idea," Roman said. "Let's throw in some weapons training. After today, there's no telling what situation may come up, and I want you to be prepared to defend yourself."

"How are your bones? Do you have osteoporosis?" Gage asked.

"I'm sure I've lost a bit of bone density because of my sedentary life," Ari said.

"Why don't you schedule a bone density scan?" Gage said. "That way Sherm will be aware of any problems and he'll create a safe level of training to start you with so you don't get hurt."

Ari's phone dinged a message. She glanced at her phone. "Oh, no. Kevin was downsized."

She fretted over her youngest son.

"We should be able to find a place for him," Roman said. "He installs cable, right?"

"Yes, he wires offices and things," Ari said. "He's the quiet one, so I don't know details about what he does."

"Send him my phone number and tell him to call me next week," Roman said.

Ari got busy texting her son.

"Fire up that grill, Roman," Gage said. "I could eat a horse!"

THE SCREEN across the open sliding glass doors let in the cool night air.

They lounged in the living room turning pages in their ancient books.

Ari wore a white thigh-length jersey tank and tiny white lace panties.

The guys sprawled in pajama pants while sipping their drinks.

Gage sat up. "Come look at this!"

Ari crawled across the sofa and Roman got up and sat on the other side of Gage.

They stared at the sequence of sketches that took up the entire page. Pictures showed a baby, a toddler, a boy, a teen, then a young man, and finally, a wolf.

There was also a sketch of a pregnant woman, and a wolf nursing pups.

"What does this mean?" Ari asked. "This is so frustrating because we can't read the text."

"I don't see the significance," Gage said. "Does this mean that the woman is a female wolf and she gives birth to wolf cubs?"

"I wonder if the boy has to be a certain age before he turns," Roman said. "He looks around twenty in that last picture. That's how old I was when I shifted for the first time."

Ari scooted away, picked up her book and placed it on the coffee table. "I'm going to bed. This day has worn me out. Maybe I need special energy?" She raised her eyebrows at them.

Gage shut the door and locked up. They trotted upstairs to the first bedroom they'd settled in earlier when they arrived. Ari crawled onto the bed and flopped down in the middle. A warm body joined her on each side.

"When do you think Sherm will let you know about those men?" Ari asked.

"Tomorrow morning," Gage said. "It doesn't take long to interrogate or go over a vehicle."

"Don't worry about it," Roman said as he nuzzled her neck.

Ari turned to him and they kissed. "Mmmm," she murmured as the kiss deepened.

She turned to Gage, and they kissed. His lips devoured hers. They parted.

"Hurry!" Ari said with need.

Gage slipped his pants off and kneeled on the bed. He hooked his thumbs into Ari's panties and slid them down her legs and tossed them on the floor. "Me first," Gage said.

Roman lifted his butt off the bed and slid out of his pants. Gage's head was between Ari's legs.

Ari's fingers grabbed Gage's hair. "Ohhh! That's what I need!"

"I have other plans," Roman said with a devious smile. He grabbed pillows, leaned Ari's torso forward and propped her up against them.

He straddled her chest and presented his cock to her mouth.

She released her hands from Gage's hair and wrapped her hand around Roman's thick shaft and she licked the pre-cum off the head.

Roman kept his weight off her as she slid her tongue and mouth up and down and all around his throbbing cock.

"Ari!" Roman gasped. He slowly pumped into her mouth, one hand on the top of her head.

Gage sucked her sweet spot and worked two fingers inside her.

Ari stiffened her legs as she pulled her mouth off Roman's cock and moaned. Her hand found Roman's slick shaft, and she stroked him.

A long whine turned into a screaming orgasm. Roman got up and slid down to lie beside Ari. He sucked on one nipple then the other, teasing it with his tongue while Ari bucked into Gage's mouth.

THE ROOM beyond the gym held the dojo where Sherm and his team kept in shape.

Sherm instructed Ari in the correct stance as they moved through several exercises. Most of the time, Ari ended up on the floor and Sherm looked a little too happy.

Ari got to her feet and brushed herself off. "Just wait, Sherm. One of these days payback will be hell."

"Looking forward to it!"

CHAPTER EIGHT

FIVE BLISSFULLY HAPPY YEARS PASSED. As they celebrated Ari's seventy-fifth birthday at Pomodoro's, Jason voiced a startling observation.

"You know what, Mom?" he said as he tucked a wisp of hair behind her ear. "I realize we've got great genetics, but I swear it seems like you're getting younger, not older."

"Cut it out, Jase," Ari said. She leaned into him and pushed his shoulder.

Roman, Gage, and Kevin studied her face. "Nah, she's just not wrinkling," Roman said.

"It's all the workouts and eating right," Gage said. "You two have something to look forward to."

Kevin worked with Sherm's group. His cabling skills morphed into everything electronic, not just wiring. He traveled with the team across the globe, doing things his mother would never approve of. She didn't need to know about his special talents. He could break into any safe, eavesdrop on anyone with high-tech equipment, or route a phone call or email to wherever the team needed it to go.

Jason had a head for people and business. Roman had paired him with Sandy Turner, and she showed him the ropes. In the four years he had been with the firm, he excelled at everything he did. He had replaced the obsessed Celeste within two years.

Even though her old friendships drifted apart, Ari never felt lonely. Her days were filled with her men, her sons, and the friends she made within the company.

Ari adored Sherm and spent many hours in his domain. She loved finding the secrets in cooked books their company was hired to investigate.

"Let's go get ice cream," Roman suggested. He stood and pulled Ari's chair back.

"I've got to get back to work," Kevin said.

"You realize I can give you a 'get out of work' pass," Gage joked.

"I promised someone I'd help her." Kevin blushed a deep red.

Jason poked his brother. "That's code for *I'd better run to the drugstore and get some condoms before Amanda and I go at it.*"

"Jason!" Ari stormed. "Don't be so crude and don't give your brother's secrets away so publicly."

She turned to Kevin, leveling her eyes at him. "You have a girlfriend?"

Kevin blushed deeper. "We've been seeing each other for a couple of months."

"We guess her name is Amanda?" Roman asked.

"Gaa! The inquisition!" Kevin said.

Gage threw an arm across Kevin's shoulders. "It's okay. We love you. Go see your girl."

"Bring her home sometime so we can meet her," Roman said. "I'll bet she's cute."

Ari's sons left.

Kevin socked Jason in the arm as they left the restaurant. "Ow!" Jason rubbed his arm.

The server cleared the table. Gage signaled for the check.

He turned to Ari. "Jason has a point. You don't appear to be aging—at all."

"How is that possible?" Ari asked.

"I'm not sure. Maybe we're rubbing off on you," Gage said with a wide grin.

They finished their wine and Roman paid the server.

Gage left a generous tip on the table and they left the restaurant.

While they weren't married, Roman and Gage had presented Ari with a set of rings on their first anniversary.

She rarely removed the white gold band, and the three entwined diamond hearts on another band, even doing dishes or bathing.

No one questioned their relationship with raised eyebrows anymore, but a few tongues had waggled when Ari started wearing the rings.

Two years ago, she donated a foot of her hair for a hair drive for wigs to benefit cancer patients. She thought Gage would cry, but her hair grew back to her waist, and she promised him she'd never do that again.

They walked next door to the ice cream parlor.

ARI PUT her purse in her room and joined Roman in the living room.

He was stretched out on the sofa with his feet on the coffee table.

Gage walked into the room holding a photo album. He plunked down on the sofa and Ari wiggled in between them.

Gage put the album in Ari's lap and opened to the first page of photos. His neat handwriting showed the date when they met five years earlier.

As Ari flipped through the pages, she recalled many of the situations captured in pictures. They laughed and joked as they flipped through the book.

About midway through, Ari sobered. "I look the same," she said.

She contemplated for a minute. "My mother didn't start to wrinkle until she was sixty-eight or seventy, then it seemed like she aged ten years overnight."

Roman took the album and flipped back several pages, then forward. He picked up his phone and took a picture of her.

"I would have to agree with Jason. You appear to be reversing your age. You seem younger now than you did two years ago. Look here."

He flipped the pages to their third year together and held his phone with the picture he just took beside a photo in the book.

Ari jumped up and hurried to the bathroom. She turned on the light and stared into the mirror, touching her face.

Roman and Gage joined her and all three leaned toward the mirror.

"This may be the stupidest thing I've ever thought or said out loud, but what if when we come inside you something happens?" Roman shrugged at the absurdity of what he said.

"That sounds rather science fiction-like, but we're approaching one hundred," Gage said. "How are we supposed to figure this out? It's not like we can go to a doctor who specializes in shifters and weird genetics."

"There are scientists who specialize in genetic oddities. I wouldn't suggest it because we'd end up as the government's lab rats," Ari said. "We can't afford to have anyone document these things. I feel guilty that my own sons don't know about you two."

"We should tell them," Roman said.

Gage fidgeted. "We should wait for the right situation."

"It's been five years. What situation are we waiting for?" Roman asked.

"I'm not sure," Ari said. "Don't you think that would make things awkward? Especially after today's conversation?"

"Well, it's coming," Roman said. "They're grown men."

ARI WORKED out with Sherm in the dojo. She easily threw him to the mats... fast, calculating every move.

He grinned, nodding. "Think you're something else, huh?" Sherm caught her off guard with his fancy footwork, flips and what seemed like impossible acrobatics. In a blink, she was on her back.

"Don't look so smug. One of these days I'm going to catch up," she said.

"Go change. Let's head over to the gun range," Sherm said. "I want you to practice with the shotgun some more."

THE NEXT DAY Ari kissed Roman then Gage. "I'm going across the street. I'll be back in an hour." She grabbed her purse and her empty canvas book bag.

"I'll be downstairs. Jason has some papers I have to approve," Roman said.

"I'm taking a nap," Gage said. He hunkered down on the sofa.

Ari and Roman got in the elevator and left the penthouse.

Roman kissed her goodbye at the thirtieth floor and Ari continued the descent to the ground floor.

Alex, the doorman, opened the front door for her. "Morning, Miss Ari," Alex said. "Supporting the bookstore today?"

"You bet, Alex. Someone has to keep the mom and pop stores alive," Ari said.

She stood at the curb and waited for walk signal, and for traffic to clear between cycles of the traffic lights.

A white van screeched to the curb. Ari hollered and jumped back a little.

The side door slid open with a loud slam.

Arms grabbed Ari and hauled her inside. She screamed as she grabbed a hold of the doorframe then kicked viciously at her abductor.

"HELP! Someone call the police! Help, police!" Alex yelled.

Alex pulled a gun out of his uniform and shot at the van. Glass flew.

The van screeched away.

Alex pulled his phone out and frantically pressed buttons.

"Mr. Gage! Miss Ari's been kidnapped!" Alex yelled into the phone. "I'll call the cops."

Alex fumbled with the keys and got 9-1-1 on the phone and reported the incident.

THE VAN SCREECHED AWAY from the curb.

Ari's arms flailed as she was dragged into the vehicle and the door slammed shut.

ROMAN! GAGE! HELP ME!

She stomped down on her assailant's foot, rammed her elbow into his ribs and grabbed him around his neck.

A bullet came through the back window and nicked her shoulder making her slack on her grip.

The fifty-year-old man slugged her in the face, threw her to the floor and leaped on top of her.

Ari attempted to flip him, but couldn't dislodge him. She rammed her heel into the back of his calf.

He grunted in pain, stretched for a white cloth on the floor and shoved it over her mouth and nose. "Go to sleep, you whoring bitch!"

Ari tried to hold her breath and fight him off, but the ether-soaked cloth knocked her out.

GAGE, Roman and Sherm stampeded out of the door.

Sherm barked orders into the phone. "Grab all cameras in a five-mile radius. Try to track that white van. Have someone look for anyone who has shown any interest in Ari for the past week. Same with the satellites."

Alex, gun still in hand, snatched Ari's book bag from the side of the road.

"Do you see her purse?" Gage asked. He looked around, frantic.

Ari! Can you hear me? Where are you? Gage sent.

"I tried to hit the driver, but my nerves were wrecking," Alex said. He removed his doorman's hat and wiped his brow.

"Did you hit the van anywhere?" Roman asked.

ARI! Ari! Roman sent.

"Yeah, back right window," Alex said. He holstered his gun.

He pressed buttons on his phone. "Got a partial picture of the license plate."

Alex pulled up the picture.

They saw HV8 along with the driver's side of the white van with a little dent at the quarter panel.

Cop cars screeched to the curb along with an unmarked black car. They piled out of their cars.

"Alex, send the picture to Lonnie," Sherm took charge. "Find out where those two guys are from the cabin incident," Roman said. "Could be they weren't as innocent as you thought."

Jason came running out the door, breathing hard. "Kevin texted me someone kidnapped Mom!"

Gage paced on the sidewalk as a crowd drew near. He approached Jason and put his arms around him. "It's going to be okay. We'll get her back."

Roman joined them while Sherm dealt with the police. "The team's trying to track the van. Alex got a picture—a partial picture of the license plate. The cops will put an APB out, but we'll most likely find it and her before they do."

ARI! Gage and Roman sent.

Kevin flew out of the building. "Why's everyone standing around? Shouldn't you be looking for that van?"

Sherm placed a hand on Kevin's shoulder. "Think of this as one of your assignments, Kev. Calm the fuck down. Lonnie and the guys are examining every camera in the area, and they're checking the satellites."

Kevin let out a breath, then joined his brother.

CHAPTER NINE

JASON FREAKED OUT. "Why would someone want to kidnap Mom? She's seventy-five for fuck's sake!"

"Doesn't appear to be planned. How could anyone know your mom was going over to the bookstore across the street unless they could read her mind?" Gage asked. "It seems like a random opportunity."

Sherm approached them. "Lonnie said it wasn't those two guys in the woods."

"What guys in the woods?" Jason asked.

Roman filled Jason and Kevin in about the house in the woods.

"How come you never told us?" Jason asked, furious.

Gage fumed.

His anger spiked.

Gage snarled. "If either of you would take the time to call your mother, you'd get details. It's not like you've got after-work family duties. Neither of you is married with kids."

Roman's nerves were shot.

He jumped into the finger-pointing. "You two don't give a

shit about anything but yourselves. Would it kill you to text her a good morning every day? Maybe call at least once a week?"

Sherm got between the four of them and pushed each faction away from each other.

"Look, this *woulda, coulda, shoulda* crap isn't doing anyone any good right now. The cops have the picture of the van. They've got Ari's picture. We've got the cameras and satellites being monitored. The cops put out an APB. There's not much more we can do. We're going through the DMV searching the database for the license plate."

Gage sucked in a deep breath and exhaled. "Can you track her phone, Sherm?"

"Only if it's turned on," he said.

"She took it off the charger before she left, but I don't know if she turned it on," Roman said.

A detective and a police officer approached.

"This is Detective Valk. He needs to talk to all four of you," Sherm said. "Why don't you go inside?"

Detective Valk nodded to the four. "Can we go somewhere quiet?"

They went inside, and Roman slid his cardkey into the slot, and they rode up to the penthouse.

Detective Valk took in the living room with his eyes. "Nice setup, but aren't you worried about unauthorized access to your living quarters?"

Gage explained about the app on the cellphone.

"If they've got Ms. Davis' cellphone and cardkey, they have access to your space," Valk said.

"I'll get the cardkeys and the app reprogrammed," Sherm said.

He texted Lonnie.

A few minutes later George, a team member, arrived via the elevator.

Roman and Gage handed over their cardkeys.

"George can go into the elevator app and change the code." Sherm said as he nodded to George.

"Sure thing, boss. I'll text you guys the new code," George said. He turned around, got into the elevator, and rode back down to the twenty-eighth floor.

Gage herded everyone over to the living room. He sat on the long sofa before he fell down from the shock of losing Ari.

Roman sat beside him and Kevin and Jason filled up the rest of the sofa.

The detective sat opposite while the cop stood nearby. Sherm stayed in the foyer manning his phone.

"Arianna Davis is your mother?" Detective Valk asked the four.

"She's our mother," Jason said. He pointed to Kevin and himself.

Detective Valk turned his interest to Roman and Gage.

"Ari works for us. She's our personal assistant," Roman said.

"She lives here?" Detective Valk asked.

"Yes," Roman said.

"Isn't that a little unusual?" Valk asked.

"How's that?" Gage said. "A lot of housekeepers and personal assistants are live-ins."

"What exactly is her function here?" Valk pushed.

"She keeps track of us. Ari makes sure we get to our board meetings on time, she keeps us organized, and she cooks all our meals," Roman said.

"Do you sleep with her?" Detective Valk asked.

Gage jumped to his feet. "What the fuck does that have to do with her kidnapping?"

Oh great! You just had to dump us into that now? Roman sent.

Fuck, Gage sent.

Jason and Kevin were on their feet, enraged, fists ready to fly.

"You're sleeping with our mother?" Jason yelled. His facial features contorted through an entire display of shock and anger.

Kevin grabbed the front of Gage's shirt, ready to pound on him.

Roman pulled Kevin's hand free.

"Knock it off, Kevin!" Roman said. "Now's not the time."

"You fucking sick bastards. As soon as we find our mother, she's moving the hell out of here," Kevin said.

Sherm let out a huff, shook his head, and strode across the room.

"Enough! If I'm not mistaken, everyone in this room is over forty, and Ari is seventy-five."

He poked Jason in the chest. "It's your mother's business what she does and who she does it with, not yours. She seems pretty happy as far as I can tell. I'd advise you to ask her yourself when we find her. In the meantime, everyone sit the fuck down and shut the fuck up."

Detective Valk let out a little cough.

The cop teetered from heel to toe.

"May we continue?" Detective Valk asked. His eyes drilled into Jason and Kevin. "What is your father's name and whereabouts?"

"Thomas Davis," Jason said. "But it's spelled T O M O S."

"We don't have anything to do with him," Kevin blurted.

"Was he violent? Did he abandon the family?" Detective Valk asked.

"He's a first-class bastard," Jason said. "He beat our mother and us. She filed charges against him a half dozen times before she finally broke away from him."

Roman barely controlled his rage. "He lives in Philly, but lucky for him, I don't know the address."

Gage controlled his violent thoughts so he wouldn't shift.

Roman glanced at the boys, wondering how much he should divulge. He let out a whoosh of breath and met Valk's eyes. "Ari was married briefly before Tom."

"No, she wasn't! Our dad was her only husband!" Jason bellowed.

"She was very young, and it didn't last long. She didn't think it was relevant," Gage said.

THE WHITE VAN sped through the city. Dom, barely over twenty, clutched the wheel. He turned on his directional signal and took the next right turn.

"Slow down! We sure don't need to get stopped for speeding," Eddy said.

He glanced at Ari on the filthy floor of the van. She was out cold.

Dom took another right, then turned into a driveway with a high chain-link fence covered in ivy.

Eddy swung the door open and got out and closed the fence behind the van as it drove through. The fence concealed a ramshackle building from prying eyes due to the thick ivy.

Eddy walked behind the van.

Dom parked on the side of the building while Eddy brought out a set of keys. He unlocked a heavy-duty padlock on the door.

He opened the door and flipped on the lights, continuing to an inner door, also padlocked. He opened the door and lit the room.

It told a gruesome story. An old wooden plank floor stained with blood across a good portion of it.

Grimy ropes looped over large hooks on the wall.

Knives, hammers, pliers.

A shelf with dark brown bottles of some unknown liquid stood dust-free from many uses.

An inner padlocked door.

Eddy returned to the van. He grabbed Ari and slung her over his shoulder, and carried her into the inner room. He dropped her on the blood-stained floor, his face a mask of fury just below the surface.

"You fucking whore!" he screamed. Eddy kicked her in the ribs.

He paced in agitation and pulled at his short brown hair. "We'll see how much you like this."

He pulled off her shoes and threw them against the wall. Eddy yanked down her slacks and tossed them.

He grabbed her panties and tried to rip them off, leaving a red mark on her flesh.

Eddy pulled a pocketknife out of his back pocket and cut the panties off her, nicking her skin.

Then he pulled her shirt over her head and grabbed the front of her bra and sliced the material.

Eddy got up and walked over to a shelf where a dusty metal tube of around a half-inch in circumference and three inches long sat. It had tiny, biting spikes on the outside.

He stuck his finger in the spiked tube and grabbed a filthy speculum and returned to Ari.

"Open your cunt, whore," Eddy said.

He opened her legs and inserted the dirty speculum into her vagina and opened her up. He jammed the spiked tube inside her, then pulled out the speculum.

His insane laughter echoed off the walls as blood trickled between her legs.

"We're going to have such a good time," he said. His eyes sparkled with madness.

Dom came to the doorway. "Want to get lunch?"

AN HOUR AND A HALF LATER, Detective Valk and his shadow left the penthouse.

Jason, Kevin, and Sherm stayed behind. "What are we going to do?" Kevin asked.

He looked to Sherm, Roman and Gage for answers.

"We will track down that van, one way or the other," Sherm said. "Go back to work. Make yourselves useful. There's nothing else we can do at this point. We have to hope this is a kidnapping for ransom and wait for a call."

"I'll be on that call like a tick on a deer!" Kevin said. "Come on, Jase."

Kevin and Jason left.

Sherman turned to Roman and Gage. "Can you sense her?"

"She must be unconscious," Gage said. "I've called to her a thousand times."

Roman flopped down on the sofa and buried his face in his hands. "I pray to God they don't hurt her."

DOM AND EDDY walked to the deli, separated from the decrepit old building by a vacant lot. They went inside and ordered sandwiches.

Eddy looked down at his hands and walked to the bathroom to wash.

They ate their lunch at a rickety table and sipped root beer out of brown bottles.

ARI'S HEAD MOVED SLIGHTLY.

She moved a leg and screeched in agony. Blood spilled from her pelvic area.

Ari took in her surroundings, her nakedness. Her clothes against the wall, the rope and other things she could see from where she lay on the floor. Then she noticed the blood-red floor around her. She tried to move, and the internal pain almost knocked her out.

ROMAN! GAGE! HELP! HE'S GOING TO KILL ME!

Her hand touched her pelvis, and she wiped it across her labia. Her hand was bright red with blood. She stuck a finger into her vagina and felt the tube. She tried to trace around the circumference but was nicked by a spike.

"Oh my God, what have you done to me?" Ari's eyes were wild. She tried to roll to her hands and knees. She screamed in agony as the spikes dug into her vaginal walls.

The slightest movement hammered the spikes into her tender core.

ROMAN! GAGE! FIND ME!

"Please find me," she whimpered.

WHEN THEY FINISHED LUNCH, Dom gathered the two baskets. He dumped crusts and paper in the trash and stacked the baskets onto the pile on top of the trash receptacle.

They walked back to the building.

Eddy unlocked the gate and Dom locked it behind them.

Eddy unlocked the padlock and entered the first room. He heard her scream.

"Oh, good. Fun's about to begin," Eddy said.

Dom flopped down in a chair and played video games on his phone.

"GAGE!" Roman screamed. "Gage! I heard Ari! She's in pain! She said he's going to kill her!"

Gage came running from his room. "I'm going to try to track her."

"Take to the air. Try to find her!"

Gage stripped his clothes and shifted.

Roman opened the patio door. "I'll call Sherm. He'll have a team standing by."

Gage walked out to the patio on his thick legs, fluttered his wings and took to the air.

Roman contacted Sherm. He reiterated what they picked up from Ari and what they sensed. "Gage took off to try to find where she is."

"You let him fly from your patio? That's risky," Sherm said.

"Not much of a choice," Roman said. "I wish I could shift, but I don't think people would take too kindly to a half-insane panther running around the city."

"We'll be ready," Sherm said.

"WHAT DO YOU WANT?" Ari asked Eddy. She panted through the pain. "If you're looking for money, we can pay whatever you want—millions even!"

Eddy looked at her with pure evil in his eyes.

"You think I want your whoring money? No, you're going to pay with your blood."

He screamed the word *blood* like a maniac from Hell. Then he punched her in the face, arms, and ribs.

Ari grabbed for him, but screamed as the metal spikes dug into her.

He stomped on her shoulder.

ROMAN! GAGE! HURRY!

He wrapped her hair around his fist and dragged her around the room.

Ari screamed as blood poured from between her legs. Then she passed out.

ROMAN RAGED AS HE PACED. Ari's scream almost knocked him off his feet. He felt sick from pain.

He's hurting her! We've got to find her before he kills her!

Gage soared, his mind open. He mentally called out to Ari to no avail.

She must be out again. I haven't picked up on anything in the past ten minutes, but she's somewhere in the northeast. Find us somewhere we can set up base and monitor for her.

If anyone noticed the rather large eagle flying over the city, no one posted a video to social media or YouTube.

Roman took the elevator down to Sherm's office and passed along what they overheard and what Gage said. He paced, freaked out.

"I think that time has arrived. Kevin and Jason need to know about our animals. Get our special detail team together."

Sherm buzzed Lonnie. "Find us a low-end hotel on the northeast side of town. Get Bruce's team together. We'll move out as soon as everything's set up."

Lonnie understood the message. Bruce's team knew about the shifters. They were sworn to secrecy and paid well for their loyalty. Plus, they loved being around Roman's panther and Gage's eagle.

Ten minutes later, Sherm received a text.

Moonlight Hotel on Draper Street.

"Roman, grab Gage's clothes and meet us in the garage."

Sherm opened a closet and pulled on his commando gear. He stuffed guns and knives in their respective places.

THE MOONLIGHT HOTEL was a prime location for hookers, addicts, and the downtrodden. Beige bricks had mildewed over a decade earlier, which created an interesting pattern that wasn't unpleasant to look at.

The Pakistani clerk's eyes bulged when a geared-up Lonnie entered his establishment.

"I called about getting three rooms next to each other in the back," Lonnie said.

The clerk bobbed his head. "Eighteen, nineteen, and twenty. Are you army? Special forces? You pay ahead of time. You wreck the place, you pay!"

Lonnie counted out five hundred-dollar bills. He slid them across the counter to the clerk. "I'll pay per day."

The clerk pulled three keys off a pegboard on the wall behind him and handed them to Lonnie.

"There'll be a bonus if you keep your mouth shut. You never saw me, or anything else. You won't hear anything. Do we understand each other?"

The clerk took in Lonnie's size. His weapons. His big boots. He nodded.

Lonnie walked out the door to the black SUV. He opened

the passenger door, and they drove around to the back of the hotel. Lonnie stepped out of the vehicle and approached the door. He unlocked each room and swung the doors open.

"Better let 'em air out a minute."

Bruce's team piled out of another SUV. Six big brutes. Most with military backgrounds and special training. One was a former convict who now channeled his aggressiveness when it was required for the assignment.

Another SUV approached and parked. Roman, Sherm, Kevin and Jason got out.

"How do we know Mom's close by?" Kevin asked.

"You'll find out soon enough," Roman said.

He grabbed a weekend bag and walked to one of the open doors.

"Where's Gage?" Jason asked.

"He'll be here soon," Roman said.

Roman's eyes searched the sky. "Come on, we should go inside so we don't draw attention."

They filled the three small rooms.

CHAPTER TEN

KEVIN AND JASON sat on a lumpy love seat.

Roman tilted the mini-blinds and looked outside. "Gage's here," he said.

The door opened and Gage entered, naked.

"What the fuck?" Jason said. "Where's your clothes?"

Jason and Kevin did not notice that Lonnie and Sherm stood in back of the love seat where they sat.

"It's time you understood why your mother is with us. We're bonded to each other," Roman said.

"What the fuck is that all about?" Kevin asked.

Roman undressed.

"What the hell are you doing? Are you two going to get it on or something?" Jason asked.

His eyes bugged at the two men he thought he knew so well.

Jason attempted to stand.

Lonnie grabbed his shoulders and pushed him back onto the love seat.

"Don't move a muscle, understand?" Lonnie asked. "Watch."

Gage and Roman shifted.

Jason and Kevin tried to jump to their feet. Lonnie and Sherm restrained them.

"What the fuck?" Kevin yelled. "What just happened?"

Roman paced the small space. He snarled at Kevin and Jason. Gage shifted his head and stared down Kevin.

"When Roman said they were bonded, this is what it means. Roman and Gage are shifters. They bonded with your mom—and she bonded with them—immediately," Sherm said. "That's why she ran away to Mexico five years ago— she was as confused as they were. You could no more pull them apart unless you killed all three of them."

THE WOOD FLOOR had a fresh smear of blood. Ari was sprawled on her back, her hair soaking up blood.

Roman, Gage she barely whispered.

Eddy stood over her. "Whore! Whore! Whore!" he shouted with every kick and punch.

Blood flowed freely from between her legs.

ROMAN AND GAGE DRESSED.

Kevin and Jason sat, shocked into silence.

"I haven't heard her in the past half hour," Gage said.

He ran his hands through his hair, then down his anguished face.

"What do you mean?" Jason asked.

Roman sat on an overstuffed chair, his arms on his knees, head in his hands.

"Why can't we hear her? What have they done to her? What if she's dead?"

"Listen, I realize it sounds bad, but maybe they've drugged her and she's out," Sherm said. "You can't jump to conclusions. It's too soon."

"We are aware there's at least two of them," Lonnie said. "Someone driving the van and somebody else who dragged her inside. No one has made demands. You haven't had as much as a call from a telephone solicitor on the home phone. Nothings come through the company switchboard—everyone in the company is on high alert."

"They might be thinking of their options," Sherm said.

"Shh! I heard something!" Roman jumped to his feet and turned to Gage.

Gage stripped off his clothes and shifted. His eagle screeched.

Roman yanked the door open and Gage took to the air.

Kevin and Jason stampeded to the door and watched as Gage's eagle flew into the twilight sky.

"I can't fucking believe it," Jason said.

Kevin swung his attention to Roman. "You can hear our mom in your heads?"

Roman nodded. "It's part of the bonding. We never realized we could communicate with humans while we were in our animal forms until we bonded with Ari."

"Humans?" Kevin asked. He became pensive. "Yeah, I guess you two are definitely outside that category."

"Please, everyone be quiet so I don't miss something from Ari or Gage," Roman said.

He paced, frantic.

GAGE SOARED over the area intent on locating Ari. He picked up a tiny sound in his head and dove toward it.

There was a dilapidated structure. The white van was not present.

He landed on the roof of the place and listened. He picked up a whimper.

Roman! I found her! I'll lead the team here.

It tugged at his heart to have to take to the air, but he wasn't prepared to break in. He couldn't even tell them the street address.

His massive wings brought him back to the Moonbeam Hotel. He floated overhead as he witnessed the entire team getting into the vehicles.

"Tell Gage we'll try to track him and get GPS directions to the location," Sherm said.

They were the lead vehicle.

Roman's head was outside the passenger window.

Kevin and Jason hung out of the back windows watching the sky.

"He's flying east," Roman said.

"I wonder if he's over the place, or just waiting for us to catch up," Jason said.

The three black SUVs roared down the streets. "Slow down, it's right up ahead," Roman said.

They watched as Gage spiraled down behind the ivy-clad high fence. The SUVs piled into the driveway and stopped.

Everyone got out.

"The white van isn't here," Roman said.

"Okay, here's the plan. Get this gate unlocked. Make sure there's no telltale sign," Sherm said.

One of the guys approached the fence. He picked the lock and hung the padlock on the fence.

Two men opened the gate.

They drove the SUVs inside the gate and shut it behind them.

Gage fluttered down from the roof of the structure.

Roman returned to the vehicle and retrieved Gage's clothes.

"I don't detect anything now," Gage said.

Roman shook his head. "Me neither."

The same guy picked the lock on the front door.

"Gonzalez, you and Jones document every inch of the place," Lonnie said.

Gonzalez carried a Nikon 36-mega-pixel D800E camera, and Jones carried a high-end commercial-grade video camera.

They already started work documenting the exterior of the place.

"Jake, get your kits. You guys collect everything you can. The cops won't share with us," Lonnie said.

Lonnie dropped a case on the ground at the open door. "Listen up. Everyone grab gloves and booties. We can't contaminate the crime scene."

Lonnie rolled out clear plastic and covered the doorstep and five feet in either direction. He slipped on gloves and secured booties over his boots.

Gonzalez and Jones geared up, stepped inside, and documented the room.

Lonnie stepped inside when the photographers were finished.

Sherm, Roman, Gage, Kevin and Jason followed suit. It was a nondescript room with old furnishings in poor condition.

The padlocked door was unlocked. When Lonnie opened

the door, a loud gasp escaped him. He grabbed the doorknob and slammed the door shut.

"Gonzalez and Jones, get in there," Lonnie directed. "Everyone but Jake and his team, back up to over there," he commanded as he pointed to the far end of the room.

Sherm's team restrained Roman. "Let me in there!" He fought to get free.

"Sherm, we're going to have to call in the police. We need an ambulance and a doctor—not just EMTs, and a whole forensics team," Lonnie said.

Sherm motioned to his commando team. "Don't let these four near this door, understand? I don't care if you have to shoot them in the knees."

Sherm stared at Lonnie. "Let me see what's going on." Lonnie opened the door.

Sherm was speechless.

He nodded at the four being restrained. "They don't need to see this."

Sherm and Lonnie entered the room with their own CSI team.

They whispered mutterings of *God Almighty*. Lonnie closed the door after them.

Sherm pulled out his phone and called Detective Valk.

He took a picture, filled him in, sent the picture, then disconnected the call.

Lonnie squatted over Ari and checked for a pulse. She was barely alive.

"She's alive," Lonnie called out—loud enough for them to hear in the other room.

Lonnie and Sherm noticed the blood pooling between her legs.

"What the fuck did they do to her?" Lonnie asked. He was shell-shocked.

Sherm was thoughtful for a moment. He turned to Lonnie.

"Let Roman and Gage in here. Their senses are far greater than ours and could be helpful." Lonnie left the room.

"Roman, Gage, come here. You two stay there." He pointed to Kevin and Jason.

Roman and Gage shoved past the team.

Roman yanked the door open. "OH MY GOD! ARI!"

Gage clutched his head and wailed at the scene before him.

Lonnie shoved them into the room and slammed the door. He stayed in the outer room, waiting for the ambulance and police.

He pointed to Ari's sons and motioned to the team. "Take them outside."

The team dragged Kevin and Jason out of the building by force while they yelled and fought. Tears streamed down their faces.

They comprehended whatever was behind that door was horrifying, and they feared for their mother's life.

Sherm's two teams were methodical.

They documented every square inch of the inner room. The CSI team collected scrapings from every surface, every board.

Roman and Gage hovered around Ari.

"Don't touch her," Sherm said. "You need to get the scent of whoever did this, then you need to go to the boys. They desperately need you."

"I picked up two distinct scents in the outer room," Roman said. "There's only one scent besides Ari's in this room. I WILL KILL THAT FUCKER."

Roman's panther showed through his eyes. His hands morphed between fingers and claws. He was enraged to the point where he could barely stop himself from shifting.

"That's what you will focus on, Roman—the scent," Sherm said. "Gage will be the eyes in the air."

Roman and Gage stumbled out of the room.

Sherm approached the padlocked door. "Get this door open."

One of the guys picked the lock and opened the door. Stairs led down to a dark basement.

"Looks like a cellar," the guy said.

The approaching ambulance wailed. A dozen cop car sirens sounded close.

"Someone flag down the cops and open the gate!" Sherm called through the closed door.

Sherm looked for a light switch. He found it inside the stairwell and flipped it on.

The downstairs lit up.

He went down the stairs and stopped.

"Good God!" Sherm ran up the stairs, stared at Ari on the floor amid her blood. "Thank God we got here in time."

Feet stormed into the outer room.

Lonnie opened the door for the police and Detective Valk.

They stopped dead in their tracks. "Is she alive?" Valk asked.

"Yes, barely. We're not sure what he did to her, but most of the blood is from between her legs," Lonnie said. "Listen, I don't want to tell you your business, but I don't want the scene contaminated. I've got booties and gloves."

Valk grabbed booties and slipped his shoes into them. He donned gloves.

"No one goes in this room without gearing up, understand?" Valk said.

"Valk, there's more bodies downstairs," Sherm said.

"Jesus," Valk said.

He followed Sherm to the door, and they went down the stairs followed by a couple of cops.

A special EMS team entered the outer room, which included a doctor. They booted up and entered the inner room.

"JESUS! WHAT HAPPENED HERE?" he asked. "I'm Doctor Tanner."

"Let me have some plastic to kneel on," Dr. Tanner said. "I don't want to move her until I can see what's going on."

One of the CSI team pulled out a roll of clear plastic and cut off a large piece. Dr. Tanner kneeled and gently pushed Ari's legs further apart.

He double-gloved his hands.

"I need a powerful flashlight," Dr. Tanner said, glancing around the room.

"Do you want a hand-held light, or I can hold this for you?" a CSI team member said.

"I need both hands," Dr. Tanner said.

The CSI guy kneeled on the plastic and positioned the light. Dr. Tanner spread Ari's opening with his fingers.

"I need more light," he said. "Can someone go into my kit and get out the speculum? It's that metal clamp-like thing."

One of the EMS handed the speculum to the doctor.

Dr. Tanner carefully inserted it into Ari's vagina. "Shine the light here—maybe get that hand-held flashlight. I need to see what's going on inside her."

The CSI guy got the light and maneuvered around the doctor's head and shoulders.

"Oh, my God!" Dr. Tanner said. "There's something inside her!"

"Can I get a picture?" Jake asked. "We should document everything before whatever you remove from her."

"Sure," Dr. Tanner said. He adjusted the speculum to open Ari as wide as possible. He moved out of the way.

Jake grabbed his camera and kneeled on the plastic. He took several shots and got out of the doctor's way.

Dr. Tanner studied the situation he had to deal with. He reached inside with two fingers and carefully pried the spiked tube away from the walls of Ari's vagina. Blood flooded the floor.

"I need a sterile bag!" Dr. Tanner yelled.

One of the CSI members pulled a bag out of a case, opened it and held it out. Dr. Tanner inched the tube out and dropped it in the evidence bag.

"Better double-bag that, or better yet, put it in some type of case," Dr. Tanner said.

"God Almighty!" Lonnie said. "What the fuck kind of monster are we dealing with?"

"A sick fucker," the CSI guy said.

VALK AND SHERM looked around the cobwebbed basement. There were several skeletons amid bodies in different stages of decomposition.

"Looks like he's been at this for quite some time," Valk said.

He pulled out his phone and got the medical examiner on the line, then the police chief. Valk outlined the situation. He turned around and climbed the stairs. "The chief's calling the mayor."

Valk looked over the entire room: ceiling, floor, and walls. "Scrape and identify as many layers as you can. There may be places where individual blood samples are not contaminated by another victim's blood. We've got fourteen dead women down-stairs. Their blood is in this room. They deserve a final resting place with their families in attendance. I want everything in here bagged. If you need more help, call them in. This is a priority over anything else."

Sherm and Valk walked into the outer room.

"Lonnie, did you find out who owned this place?" Sherm said.

"Yeah. Tax rolls show Helen Brindlethorpe with an address over on Jackson Square," Lonnie said.

Valk, Lonnie, and Sherm walked outside.

Valk signaled to four of the cops. "We're going over to Jackson Square to talk to the owner."

Valk talked to someone on the phone about getting a search warrant.

"We'll follow you, but we won't interfere," Sherm said.

He motioned for Roman to accompany him. "The rest of you stay here in case you're needed."

Roman and Sherm climbed into one of the SUVs and fell in back of Detective Valk's car.

"When we get there, we need to stay in the car. I'll roll down the windows so you can see if you pick up any scents from the building," Sherm said.

THE EMS TEAM rolled the power stretcher into the inner room. They took in the room with wide eyes.

"What the fuck!" one of the EMS techs exclaimed.

Dr. Tanner spoke to the EMS team. "I've packed her vagina with sterile gauze to stanch the bleeding until we can get her to the hospital."

One of the EMS guys lowered the power stretcher to its

lowest level. They carefully placed Ari on the stretcher, covered her with a sheet, secured her in place, and raised the stretcher.

"Let's go," Dr. Tanner said. "She's lost a lot of blood."

When they rolled the stretcher outside, Gage, Kevin, and Jason ran to them.

Ari was covered in blood. Her hair was no longer white. Both eyes were swollen shut, and her face and neck were heavily bruised.

"MOM!" Kevin screamed. "OH, MY GOD!"

"NO!" Jason screamed.

Gage and Lonnie grabbed Kevin and Jason and pulled them away from the stretcher.

Lonnie took command. "Let them get her to the hospital. There's nothing you can do for her now. Time is of the essence."

The EMS attendants moved the stretcher inside the ambulance. Doctor Tanner and one of the EMS guys climbed into the back with Ari. They got an IV started. The others rode up front. The ambulance left, lights flashing and sirens wailing.

Gage, Jason, and Kevin piled into one of the SUVs and followed the ambulance.

"She's most likely going to need a lot of blood," Gage said. "Between the four of us we should have the right blood type, but mine and Roman's would be better. As shifters, we have healing abilities. I'd rather not have her get a blood transfusion from the general population.

"In case there's an issue of next of kin—if Roman and I don't qualify—you two need to be adamant about the blood transfusions. You are NOT to make any medical decisions without consulting myself or Roman. Do you understand?"

Numb with shock, Jason and Kevin nodded.

"How could this monster hurt her so badly in such a short time?" Kevin asked.

Gage stole a glance at Kevin. "You two might have thought Roman, and I were the monsters, but we live among monsters. You never know who your neighbors or coworkers are. Who is that clerk at the counter, the person who delivers stuff, the business owner? They may seem like normal everyday men, women, and children, but some are horrible monsters like these people who hurt your mother."

"What's going to happen?" Jason asked.

"They have to do a full body scan to find out if she has broken bones and if there's significant internal damage. She'll need blood—lots of it. They'll have to operate to repair any internal damage, broken bones—" Gage said.

"That's not what I meant," Jason said. "What about this fucker who hurt Mom?"

"Sherm took Roman with him so he could catch any scent —to see if they've been there recently," Gage said.

He looked in the rearview mirror at Jason.

"Don't stand between me and Roman because there will not be an arrest or trial. We're going to tear these bastards apart, limb by limb."

CHAPTER ELEVEN

DETECTIVE VALK KNOCKED on the door of the one-story house.

An elderly woman cracked the door open as wide as the chain allowed. She stared at the cops and the man at her door.

"Helen Brindlethorpe?" Valk asked. He held his credentials up to the door.

She nodded, fright masking her face.

"May we come in, please?" Valk asked.

The door closed, and the chain slipped off its track. She opened the door and stepped aside. "Please wipe your feet so you don't track in dirt."

Valk proceeded inside after he scrubbed his feet along the doormat.

The two cops followed his actions.

Two police officers walked around the perimeter of the property, guns drawn. The small lot only held the house and a one-car garage.

SHERM LOWERED ALL the windows in the SUV. Roman pulled in a deep breath.

"Faint. I'd say he hasn't been here in a while," Roman said. "Can I stand outside the car? I may get a better sense of things."

Sherm opened his door. "Yeah, but we need to stay near the SUV. I can't let you walk the property while the police are here."

THE INSIDE of the house was spotless. The furniture was dated but in pristine condition, showing little wear except for a recliner. It appeared that the woman spent all of her time in that chair.

"Is it Mrs. Brindlethorpe?" Valk asked.

"Mr. Brindlethorpe passed away over a decade ago," she said.

"I'm sorry for your loss," Valk said. "Mrs. Brindlethorpe, the reason we're here is to ask you about the property on Cooper Street on the northeast side of town."

"That old place? My son Eddy maintains the property," Mrs. Brindlethorpe said. "I don't know why I keep paying the taxes on it. My husband bought the place back in the fifties for his machine shop. We sold all the equipment when he died."

"Do you have a recent picture of Eddy?" Valk asked.

"What did he do?" Mrs. Brindlethorpe asked.

"We want to question him about an incident at the building," Valk said.

"There was an incident?" Mrs. Brindlethorpe asked.

She walked to a side table where framed photos jammed the surface. She picked up a framed picture and brought it to the detective.

"This is my Eddy and his little friend, Dom. The boy

doesn't have a family, and Eddy helps him with work and things."

"That's very charitable of him. May I take the picture out of the frame? I'll snap a picture with my phone so you can hold on to the picture."

"Oh, sure," she said.

Detective Valk took a photo with his smartphone. He sent the picture to Team and Sherm from his contacts. He handed Mrs. Brindlethorpe his card. "Do you have Eddy's address?"

"Yes," she said. She stepped over to the side table by her recliner and pulled open the drawer. She pulled out an address book. "2314 Ledger St. It's a white house with blue shutters and flower boxes on the porch. He loves those flower boxes."

"What type of work does Eddy do? Does he have a regular job?" Valk asked.

"Oh, yes. He's a supervisor at the D & H Lumber store. He was the employee of the month in January," she boasted with pride.

Valk wrote the address and the employment in his notebook. He handed her his business card.

"If Eddy should show up, please call me. Thank you for your time Mrs. Brindlethorpe."

VALK APPROACHED SHERM AND ROMAN. "You receive the picture? Eddy Brindlethorpe is the older guy and Dom is the kid. We're splitting up. I'm heading over to Ledger Street where he's supposed to live. My boys are going over to D and H Lumber where he works."

"Let me know what you find out," Sherm said. "We're heading over to the hospital."

Valk and his team left.

Sherm nodded to Roman. "Make it quick."

Roman took off at a trot. He travelled down the cracked driveway to the garage at the rear of the lot. He sucked in air to no avail. Roman returned to the SUV.

"He definitely doesn't keep his mother company," Roman said.

They got into the SUV and headed to the hospital.

ROMAN, and Sherm entered the hospital and found Gage, Kevin, and Jason in a waiting area.

"What's happening?" Roman asked.

Gage, Kevin, and Jason got up and stood before Roman and Sherm.

"They're taking scans to determine the extent of the damage. I've donated blood. You should too," Gage said. "Ari's going to need our blood to get through surgery and to heal faster."

"Did you find the guy?" Kevin asked.

Roman detected waves of murderous rage rolling off Ari's quiet boy.

"Valk spoke with his widowed mother. The cops are searching his house and work," Sherm said.

Doctor Tanner came down the hall and approached the group. He shook hands and introduced himself.

"We've taken scans and determined Ms. Davis has a broken cheekbone, nose, right arm, four broken ribs, and a dislocated shoulder. There's extensive internal damage to her vaginal walls. She's going to need a lot of blood."

"I can donate—we're compatible blood types," Roman said. "Gage and I can donate as much as she needs."

"Will she require cosmetic surgery to repair any of the

damage to her face?" Gage asked. "Money is no object. Not only do we have a great hospitalization plan, we'd even consider donating a wing to the hospital. Whatever is required to make her whole again."

"You really think cosmetic surgery is necessary?" Kevin asked.

"She shouldn't have any physical reminders of what she suffered through," Roman said. "It may take months or years of therapy to help her work through this."

"That makes sense." Kevin looked pained.

"Can we see her before surgery?" Gage asked.

"Sure," Dr. Tanner said. He pointed to Roman. "We need to get started with your blood."

They all followed Dr. Tanner.

LONNIE ENTERED the waiting room with bags of food. He spread everything out on the table. "You need to eat to keep your strength up. Especially you and Gage. Your animals need to be fed."

Lonnie eyed Roman. "Eat as much as you can. When you need more, text me."

"Any word?" Gage asked.

"They must have approached the building and seen their number was up. There's no one at the house and Eddy wasn't at work," Lonnie said. "Valk got a search warrant and they're going through his house. D and H Lumber allowed the cops to look at Eddy's locker, but they didn't turn up anything. No one there had any knowledge of his personal life or that of the kid."

"If either of you is going to shift, eat first. You've been running on adrenaline for a while now, and you'll crash if you don't get some food in you," Sherm said.

"Can you see at night?" Jason asked Gage.

He looked out the window. Twilight was turning into a night sky.

"Normal eagle vision is anywhere from four to eight times better than humans. Because of my shifter heritage, my vision is almost ten times greater than a human's," Gage said.

"Animal infrared eyes," Roman said.

"What's the plan?" Kevin asked.

"Gage will try to find the van, or pick up a visual of either of them," Lonnie said. "No one ever suspects they're being watched or hunted from the sky if they don't hear a chopper. They expect to see cop cars or someone following them on the ground."

Roman dug into one of the bags from The Burger Grill and pulled out a triple-decker beef burger with bacon and cheese.

He nudged bags toward the others as he took a huge bite of his burger.

He pulled out a bag of fries and shoved several into his mouth. "I can't wait to get my claws into that fucker."

"Where can I shift?" Gage asked between stuffing his mouth with a burger and fries. He sucked down a milkshake.

"The roof should be safe," Sherm said.

Gage nodded. He ate another burger and another bag of fries. "Let me see that picture again."

The news came on the TV.

Kevin searched for the remote and adjusted the volume so they could listen to the broadcast.

The picture of Eddy and Dom came on the screen.

An external picture of the building was on the screen along with the coroner's office removing bodies from the basement. Cops all over the place. News teams vying for the best place. The police chief getting PR time.

A newscaster reported Eddy's new status in life: serial

killer. Now all the world would see his picture—the tip line would light up with calls.

"They'll be going to ground unless they're stupid," Sherm said.

He pulled up the picture of Eddy and Dom on his phone so Gage could get a better look.

Gage memorized every feature of the two suspects.

"If you find them, don't do anything until I can get there," Roman said with a low growl.

His panther wanted out.

Kevin and Jason sat back against their chairs, keeping a healthy distance from Roman and his deadly cat.

GAGE AND SHERM exited a door onto the roof of the hospital. They turned away from the helipad area and headed toward a utility shed.

Gage stripped down and folded his clothes. He anchored them with his shoes.

"Leave my clothes here," Gage said. "Tell Roman to let me know when Ari is out of surgery."

"Will do," Sherm said.

Gage stretched and let his eagle come forth. His bird walked toward the edge of the roof, spread his gigantic wings and dove off the ledge. He caught a current and headed toward the northeast.

Sherm watched as Gage became a speck in the night sky. Even though he had witnessed this dozens of times, he was always stunned speechless by the shifter's ability.

He turned, opened the door and raced down the stairs.

GAGE SOARED OVER BUILDINGS. He glided lower to get a better view of his surroundings. He located the rundown building. Crime scene tape blocked the entrance.

Gage glided around the property and landed on the roof. Not detecting anything, he lifted off and took to the sky once more. He hadn't expected to find Eddy or the boy at the crime scene, but it wouldn't be the first time a murderer returned to his lair.

Gage swooped and glided, covering blocks and miles of the old, worn-down part of town. He examined people milling about with his eagle vision from the sky.

Valk had an APB on the vehicle.

Gage knew Eddy and Dom wouldn't be stupid enough to drive it around unless they changed the plates or its appearance in some way.

Still, Gage searched for it. No one ever accused criminals of being smart. He hoped Eddy and Dom didn't have the brainpower to think things through.

ROMAN, Jason, Kevin and Sherm waited in the hospital in their own internal personal plots of Hell.

Kevin was asleep on a sofa and Jason was stretched out on a chair.

Roman stood in front of a window and stared out into the night sky.

Footsteps approached. Dr. Tanner came into view and approached them. He looked tired.

"How is she?" Roman asked.

Jason stirred. He woke and nudged Kevin awake.

"Is our mom going to be okay?" Jason asked in a sleepy voice.

Kevin rubbed his eyes, then stood.

"Ms. Davis is in recovery. She had fourth degree vaginal lacerations which required an extensive repair," Dr. Tanner said. "I discovered her spleen was ruptured, and we removed it.

"We set the four broken ribs, along with two broken bones in her lower arm—the ulna and radius. We set her nose, repaired the cheekbone, and set her dislocated shoulder. She may be out for several hours. We've got her on a morphine drip because she'll be in extreme pain once she comes around."

Roman was pensive. "Can we look in on her?"

"Sure, but you can't stay more than ten minutes. This is a crucial time."

Roman, Kevin, and Jason followed the doctor.

Gage, Ari's out of surgery. We're going to see her now.

Okay, I'm on my way. So far, no luck.

They stopped at the door to Ari's private room. Roman blocked the entrance.

"Try not to let her detect your distress," Roman said. "If you're going to cry, step out of the room. We have to be her strength right now. She's gone through a horrific experience, and no matter how much you want to wail, don't do that in the room."

Kevin and Jason nodded.

Kevin drew a deep breath. "Let's go."

SHE LOOKED SO small in the bed.

Roman was relieved they washed the blood out of her hair so it was white again. He sent pulses of heat to help her with the healing and pain.

Ari's face was a mask of stitches, along with tape across her nose.

He couldn't tell if she'd require more surgery for her cheek bone since her face was so swollen.

One arm was in a cast.

He held back so Jason and Kevin could approach the bed together. He gave them credit—they appeared calm and told her they were there for her.

She was out cold and didn't respond.

Kevin hurried out of the room.

Roman heard him break down in wracking sobs outside the door. He sent a pulse to both boys to comfort them.

Jason left the room. Sherm and Lonnie joined Jason and Kevin.

Roman approached the bed. He brushed a wisp of hair from her forehead.

"I'm here, Ari. You're in the hospital. You've had multiple surgeries. Now it's time to heal. I love you. Gage will be here soon. He's searching the skies."

The door creaked open, and Gage approached Roman. He put his arm around Roman's shoulder and gave a one-armed hug. He crossed to the other side of the bed.

"Ari, I'm here with you. I love you. We love you. You're going to heal much faster than they think because our blood is flowing in your veins. Rest and recover."

Send her comfort and healing, Roman sent to Gage.

JEFFERSON LLOYD STEPPED outside his house to go to work at seven-thirty in the morning. He liked to get there before eight so he could grab a coffee and a moment of peace and quiet.

His motorcycle was in front of his pickup truck, which was

in front of the garage, which was too full of junk to hold the vehicles. He glanced at his truck and stopped.

"What the—"

Jeff swung around to the rear of his truck and looked at the license plate. He pulled out his cellphone.

"No, it's not an emergency. Someone switched the license plates on my truck in my driveway," he said into the phone. "HV8-UU9 he called out."

He listened to the police dispatcher.

He confirmed his address.

"Damn!" He walked back into the house, which was north-northwest of the crime scene.

Twenty minutes later, Detective Valk arrived, followed by an SUV with official city plates. He approached the front door and knocked.

A woman got out of the SUV and grabbed a case. She approached the pickup truck and got to work taking pictures, dusting for fingerprints, and removing the plates.

Jeff opened the door. Valk announced himself.

Jeff came outside and stood by the truck, keeping out of the way from the CSI woman.

"I don't know why I looked at my plates this morning, but when I noticed the front plate wasn't mine, I looked at the back," Jeff said.

"We're going to have to take the plates," Valk said.

"Is this tied to that serial killer?" Jeff asked.

There was no way Valk could deny or skirt around the question. A picture of the van and the license plate number had been on every news channel around the clock. "Yes, these are the plates from the white van you've seen on TV."

"Jeez! I can't believe a serial killer came up my driveway. Never mind switching my license plates," Jeff said.

He ran his hand through his hair. That was an awfully close brush with death.

"Just be lucky you didn't have to confront them," Valk said. "At least now we have a general idea of what direction they're headed."

A news truck stopped at the end of the driveway, and the crew exited.

THIS WAS one of those times when the news broadcast was actually helpful. Gage nodded at the TV screen in the hospital waiting room. "I'll be back."

He rushed out of the hospital onto the roof, undressed and shifted.

CHAPTER TWELVE

SOMETHING WAS WRONG.

Ari didn't wake up within the prescribed time of recovery. Dr. Tanner and another doctor met with Roman, Jason, and Kevin in an office.

Dr. Tanner introduced his colleague, Dr. Moore, who hit them with unwanted news.

"As you are aware, your mother suffered severe trauma from her experience. The lengthy surgery and anesthesia didn't help her body to recover as we expected," Dr. Moore said. "At this point, it appears she has lapsed into a coma. We don't believe it's anesthesia related."

"Will she come out of it?" Roman asked. His mind reeled from the information. Tension rolled off him in waves.

"We're hopeful," Dr. Tanner said. "There's so much we don't know about comas. For Ms. Davis, this could be a protective state from being brutalized by her abductors."

"Do you think she'll realize she's safe now?" Kevin asked.

"Does she understand she's in a hospital?" Jason asked.

"When I arrived at the crime scene, she was unconscious," Dr. Tanner said. "She didn't come to in the ambulance, or during the scans, blood transfusions, or any other time. Somewhere in her brain she may think she's still back there."

Roman stood. He swiped his hands down his face.

How much more of this can I endure? We need her. We need each other. She has to come back to us.

Gage blasted into his mind. *What's going on?*

Ari is in a coma.

Roman left the room.

He wandered aimlessly until he found himself in the parking lot. He knew he was being selfish.

This devastated Ari's sons. Gage was distraught.

He turned and headed back into the hospital and found her room.

Roman sat on the edge of the bed and stroked her face. "Ari, come back to us, darling. You're safe. You're in the hospital. Come back to us. We need you."

He sent her pulses of healing energy then he kissed her cracked lips. "I love you so much, Ari."

Gage stumbled into the room.

He approached the other side of the bed. He gingerly held her fingers. "Honey, we're both here. I'm going to find that fucker..."

Roman waved his hand in the air over the bed.

What are you doing? Don't say that shit to her right now!

She needs to know we will avenge her!

Gage glared at Roman.

Kevin and Jason came into the room. They noticed the tension between the two men.

"Is everything okay? The nurse said we have to go home," Jason said.

"Bullshit," Gage said. He turned to Roman. "Let's get the spare suite set up so she can recover at home."

"Good idea," Roman said. "She'd be much more comfortable at home. She doesn't like cold air conditioning and this environment can't help."

Gage turned to Jason. "Get with Dr. Tanner. Find out what medical equipment we need at the house. I will not allow hospital rules to keep us away from your mom."

THE NEXT DAY the required hospital equipment arrived at the penthouse.

Lonnie installed a hidden camera that captured the bed and equipment.

Sherm vetted three private nurses for eight-hour shifts each. Shortly after noon the ambulance arrived, and they settled Ari into the larger hospital bed.

Gloria, the three-to-eleven shift nurse, monitored the equipment, and Ari. She pulled her knitting out of her big bag.

Roman and Gage came into the room. "Gloria, right?" Gage asked.

"Yes, are you Ms. Davis' sons?" she asked. She dipped into a little curtsy.

Did she curtsy? Roman asked Gage.

Looked like it. Wonder why? That's not a nurse thing, is it? Gage asked.

Don't be stupid! Nurses don't curtsy! Roman said.

Gloria covered her mouth and coughed. She grabbed her water bottle and took a sip. "Sorry. I had a little tickle in my throat."

"You'll meet her sons a little later," Roman said. "I'm

Roman Davenport and this is Gage Stryker. Ari lives here with us. She takes care of us."

"We couldn't tie our shoes without her telling us what to do," Gage said. He tried to make light of their arrangement.

"Oh, she's your housekeeper!" Gloria said. She studied them for a moment. "I'll just go in the other room so you can spend time with her."

"Housekeeper, admin, our go-to person when we can't figure things out," Roman said.

Gloria picked up her knitting bag and slipped into the sitting room.

Roman took one side of the bed and Gage the other. They eased onto the mattress, careful of the tubes and connections. They leaned into her so she could feel their presence.

"Hi, angel," Roman said. "You're home in the spare room. Gloria's the nurse that's looking after you on this shift. You'll meet Beverly and Janet on their shifts." He carefully placed his arm across her waist and kissed her temple.

Gloria shook her head when she spied them in bed with Ari. *None of my business.*

Roman caught Gloria's thought. He made a face and shrugged at Gage.

Gage shook his head in resignation.

"The boys will be here when they get off work," Gage said. "I'm not sure if they plan to stay here, or just come up every day."

He brushed a soft kiss on her neck. "They're doing okay... coping."

"Don't stay locked up inside," Roman said. "You need to understand that you're home and you're safe. We need you— all four of us need you, honey, so come back and take care of us."

Gage looked across the bed. "It's time to fly." Roman caught the burning rage in Gage's eyes. They both got up and took turns kissing her.

"We'll let you rest now," Roman said. He stopped at the sitting-room door. "We'll be in and out. Do you have the list of contacts?"

"Yes, it's taped on the wall by the equipment," Gloria said. She stood and joined them in Ari's room.

"Okay. The boys have their own cardkeys so you won't have to worry about letting them in," Gage said. "This floor is secured. No one can just ride the elevator up to the penthouse. They have to be announced first. Then someone here with the app on their phone has to code the elevator to let them in."

"If there're any problems whatsoever, or you have a family emergency when we're not here, you're to call Sherm or Lonnie, on the list. Beverly should be here fifteen minutes before the end of your shift."

"Lonnie went over the details, but thank you for explaining about the elevator again," Gloria said. "I'm so sorry Ms. Davis has suffered so. I hope the police find those monsters. They said there were fourteen bodies in that basement. Uh... uh... uh. They deserve the death penalty."

Not if we can help it. Those fuckers will receive OUR justice. Out loud Gage said, "Let's hope they catch him soon."

Roman's phone rang. He glanced at the screen as he walked out of the room. "Hey, Kev. You coming up?" He listened a minute. "That will do you good. We'll keep you up to date. You coming up before you leave?"

Gage caught up with him in the living room. "Is Kevin going on an assignment?"

"Yeah, he'll be here in a little while, then his team's heading out to Central America. This will be good for him. He needs distance from all the grief, and his teammates will be able to help with that," Roman said.

The elevator dinged Kevin's arrival.

The doors slid open and both of Ari's boys stepped into the foyer.

Kevin was in dressed-down commando gear that was free of any visible weapons, but Roman suspected some were tucked away. Sherm's guys felt naked without the bare minimum of weaponry against their bodies.

Jason wore his regular office attire: slacks and a long-sleeved dress shirt open at the neck.

They entered the living room and exchanged hugs with Roman and Gage.

"So, how long will you be gone?" Gage asked.

"Lonnie said three weeks." Kevin fidgeted, picking a thread on his camo shirt.

Roman gripped Kevin's arm. "Listen, you need to get back to work. Gage, Jason, Sherm and I will be here for your mom. She'll recover."

"You don't hate me for going—for wanting to go?" Kevin said.

"No, it's best you get away. This assignment will help you," Roman said.

"Don't worry, Kev," Jason said. "We'll keep you updated."

Kevin nodded, losing some of his guilt. "I'd better go see mom."

Jason and Kevin entered the spare room. They stopped inside the room and stared at the equipment.

Kevin cringed.

There were several tubes hidden by the top sheet: A feeding tube snaked under the hospital gown and was in her bellybutton. A catheter was connected as well. An IV tube was in her arm, and a face mask provided oxygen.

The penthouse was quiet.

Gloria sat knitting beside the bed.

Ari's boys had left before they became emotional, and she didn't know where Roman and Gage were.

ROMAN WAITED as Sherm finished talking to a prospective client.

"Mr. Johnson, we're a billion-dollar security services conglomerate. Panther Securities doesn't need you as a client, but you need our services. You don't dictate rules to us. This company has been in business for a good long time. We have over two thousand happy domestic and international clients for references," Sherm said.

"We're not mercenaries. Our employees don't run around killing ex-husbands, wives, or bad bosses. We do extractions, protection, recovery and other services. If you want to get on our calendar to discuss your situation, we'll be happy to talk to you. But if you think we'll shoot one of your competitors, go find that mercenary."

Sherm ended the call. "Some people..."

"Who was that?" Roman asked.

"I could backtrack the call, but I'm not all that interested. Johnson was most likely a fake name," Sherm said. "Where's Gage?"

"Flying. He'll find them," Roman said. "The police never recovered Ari's purse. It may be in that van."

"We've already shut down all the credit cards and her card-key," Sherm said.

"She wasn't wearing her rings when we recovered her," Roman said. "I want to go back there and search."

Sherm thought for a moment. "Let me call our forensics team and the police CSI team. They might have found them. I have a picture of the rings in the insurance file I can send them."

He picked up the phone and pressed a speed dial number. "Hey, by any chance, did you find and bag a set of rings? I'll send you the picture, but Ari wasn't wearing them, so they've got to be among evidence."

He repeated the call to the police department and Detective Valk. No one had discovered any rings during their extensive search of the building.

"Let's go out there and search," Sherm said.

Gage, Sherm and I are going to the building to search for Ari's rings.

She wasn't wearing her rings?

No. They've got to be in that building somewhere, Roman sent.

Sherm and Roman rode the elevator down to the garage and got in one of the SUVs and headed out. They arrived at the building. The gate was standing open, so they drove in, parked and got out of the truck.

Roman grabbed Sherm's arm and hauled him to a stop. He sucked in air through his nose.

"Someone's inside."

Sherm pulled his Glock 17 9mm pistol out of his holster. He approached the handle side of the door and motioned for Roman to take the hinge side.

He reached up and grabbed the door handle and pulled the door open. They entered the building without making a sound.

Roman sucked in a breath, turned his head and pointed for Sherm.

They found Dom huddled in a corner. "Don't move or you're dead," Sherm said.

He grabbed his phone and pressed star-eight. "Valk, we've got the boy. He's at the building."

Roman grabbed Dom by his jacket collar and hauled him from his hiding place. Fury blinded him. He pounded Dom relentlessly.

Dom got in one good slug to Roman's jaw but he was no match for the bigger, stronger man.

Roman beat him down until Sherm pulled him off his victim.

"Knock it off. Get yourself under control," Sherm yelled.

Roman's panther wanted out in the worst way. A loud growl escaped him.

Sherm grabbed Dom and tossed him into a chair. "Where's Eddy?"

"I don't know," Dom said. He was full of attitude. His eyes were wide as he searched the room for a wild animal.

Roman glanced at Sherm. He was borderline in control, but wasn't sure how long he could contain his vicious feelings.

"You've got time, but I don't suggest it, Roman," Sherm said. "We'd never be able to explain that away."

Roman's panther was reflected in his eyes. The cat mentally clawed for access to the boy. Roman pushed the cat back. *No! We have to let him live for now.*

Gage piped in. *You talking to me? What's going on?*

Sherm and I are at the building. The boy is here.

Kill that little fucker! Gage raged.

Can't! Cops are on the way—how would we explain him being mauled by an animal? It's for the best—the little fucker needs to suffer. See what he was a part of? There's no forgiving Eddy. You'll have to be satisfied with that.

Gage's eagle screeched in a rage in Roman's mind. He cringed while Sherm studied him.

"Gage isn't happy," Roman said.

Sirens approached, fast.

Cars swept into the driveway. Doors slammed shut.

"I'll record everything," Sherm said. He enabled the voice recording function on his iPhone.

Valk charged into the building. He looked over at the battered and bruised young man on the chair whose right eye was swelling shut and lips were bloodied.

His eyes darted to Roman. His chest was heaving and his hands were clenched at his sides.

"I'm surprised he's still alive," Valk said.

"Not my choice," Roman said. He was barely in control.

Valk approached Dom. "Where's Eddy?"

Dom seemed about to cry. "I don't know!"

"Let me back up. You have the right to remain silent; anything that you say may be used against you in a court of law. You have a right to an attorney. If you cannot afford one, one may be appointed to represent you. Do you understand these rights?" Valk asked.

Dom stared at the detective. "I didn't do anything!"

"That's obvious, you piece of shit," Roman shouted.

"Do you understand your rights? Answer the detective's question," Sherm shouted at Dom.

"Yes!" Dom shouted.

"When was the last time you saw Eddy?" Valk asked.

"This morning, before he kicked me out," Dom said.

"Where were you when that happened? Why did he kick you out?" Sherm asked.

"We were over near Segerville. He got mad at me because I asked him why the cops were here. He kicked me out of the van for asking too many questions. I had to hitchhike back here because I didn't have any money," Dom said.

Gage! Check Segerville!

Okay. I'm on it. Not too far from where I am.

Roman nodded ever so slightly to Sherm.

Valk told Dom, "In this state, we follow the *common intent doctrine*. That means you and your co-conspirator can get the same punishment, even if it's the needle."

"I didn't do anything bad!" Dom cried. His eyes were wide with terror.

"You drove the van while Eddy grabbed these women, right?" Valk asked.

"Yeah, but that's all I did. I don't have a clue what he did with them. He never let me go in that room. He always kept it padlocked," Dom said.

Roman heard the kid's heart beat a frantic tempo. He also sensed a lie.

"Maybe you need to see your buddy's handiwork—take a look at what you were a part of," Sherm said.

He grabbed up Dom and flung the inner door open. "Here's what you played games through. See what you could have stopped fourteen bodies ago?"

Dom blanched at the blood covered floor. "I didn't know!" He wailed.

"You're lying. I can feel the lie rolling off you. How could you not tell what was going on in there? How could you have not heard screams? Women begging for their lives?" Roman raged.

Dom cried. "Eddy bought me these high dollar headphones and all these games. I thought he was screwing the women. I didn't know he was killing them!"

"Weren't you even curious when you never saw any of these women walk out of here?" Valk asked.

Dom shrugged.

"What a little sociopath in training," Sherm stated.

Valk told one of the cops, "Cuff him. He's a man; don't have to worry about juvie getting in the way."

They cuffed Dom and hauled him out to a car.

"Now, let's look for the rings," Valk said. "I don't understand how they could have missed them." Valk walked into the slaughter room and started searching surfaces and shelves.

Sherm took the broad area of the floor while Roman began at the door with a powerful small flashlight. He searched the floor against the wall. He was halfway through the second stretch of the wall when he spotted one of the bands.

"Here's one of the rings!" Roman shouted.

"Don't touch. Let me document this," Sherm said.

He took pictures with his phone from multiple angles while Valk and Roman stood by.

"I want to mark that wall and board," Valk said. "Be right back."

Valk left the building and returned with a spray can of fluorescent paint. He sprayed an arrow on the wall where Roman found the band.

Sherm pulled a baggie out of his pocket with a long-necked tweezer inside. He opened the bag and retrieved the band and dropped it into the bag.

Roman continued searching along the wall for the band with the three entwined heart-shaped diamonds.

"The other band with the diamonds isn't here. Do you think it dropped through?" Roman asked.

He turned to Valk. "Can we pull up the board and check?"

"Yeah, be right back," Valk said. He left the building and returned with a crowbar.

Valk wiggled the crowbar between the wall and the board. He eased the nails up out of the board and the board lifted. He grabbed it and set it aside.

The three men were stunned with their discovery—jewelry from the victims. Rings, bracelets, necklaces, brooches, pins, bobby pins—all sorts of items that either fell to the cracks or were intentionally hidden.

"Some of these things are too big to just fall through," Sherm said. "This fucker hid these keepsakes."

Sherm found Ari's ring. Before he bagged it, he and Valk snapped pictures of the stash.

Valk was on his phone arranging for the CSI team to return to the building.

"We never found any clothing from the vics. He might have burned it, trashed it, or stashed it under the floor. There weren't any clothes downstairs."

They all looked down. Anything was possible.

I found him! Gage blared into Roman's head.

Roman startled.

Sherm noticed.

Where?

West of Segerville in the woods. Looks like the van.

Roman stared into Sherm with intent.

"We'll leave you to it," Sherm said. "We're heading back to the house"

They shook hands with the detective and left. When they were in the SUV, Roman updated him.

"Let's head out." Sherm backed out of the driveway.

"I need to check in on Ari," Roman said. He pulled up the camera feed on his phone. He watched and listened.

[[Gloria put her knitting aside and got up. She lifted the oxygen mask and applied a lip balm to Ari's cracked lips.

"Honey, I'm Gloria, and I'll be taking care of you. You have some wonderful men in your life. Why don't you come out of hiding and live again? I know you suffered through a horrifying experience, but that's all behind you now."

She puttered around the room, checking the equipment, then attended to Ari once again. Gloria retrieved a washcloth from the linen closet in the bathroom and ran it under warm water. She wrung it out and wiped Ari's face. She fanned her face dry.

"I'm going to apply some of my natural moisturizing cream to the parts of your beautiful face where I can," Gloria said. "It will make you feel better."]]

"I want to give Gloria a bonus," Roman said.

He clicked off the camera feed and focused on where Sherm was driving.

Forty-five minutes later, Sherm pulled the SUV over to the side of the road.

"Check in with Gage and find out if we're close."

They saw Gage overhead. *One more mile. Turn left. Park.*

Roman gave Sherm the instructions. They got out of the SUV.

Gage landed on the roof.

"Hey, watch the paint job, birdman," Sherm said.

Gage squawked at Sherm. He eyed Roman.

Shift. The van is hidden in the trees. He's there. Don't bring Sherm—we don't want to implicate him in this.

Roman nodded. He passed along Gage's warning as he undressed.

"Shift already! I don't need to see your junk," Sherm said. "I'll wait here."

Roman shifted.

Gage's eagle took flight above the trees.

Roman's panther charged into the woods at a full sprint. He sucked in air and picked up the scent. The panther headed in that direction.

The van was partially hidden by branches piled on the roof and up against one side.

Roman stopped at the edge of the trees. He smelled fresh human urine.

Eddy came out of the trees opposite him, zipping up.

A low growl escaped the panther's snarled lips. He hissed.

Eddy's head jerked up.

He barely saw the panther before it sprinted across the clearing and slammed him to the ground. Eddy screamed as he flailed his arms, trying to push the beast off him.

Roman backed away. He shifted.

Eddy's eyes bugged out of his head. "What the fuck are you?" Eddy squealed.

"We're your judge and jury," Roman said.

Gage swept down to the ground and shifted.

"No human will lay a finger on you. There won't be a trial. No lethal injection. Just us. Payback for what you did to our mate, and all those other women you tortured," Gage said.

"You can't do that! I have my rights!" Eddy screamed.

"Not in our kingdom, you don't," Gage said.

Gage shifted and took to the air. He dove to his prey, talons tearing across Eddy's scalp.

Eddy shrieked as blood ran down his face and into his ears.

Gage swept in again and gouged Eddy's eyes. The man fell to the ground screaming in pain, trying to get the large bird off his face. The eagle ripped an eye out of his eye socket and tossed it aside.

Gage lifted one of his eagle feet. The deadly talons sliced an ear off Eddy's head.

Eddy shrieked as his arms flailed.

Roman shifted and let his panther have full reign.

The cat grabbed Eddy's right arm and flung him about. He ripped Eddy's arm out of his body. The panther flung it aside. Roman mauled Eddy front and back, raking his claws deep into the man's flesh and biting every surface. After a while, Eddy no longer screamed. Roman's powerful jaws clamped down on the killer's neck.

Bones crunched.

Blood squirted into his mouth and onto the man's chest.

He squeezed his jaws tighter. There was no life left in the body.

The panther dropped the body and moved away. He growled as he stared long and hard at the killer.

Revenge was theirs.

Gage squawked.

Let's go home. Don't shift here. Can't leave footprints.

Gage took to the air and flew over the trees. Roman ran back to the SUV.

They shifted. Roman was covered in blood. Gage's feet and legs were a bloody mess. Gage got in the SUV and sat naked in the back seat. Roman stared at the ground. "I'll cover our footprints."

Roman shifted. His panther scratched through all the footprints. He shifted back to his human form and got into the SUV.

"We'd better stop at that car wash we passed," Sherm said.

Sherm opened the glove box. He retrieved a burner phone and made a call.

Sherm used one of his many voices, making him sound like a teenager with a foreign accent.

"I was walking through the woods with my dog and there's this white van hidden in there. It could be that serial killer guy!"

The police dispatcher dug for more information. The "boy" gave the details of the location.

"My dad wouldn't let me call from our house. He doesn't want to get involved because of his Visa status."

Sherm disconnected the call. "Let's get out of here." He started the SUV, and they sped down the road and got on the highway. Twenty minutes later, Sherm pulled into a coin-op car wash. He fed the machine coins and hosed down Roman and Gage.

"Thanks," Gage said. "I hope that fucker rots in hell."

ROMAN! GAGE! KEVIN! JASON!

Ari's frantic voice screamed into their heads.

"She's awake!" Roman roared. He threw on his clothes. Gage shifted and took off toward their home.

Sherm threw the SUV into drive and they spun out of the car wash.

Gage will be there soon, Ari. I'm on the way with Sherm.

As they returned to the highway, a long line of police cars screamed from the opposite direction.

GAGE LANDED ON THE BALCONY. He shifted, then entered the living room.

"Roman! Gage!" Ari screamed frantically. The oxygen mask dangled below her chin.

She sobbed, loud wracking sounds as if her soul were being ripped from her.

Gloria tried to comfort her.

Gage sprinted, naked, into the room.

Gloria gawked. "Mr. Stryker!"

"Towel!" Gage barked out.

Gage wrapped Ari in his arms as best he could with all the tubes from the monitoring equipment.

"GAGE!" Ari tried to sit.

"It's okay, honey. I'm here," Gage crooned. "Roman's on his way with Sherm."

Gage pulsed soothing thoughts at Ari. His energy engulfed her with calm.

Ari leaned into him. "Gage. My Gage."

She wildly searched his face. "Where's Roman? ROMAN! ROMAN!" She shrieked for Roman, frantic.

"Shh. Shh." Gage said. "Roman's on the way. They're driving. I'm here. You're safe. You're home—this is the spare room, honey."

He brushed his hand across her forehead. Pressed his lips to hers, gently. He sent more soothing energy her way.

Ari whimpered as she clutched him. "Where's Kevin? Jason?"

"Kevin's out of town on an assignment. Jason's downstairs. I'll call him to come up," Gage said.

Gloria tossed the towel across the bed. Gage wrapped it around his waist.

"Call Lonnie, Gloria. Have him locate Jason."

Gloria picked up the home phone and pressed the code for Lonnie. She reiterated the message.

Within moments, the elevator announced a visitor. Jason ran into the room.

"Mom!" Tears streamed down his face. He almost flung himself on the bed, but caught himself in time. He sobbed as he tenderly held his mother.

Ari was out of it. Her eyes were wild.

She focused on Jason's face. "Jason!"

Then her eyes darted around the room and landed on Gage.

"Where's Roman? Where's my Kevin?"

She screeched out Roman's name again and again.

Gage pulled his hands through his hair. His pulses of soothing energy didn't seem effective. He turned to Gloria. "Call Dr. Tanner."

Twenty minutes later, Dr. Tanner, Roman and Sherm arrived. Roman flew into the room and grabbed Ari into an embrace. He cried as he kissed her face over and over.

"Roman! Roman," Ari said.

She raked her fingers through his dark hair. Then she blacked out.

Dr. Tanner pushed Roman aside.

He pulled up each of her eyelids. He took her vitals. "Looks like she's gone again. She may repeat this a few more times, but I'm confident she will recover. She just has to work through some issues."

Gage, Roman and Jason stood with chests heaving. Sherm and Gloria stood quiet, as concerned bystanders.

CHAPTER THIRTEEN

THE MEN WATCHED the news unfold in the living room. "The manhunt for Edward Brindlethorpe has ended..." one newscaster reported.

"A boy and his dog reported the white van..." a different newscaster said.

"Police indicated the suspect, Edward Brindlethorpe, accused of killing fourteen women and seriously injuring his fifteenth victim, was killed by an animal attack in this wooded area," another newscaster reported.

Police roped off the location and wouldn't allow any of the news teams access to the scene of the attack.

Roman clicked off the TV. "That chapter is closed."

TWO NIGHTS later Roman and Gage woke to whispers in their heads.

Roman, Gage...

They met in the spare room, disheveled from sleep, startling Janet, the night nurse.

"Is everything okay?" Janet asked.

"Just checking. Thought we heard something," Roman said.

He and Gage approached the bed from both sides.

Gage leaned over and ran his fingers across Ari's forehead.

"Are you awake, Ari? We thought we heard you calling out," Gage said.

Ari moved her head from side to side but didn't open her eyes.

"Just sleep, darling. We'll be here when you're ready to wake up," Roman said. He pressed his lips to her forehead.

"She's working her way through the trauma," Janet said. "It won't be long now."

THREE MORE MONTHS SLIPPED BY. Ari clung to the coma. She made periodic appearances but mentally refused to stay.

"When she finally comes through this, she's going to need a good psychiatrist," Dr. Tanner said. "As far as I can tell, she's right there, ready to get out of bed and live again. But something's holding her back."

"We've interviewed the psychiatrists you recommended and we've decided Dr. Talbotson would be the best choice," Gage said.

"Lorraine's a good doctor. I've seen her work miracles with patients," Dr. Tanner said. "It may not be a bad idea to enlist her services starting now. Maybe Lorraine can break through Ari's fear of resurfacing."

"I'll call her and set things up," Roman said. "She has the

medical records, but she doesn't have an update as to these awakening periods."

"I'll speak with her," Dr. Tanner said.

DOCTOR LORRAINE TALBOTSON just turned fifty. She was a striking woman with a rich, medium-brown head of hair with a natural wave, and warm blue eyes. She sat in a chair beside the hospital bed.

"Hello Ari. Dr. Tanner mentioned I'd be stopping by for a chat, didn't he?"

She observed Ari for any sign of a response. She didn't see any.

"My name is Lorraine Talbotson and I'm a psychiatrist who specializes in women's traumatic experiences. Anything we talk about is private between us. No matter what you want to talk about. I want you to feel safe in our professional relationship. There's nothing you could say that should cause you to be embarrassed or ashamed."

"I'm here to help so you aren't alone with your fears and terrors. The longer you stay locked within yourself, the longer you battle these things alone. You have help on this side of your eyelids."

Lorraine studied the woman who looked the same age as herself. She had a hard time believing the woman's age. Ari *barely* looked fifty instead of the seventy-five documented on her driver's license and insurance papers.

She had read the reports from Drs. Tanner and Moore. She also saw the police report along with the gruesome pictures of her new patient and the horror room. Dr. Tanner had called and detailed Ari's short awake periods.

Lorraine was not surprised Ari hid away from reality. She

read the report and watched the news. Lorraine wasn't sure if she would survive that kind of attack.

"I'll be back on Thursday, Ari," Dr. Talbotson said. "Rest up and get ready to leave that bed."

She picked up her Coach bag and walked to the living room.

Roman and Gage stood and met the psychiatrist halfway. "Anything?" Roman asked, hopeful.

Dr. Talbotson shook her head. "I get the impression she's right under the surface. Hopefully, Thursday will be better. Shall we talk?"

Roman and Gage had discussed what they would disclose to the psychiatrist. They, of course, would never reveal they were shifters.

First, who would believe them? Secondly, they'd end up as lab rats in some secret underground government lab. Probably Area 51, or wherever it was where the aliens and ships were rumored to be hidden.

But as far as their relationship, which, if they had been married, would be considered polyandry—they had no problem with the doctor knowing what it entailed.

Since they weren't married, there were no rules and they wouldn't have followed them if there were.

"What would you like to know?" Gage asked.

He and Roman bore into her eyes. They showed no signs of weakness.

"I've read the reports and all the details about her abduction, but no one provided any personal details. I'm not familiar with Ari Davis, the woman," Lorraine said. "Tell me about her life, who she is."

"As you are aware, she lives here with us," Roman said. "We all met five years ago at a restaurant. Ari was meeting her sons. Gage and I talked to her in the bar. We all had lunch together. We fell in love with her practically instantly."

"Had you memorized that little speech for me?" Dr. Talbotson asked.

"Look," Gage said.

He wasn't holding back.

"People don't understand our relationship. They don't get how two guys could share a woman without a drop of jealousy. Most nights, we all sleep in the same bed. We are uncomfortable apart from each other for extended periods of time."

Dr. Talbotson blinked as she digested Gage's words. "Are you two bisexual?"

"If Gage ever tried to kiss me or touch my dick, he'd be dead," Roman said. "I'm pretty sure he feels the same way.

"We pleasure her. She pleasures us. Sometimes together, sometimes one at a time. We're all very comfortable with our relationship."

"It isn't unusual," Dr. Talbotson said. "My professional experience has been with polygamists—men with several wives. This is the first time I've had a female client with two men under one roof. Most of the times the others don't know about each other, or if they do, they don't live together. It's more like tolerance at a distance."

"We couldn't live without her," Roman said. "I can barely find my toothbrush without her placing it in my hand. She takes care of us. She has a brilliant mind and helps on the investigative side in our many businesses."

"Does she have a background in that field?" Dr. Talbotson asked.

"Oh, yeah," Gage said. "She's a well-known forensic accountant with the nickname 'the sifter'.

"Our team loves her. She's single-minded when she's

working a case. Ari seems to have the ability to sift through things that no one else ties together."

"It sounds like you have a tremendous amount of respect for her," Dr. Talbotson said.

"We do," Roman and Gage said at the same time.

Dr. Talbotson glanced at her watch. "I have to run, but I'll be back on Thursday."

"Thanks again," Roman said.

GLORIA PULLED two items out of her knitting bag. She approached the bed. "Ari. I made you a little hat and a scarf for winter. It's cashmere—I hope you aren't allergic."

She rubbed the cap and scarf across Ari's hands. Roman wandered into the room. "How's she doing?"

"No change. I just showed her the cap and scarf I knitted for her." Gloria placed the items on the foot of the bed.

Roman picked up the cap. "This is so soft."

Gage joined them. He saw the knitted items. "Did you make these? They're beautiful—look store-bought." He grabbed the scarf and rubbed it against his face.

Gloria beamed with pride. "I wanted her to have something nice."

She glanced at the men. "There's something I want to talk to you about."

Oh, no, here it comes. She knows we're all lovers, Roman said.

Gage cringed inside. "What's that?"

"I think my grandfather can help you," Gloria said.

"With what?" Gage asked with a hint of suspicion.

Gloria chewed on her lower lip, searching for words. She finally gave up trying to be polite.

"My grandfather is one-hundred-two years old. He's Navajo and Negro—I realize people don't use that word anymore, but that's what he is. We've never set foot in Africa, so we don't understand why Black folks want to be called African-American. He's a very spiritual man, and a man of few words unless he has something important to say."

"Wow, he's old!" Roman said. "What could he possibly help us with at his age?"

"He can help you find your kind," Gloria said.

She looked from one man to the other.

Roman and Gage stood very still as they digested what they heard.

Gage went for denial. "Find our kind?"

"You don't have to worry about me giving away your secrets," Gloria said. "I've seen your animals through your eyes. You're a big black cat, and you're an eagle."

Roman dropped into a chair.

"I can see how lonely you are for your own kind," Gloria said. "But you aren't regular shifters. They hide from you—they're afraid of you. There's a lot of shifters around, but when they sense you, they take off, scared for their lives.

"So, you'd better go see my grandfather while he's still here among us," Gloria said.

"How do you know all this?" Gage asked.

Gloria let her wolf's eyes peek through. "I figured out how to shield myself from my own kind, and obviously, from your kind, too."

Roman and Gage were stunned into silence for a moment.

"You're a wolf? Where is your grandfather? When can we talk to him?" Roman asked, excitement bursting forth.

"He's in an assisted living facility where I work part time so I can keep an eye on him," she said. "I can meet you there tomorrow morning, if you like."

"Yes, that would be awesome," Gage said. He was dumbfounded.

If we aren't shifters, what the hell are we? Roman sent.

You'll find out soon, Gloria chimed in.

GAGE AND ROMAN exited the BMW in the parking lot of Singleton's Assisted Living Center south of downtown, just as Gloria's Toyota pulled up and parked.

"Come," she said. "They're finishing breakfast so everyone's alert for the morning."

They went inside.

Gloria waved to staff and patients as she led Roman and Gage down a hallway and around a corner. She tapped on an open door to the room of Ben Hatahle, as indicated by the name tag by the doorframe.

A weathered old man sat propped against pillows in his bed. He looked every bit his age, with deep lines etched in his face.

She called out to him. "Good morning, Grandfather!"

The old man smiled widely. He still had all his teeth. "Gloria! My little Gloria."

"Not so little anymore, grandfather," Gloria said with a twinkle in her eye.

She ushered Roman and Gage into the room and closed the door.

"Grandfather, I want you to meet Roman and Gage."

"What a fine eagle! Your wingspan must be immense!" the old man said. He turned his gaze to Roman. "Black leopard. I don't even see any hidden spots! A great hunter. Did you know that the leopard is the strongest climber of all cats? It's amazing! They haul their kill up into the trees so other predators can't get to it. My wolf sits and waits for us to leave, but Spirit hasn't taken us yet."

"Grandfather, Roman and Gage don't have a clue about anything regarding their kind. They need help," Gloria said.

Grandfather studied the men for a moment. "Go see Atsa. He can tell you about the Tothars."

"Is that what they call our kind—Tothars?" Gage asked.

"Yes, your species is older than the shifters. Tothars predate Egyptians. I haven't seen a Tothar for eighty years, and here's two right in front of my old eyes. I have been blessed," grandfather said.

Roman had a moment. After so many decades of dead-end searches for his people—his kind—he almost broke down and cried.

"Where can we find this Atsa?" Gage asked. "Will he talk to us?"

"You tell him Silver Wolf sent you. He's in Shiprock, New Mexico—in the Four Corners. Everyone knows him. You go there! He's an eagle, but your eagle makes his look like a chickadee." Grandfather chuckled.

"He knows about our kind—these Tothars?" Roman asked.

"Yes. Yes, you go see Atsa," grandfather said. He yawned widely.

"We'd better let grandfather take his nap," Gloria said.

She fussed over him, pecked his cheek.

"Thank you, Silver Wolf," Roman said. "You've lifted a weight off my heart."

Grandfather gave a little snore. He had already drifted off to dreamland.

"We need to get back and check on Ari," Gage said.

A snort from grandfather. "Your companion will be okay. She needs a little more time."

ON THE DRIVE back from meeting Gloria's grandfather, Roman worked his phone. "We'd have to fly into Four Corners Regional Airport in Farmington, New Mexico. Lonnie can have a car standing by."

"We'd better plan on being away for at least two days. We don't know what we're going to find when we get there," Gage said.

He fidgeted, drumming the wheel with the fingers of his left hand. "Two days—I don't know, Roman."

He looked uneasy.

Roman set his phone on his thigh. "Let's wait until Ari can come with us. Two days away is a long time."

ARI DRIFTED among the beeps and lights of the monitoring equipment.

Behind her eyelids, a loop of events replayed. She didn't want to see them anymore.

Ari mentally probed her body. She understood she was physically healed from the damage that had been wrecked on her.

She kept asking herself why she didn't wake up. Why she wouldn't return to her lovers, her sons.

Ari rationalized that no one would blame her for what happened. She was the victim. She understood that—she didn't have a problem with putting the blame on her abductors. So, then, why couldn't she open her eyes and leave this repeating horror behind?

Ari missed Roman and Gage. Her guilt was that she missed them more than her sons. Kevin and Jason were adults with busy lives, full-time jobs, and activities. Ari didn't want them to call or visit her because they felt obligated.

She wanted to meet their girlfriends—at least Kevin had a girlfriend—Amanda. She didn't think Jason had met anyone yet.

Ari wanted her life back with Roman and Gage.

Why couldn't she function? She was determined to solve the problem of letting go and waking up.

Her poor nurses.

Beverly, the first shift nurse had prepared to sponge her off when Roman and Gage took matters into their own hands.

They had arranged extra-long cords on the equipment when the room was set up so they could carry her into the shower.

ROMAN, in cutoffs, lifted Ari while Gage, in his bathing suit, and Beverly helped maneuver the cords and tubes. The shower water was already flowing when Roman entered the large stall.

Gage let his fingers untangle Ari's hair and made sure it was thoroughly wet. He shampooed her hair and scrubbed her scalp and behind her ears. It took a while to rinse her long hair, which was now below her waist.

"Switch," Roman said.

He handed Ari off to Gage.

Roman applied body wash to her skin, rubbing up and down her arms, avoiding the IV tube, bending her elbows. He maneuvered her wrists and flexed her fingers and thumbs.

He repeated the process for her legs and feet, then tackled the trunk of her body, avoiding the feeding tube, not missing an inch.

"She's shrinking," Roman said. "We need to talk to Dr. Tanner about nutrition."

Gage's eyes roamed across her breasts. "I noticed her breasts were smaller. We need to flex her joints."

They finished her shower.

Roman wiped her back and the back of her legs, then the front of her that wasn't against Gage. He threw the towel on the floor, retrieved a dry one and patted the excess water out of her hair.

"Let me put a towel on her pillow. Do you think we can lean her on her side?" Roman asked. "I want to dry her hair some more, then braid it."

"Beverly," Roman called out. "Do we have a clean hospital gown?"

Gage carried Ari to the bed.

Roman covered the pillow with a thick towel.

"Here you go," Beverly said.

She helped Roman dress Ari.

Gage laid Ari on the hospital bed.

Roman grabbed the side of the gown and pulled it to connect the Velcro straps to keep the back closed. They gently rolled her onto her side while Gage combed her wet hair, patted it dryer, then braided it.

Her men took care of everything. Ari longed to touch them.

CHAPTER FOURTEEN

DR. TALBOTSON STEPPED off the elevator into the penthouse foyer just as Jason headed to the living room. "Hi, Dr. Talbotson," Jason said. "Mom's been restless, but she's still not out of it yet."

"Restless is a good sign," Dr. Talbotson said. "It sounds like she's ready. Perhaps today's session will open the door all the way."

Gage and Roman wandered from their rooms to greet the psychiatrist.

"Hello, Lorraine," Roman said. "She's muttering and twitching."

Gage wiped his hand down his face. "I hope she comes out of this soon. I don't know how people can cope with their loved one's in deep comas."

"Let me get in there and see if she wants to engage today," Dr. Talbotson said.

She walked down to the hallways and took the third to the spare room. "Hi, Gloria."

"Hi, Dr. Talbotson. Fingers crossed," Gloria said. She exited to the sitting room and pulled the door shut.

Dr. Talbotson pulled the chair and repositioned it to better monitor Ari's face.

"Hi Ari," she said.

She watched Ari's face for a response.

Dr. Talbotson witnessed Ari's lips move under the face mask in a silent *Dr. Talbotson.*

"Did you just greet me, Ari? It looked like your lips said my name, but you didn't speak out loud," Dr. Talbotson said.

Ari's fingers jumped.

"How about coming back for good?" Dr. Talbotson coached. "Your butt must be awfully tired of that bed."

Ari's face went through several twitches. A sigh escaped.

"Come on out of there," Dr. Talbotson said. "I can tell that you want to return, to get back to your life."

Ari made stress noises—little groans, almost growls, gasps.

Her body twitched.

Her eyes blinked fast, then opened.

She stared at the doctor. In a rush, she must have realized she was awake, alert. She let out a strangled cry.

"Welcome back, Ari," Dr. Talbotson said.

Gloria opened the door. She stayed in the doorway, hand on her heart.

Roman, Gage, and Jason rushed into the room. They flocked to the bed.

"Ari!" Roman said. "Oh, Ari, please stay."

"Mom!" Jason gasped.

"Ari, do you want to sit?" Gage asked.

"Don't overwhelm her," Dr. Talbotson said. "Call Dr. Tanner."

DR. TANNER CHECKED ARI OVER. He was happy to see she was cognizant.

"Can you disconnect her from the equipment?" Roman eyed the tubes with disdain.

"Let's make sure she wants to stay around this time," Dr. Tanner said. "If she's still with us after a nap, we can set her free. Until her muscles build back strength, you'd better have a wheelchair handy, even a good sturdy cane."

"I'll get one ordered," Jason said. He attacked his phone, fingers clicking and swiping through screens. "I found a wheelchair that's adjustable—it reclines for patients if they get tired of sitting."

Roman and Gage studied Jason's phone screen.

"Yeah, that looks like a good choice," Roman said. "Find out if they can deliver it today, tomorrow at the latest. Check their site for canes as well."

Jason walked out of the room and placed a phone call.

ARI WAS BACK.

Dr. Tanner removed the feeding tube, the IV tube, and the catheter.

Within a week, Ari could eat soft food. The first time she tried to pick up a spoon, it clattered to the table.

She stared at her fingers in disbelief. "Why can't I hold a simple spoon?"

"Don't stress out about this," Gage said. "It'll take a little while until your muscles respond."

"Ari, you've just left the bed after all these months. Give your body a chance to catch up," Roman said.

Carlos, a physical therapist, replaced the three nurses.

They scheduled him three times a week to help her regain the strength in her limbs.

Roman, Ari and Gage slept in Roman's bed for the first time in almost five months.

Roman and Gage slept lightly, listening for any telltale sign of distress. They hovered, worried she wouldn't wake up again.

At two o'clock in the morning, Ari woke up screaming for her life.

"Shh. Shh. It's okay, it's just a nightmare," Roman said.

Gage brushed her hair off her face. "You're home. Safe."

Her eyes searched each of their faces. She clutched one of each of their hands and sobbed. "What if he finds me again?"

Roman and Gage exchanged concerned looks over her head.

"You don't have to worry about that," Gage said. "He's dead."

"But he was here—" Ari sobbed.

Roman brushed his fingers down her cheek. "You only dreamed his image in your head in a nightmare. He's dead, Ari. We killed him. He'll never hurt anyone ever again."

THE NIGHTMARES CONTINUED for weeks regardless of the sessions with Dr. Talbotson and the reassurances from Roman and Gage that she was safe.

"I want to move back to my bedroom," Ari said one morning at breakfast.

Her jaw was firm. She avoided their eyes.

Roman saw the crisis in Gage's eyes and knew he was on the brink as well.

They hid their emotions as best as they could—shell shocked at her request.

It wasn't a suggestion.

"You don't want us in bed with you?" Gage asked. He struggled to keep the neediness from his voice, along with the strangled choke that wanted to escape.

Ari shook her head.

"Sure, if that's what you want—if you think you'll sleep better," Roman said. "I'll put fresh linens on your bed."

He fled the room. Gage's head reeled.

Their dynamics had changed.

Gage didn't know if that other Ari would ever return to them.

While their blood had the ability to heal her physical wounds, there was nothing they could do about the terrors in her head. None of the energy, comfort, and soothing thoughts helped in that regard.

CHAPTER FIFTEEN

TWO TENSE MONTHS passed since Ari moved back to her own bedroom. She was walking with a cane and puttered around the penthouse. She hadn't returned to the bookstore across the street. Ari almost had a panic attack when her lovers brought her to the psychiatrist's office for her appointments.

Ari occasionally picked up a stray thought from Roman or Gage. She realized she was causing them pain, but she didn't know what to do about it.

The nightmares still made an appearance, but they were slowing down.

Dr. Talbotson said that was a good sign. Her psyche was healing.

Ari tried to remember the last time her men kissed her with unbridled abandon. The last time they made love. She was pretty sure it was six months ago, but it might have been longer. It wasn't Roman or Gage's fault. Ari panicked when they tried to hug her. She no longer tolerated being sandwiched between them, standing or lying in bed. She felt trapped and she couldn't free herself from the panic.

They all suffered, and she was the key. Ari had to push through the anxiety, grief, and terror. Sometimes she experienced phantom pains from her excruciating ordeal. Even though she determined she was one-hundred percent healed, her psyche was so damaged that it held onto that horrifying pain. Drs. Tanner and Moore repaired all the tissue inside her on the operating table.

Ari wanted to make love with Roman and Gage in the worst way. She longed for their hands and lips on her; she needed their kisses.

Needed them inside her.

Why couldn't she push through this barrier?

Roman and Gage picked up on her anguished thoughts.

It tormented them, but they didn't know how to help her.

They understood what she wanted and what she needed, but they also comprehended that she would have to initiate any physical contact. And even that was no guarantee Ari would want them again.

THE LOBBY CALLED. Gloria was downstairs.

Roman approved of her coming upstairs. He hit the phone app, and the elevator opened and Gloria stepped out to the foyer.

"Hello!" Gloria announced. She swung her arms wide, exuberant, her face lit with a smile.

Roman and Gage were in the living room. Ari wasn't around.

They stood and hugged Gloria, then they all sat.

"Where's Ari?" Gloria asked.

Sadness swept across the men's faces. "She's in her room," Roman said.

Gloria nodded. "I sense the pain and suffering—on all three of you."

"We can't figure out what to do," Gage said.

"Do you ever leave the penthouse? The building?" Gloria asked.

"We take her to Lorraine's office," Roman said. "She refuses to go anywhere else. Almost begged Lorraine to come here for her sessions, but Lorraine won't give in to her."

"Look, you need to drag her out of here. Go out to eat. Go to the beach, the mountains—get her out of this place!" Gloria said. "She needs something fun in her life instead of being drowned in your sorrow. It's rolling off you two like a tsunami."

"Perhaps we should go to the house in the woods," Roman said.

Gage snorted. "Only if we don't have hunters intrude."

"You could always take that trip to New Mexico and meet Atsa," Gloria said. "Grandfather keeps asking why you haven't gone yet."

Gage's face lit up. "Perhaps we should take Ari to meet your grandfather!"

"Let's go!" Gloria said. She jumped to her feet. "I'll go get Ari moving."

AFTER ARGUMENTS AND CAJOLING, Gloria convinced Ari to get dressed so she could meet her grandfather.

Ari was deathly afraid to leave the security of the building, but they loaded her in the BMW and the four set out.

They arrived at Singleton's Assisted Living Center. Ari clutched onto Roman and Gage as Gloria led them to her grandfather's room. She warily looked around, distrustful of the patients, staff, and visitors.

Silver Wolf sat propped against pillows, licking vanilla pudding off his spoon.

"Gloria!" he called out. "You brought back the panther and eagle!"

Ari's eyes widened. She noticed that neither Roman nor Gage were concerned that this old man recognized they were shifters.

Maybe he's a shifter?

Grandfather Silver Wolf noticed Ari. "Ah! Who is this?"

Roman and Gage approached the bed and shook grandfather's hand.

"Hello Grandfather Silver Wolf," Roman said.

"Hi Silver Wolf," Gage said. "This is Ari."

Ari stared at the old man. *Why did they bring me here? Who is this old man?*

Roman put his arm across her shoulders and urged her forward.

"Ari, this is Grandfather Silver Wolf, Gloria's grandfather. He's part Navajo."

She resisted moving at first, but finally took a few more steps. "Hello."

"Come, come. Don't be afraid!" Grandfather Silver Wolf said as he waved her forward. "What a vision I see before me! It's not every day that a beautiful woman pays a call."

Ari plunked down in the bedside chair. She clutched her purse to her as if it would protect her from harm.

"It's hot. Go make us some iced tea," Grandfather Silver Wolf said. He waved his hand at Roman, Gage, and Gloria to shoo them out of the room.

Gloria quietly closed the door behind them.

Ari had a moment of pure panic at being left alone with the stranger.

"What troubles you so?" Silver Wolf asked Ari. "I can see

you trapped in your body when you want to come out and play. You suffered a great personal tragedy, but you survived."

Ari stared at him.

Why am I here? Who is this old man who wants to talk about my personal history?

"There's nothing you can tell me that I don't already know from hearing your thoughts," Grandfather Silver Wolf said. "I want to help you live again."

Ari balked. *Did he just read my mind?*

"Shifters have that ability. You know that already," Grandfather Silver Wolf said. "You're not a shifter, or a Tothar, but I sense you're something not quite human. Do you sense the difference?"

Curiosity washed across Ari's face. "We bonded so quickly. The three of us—Roman, Gage and me. My sons said I appear to be getting younger. I don't look seventy-five."

"No, you don't. I suspect you will discover answers when you go to New Mexico with your men."

"New Mexico? What's there?" Ari asked.

"Atsa. He's an eagle. He will help your men learn about their heritage," Grandfather Silver Wolf said. "But for now, you need to let go of all your fears. That bad man is dead. Your men love you. No one will ever hurt you again."

Ari flushed, her eyes filled with tears. She wiped her face as a stream flowed down her cheeks. "I know," she barely squeaked out. "I can't seem to get back to who I was. It's as if I'm trapped, and I don't want to go on like this."

"Well, then don't," Grandfather Silver Wolf said. "You must face your fears in order to survive. Let your inner warrior out. She will protect you."

"My inner warrior?" Ari asked. She gazed at the old man in confusion.

"Yes. That part of you that can vanquish all that fear and help tear down those walls you've constructed," Silver Wolf said. "She can also protect you when you understand how to pull her forward."

Ari considered all he said.

The door opened and Roman carried a tray with glasses of iced tea.

Gage rushed over and kneeled before Ari as she wiped her face. He was stricken with anxiety that they made a mistake forcing her to come here.

"She's okay," Grandfather Silver Wolf said. "She's releasing her fears."

He latched onto the glass Roman handed him. "Is this sweet tea?"

THE RIDE back home was quiet. Roman sat in the back seat with his arm around Ari.

At first, she kept her body stiff when he pulled her to him, then she slowly relaxed.

Roman blocked her. *She's opening up, relaxing.*

This was the best decision we've made lately, Gage said.

"He's a very sweet man," she finally said.

"Yes, he is," Roman said. "He so wants to see our animals, but I don't think it would be a good idea for us to shift in his room."

"That would not go over very well," Gloria said.

Gage eyed Ari in the rear-view mirror.

"He said I wasn't entirely human, but I wasn't a shifter or Tothar," Ari said. "How does he know?"

Gloria turned in her seat. "Grandfather is very spiritual. In his one-hundred two years on the planet—this time—he's seen a lot of things and talked to a lot of our kind. If he said you're not all human, you can take that as the truth."

"How do I find out what I am?" Ari asked.

"You need to talk to Atsa. He will have answers grandfather can't remember," Gloria said.

Gage pulled the car into the parking garage.

Gloria walked to her car. "Make that trip soon," Gloria said. She waved goodbye, got in her car and drove off.

"Want to go out to eat?" Gage asked.

Ari chewed her lip.

Roman decided for her. "Let's go to Pomodoro's."

Gage started the BMW, and they pulled out of the garage.

ARI DROPPED her purse in her room and took off her shoes. She sat on her bed a moment, contemplating the old wolf and his words.

She felt better. Looser. Not as clenched inside. Maybe she could finally move on. Open up. Live.

She wandered back to the living room, barefooted.

Roman's long legs were spread out before him as he lounged on the sofa.

Gage had his stockinged feet on the coffee table on the other end of the sofa.

They followed her with their eyes. They expected her to sit on the sofa across from them to keep her distance, as had been customary for the past couple of months.

When she changed her trajectory, Roman moved his legs and Gage's feet left the coffee table. They sat up, anticipating. Nervous.

Ari settled between them, a little hesitant.

They sensed a difference in her, but they were wary of misinterpreting any sign of invitation.

Roman reached out and ran his hand through the hair on the side of her head.

Gage leaned over and kissed her cheek.

"Did you have a good day today?" Gage asked.

She turned to look at him. "Yes, it was a good day. I enjoyed meeting Gloria's grandfather, and dinner was nice."

Roman stood. "I'm heading to the shower."

He looked at Gage and Ari, leaving the invitation open. He walked out of the room.

Gage held his breath.

He saw emotions flashing through her eyes. He realized everything had to be on her terms so she didn't revert back inside herself and lock them out.

Gage prayed today would be the day she would come back to them.

Return to their bed.

Not just for sex, but to ease the separation that was hurting them.

Ari made up her mind, then stood. She was nervous. Even though she was one hundred percent healed *down there*, it scared her. She reached out her hand to Gage.

He stood and allowed her to lead the way.

ROMAN'S CLOTHES were on the floor. He stood naked before the mirror, shaving his five-o'clock shadow while the shower water steamed the room. He finished and wiped his face. His eyes went from Gage to Ari in the mirror. He stretched out his senses to test the emotional atmosphere.

He determined Ari was tense but was struggling to release her ironclad resolve.

Roman turned from the sink and walked over to Gage and Ari. The three of them sandwiched together in a loose embrace. The men lavished her with kisses across her face and down her neck while lightly running their hands over her breasts and up her arms.

"Ari. Ari," Roman said.

Her lips parted. They felt her passion building as they undressed her.

Gage stripped his clothes off. They entered the shower.

Roman pressed his lips to Ari's. He knew she missed kissing. She loved kissing. He let his mouth devour hers while he held her face.

She wrapped her arms around his neck. Latched her fingers in his thick, black hair.

Gage pressed against her back, his erection between them, his hands sliding down the sides of her body, brushing against her breasts.

Ari pulled away from Roman, turned around and sought Gage's mouth.

He didn't hold back.

"Oh, Ari," Gage said. "I've missed you so."

Ari pulled her mouth away from Gage. She reached out and grasped their cocks. She tilted her head back. An anguished moan escaped her lips.

Roman braced himself against the shower wall with one arm. "Ari, tell us what you want. We're afraid, and we don't want to hurt you or frighten you by going too fast."

As water poured over her, she faced them both.

"I'm scared. What if they didn't get everything out of me? What if it hurts? I feel all healed, but I haven't even touched myself because I'm so afraid."

They huddled in an embrace.

Roman and Gage stared at each other. They didn't exactly know how to proceed.

"Let's just touch," Roman said. "Get your juices flowing again."

CHAPTER SIXTEEN

AFTER THEIR SHOWER, Roman poured wine and Gage lit a fire in the fireplace. They sat on the sofa in their pajama pants with Ari in her baby-dolls and a loosely belted short robe. They sipped wine and cuddled.

Gage drew in a breath. So far, Ari had not responded the way she used to.

She wasn't getting wet. Something was still off.

Gage suspected the fear she mentioned—of something being left in her core that would hurt her. He couldn't determine how to approach that fear without pushing her over the brink.

It was difficult for Roman and Gage to keep their hands off her. They had had five wonderful, glorious years. They wanted that again. And they knew Ari wanted the same thing. They read her thoughts and her darkest secrets.

They all slept in Roman's bed for the first time in over two months. Just the relief of being close again put them under.

Gage woke first. He inhaled deeply, disappointed. Ari was

dry. He stared at the ceiling, got up and went to the bathroom, took a piss, then returned to bed.

Roman stirred. He met Gage's eyes, saw his sorrow.

He crinkled his forehead. Roman blocked Ari as he sent a message to Gage. *We've made progress. She's in the bed with us again.*

Ari turned over on her side, facing Gage. Her eyes fluttered open.

"Morning, beautiful," Gage said.

She reached out and touched his face. "Good morning."

"Did you sleep well?" Roman asked.

He hadn't sensed any turmoil or nightmares. She seemed to have slept soundly.

Ari turned over on her back. "I slept really well. I missed this."

"It felt good waking up beside you," Gage said.

He lowered his mouth to her neck and kissed her. Gage slid his tongue down her neck. He remembered it used to turn her on.

Ari's nipples stood at attention. She purred a little moan.

Roman's teeth scraped a nipple, then his mouth sucked while his tongue teased the tight tip.

Gage attacked the other nipple. Ari gasped. She couldn't lie still. Gage drew in a breath.

Her juices were flowing.

He silently rejoiced.

His hand slid to her folds. Two fingers touched her entrance.

Ari grabbed his wrist. "NO!"

Panic flooded her face. She scooted up the bed slightly.

Roman sat up. He glared at Gage. *What the fuck are you doing?*

"I can hear you, you know!" Ari said.

She breathed rapidly from the fear of being penetrated in any form.

"Let me try," Gage said. "I'll be gentle. We'll be able to find out if anything is wrong."

After several long moments, she nodded. "Be careful!"

She gripped his hand as Gage slowly inserted one finger inside her. He inched forward until he was in all the way.

Gage and Roman studied her face for a response.

She held her body stiff, unable to relax. Her hand clasped his like a vise. Waiting for something—anything horrendous to happen.

When she realized that nothing hurt, she relaxed her hand on his, but didn't let go. Not quite trusting her body — waiting for a betrayal from somewhere inside.

Gage slowly moved his finger in and out. She relaxed even more. She was getting wet. "Do you like that?"

Ari sucked in air. "Yes!" She practically screeched the word. "Don't stop!"

She pulled Roman's mouth to hers. "Roman!" She moaned into his kiss, mindless with an urgent need for release.

Ari wanted everything, and she wanted it now.

Gage withdrew his finger and replaced it with his mouth. He wrapped his arms around her hips and buried his face in her.

Ari grabbed Gage's hair with one hand, needing him to stay right where he was. Her other hand was in Roman's hair as his lips and tongue made love to her mouth. She missed his kisses so much. She didn't want him to stop.

She was so wet.

Gage was so happy.

Ari was like a wild woman that had been starved and presented a buffet. She pulled back from Roman and screamed as her first orgasm hit long and hard.

"I want you both," she repeated over and over as her orgasm crashed over her like a tidal wave pounding the beach.

Gage slid inside her. He kept his thrusts at a gentle pace. He realized this time he wouldn't be able to sustain himself—it had been so long since they had made love. It was all he could do to not lose it within the first few minutes.

Ari wrapped her legs around his hips, her heels digging into his butt, holding him in place. Her hands wrapped around his shoulders as she babbled nonsensical words, lost in the passion.

When another orgasm clenched down on his cock, Gage exploded. After a moment, he kissed her lightly on the lips.

She unwrapped herself from Gage and turned to Roman.

Roman devoured her mouth, then her breasts. He slid inside her and lay still for a moment, testing to make sure everything was still okay.

"It's okay, Roman. It's okay!" Ari practically yelled.

When he started a tempo, she wrapped her legs around him.

"Harder! Faster!" She begged. "It's okay."

Roman pumped into her, his mind gone. He lasted longer than Gage, but not by much.

When he blew his load, he let loose a groan of immense pleasure.

They all chuckled, then belly-laughed.

"Oh, my God, that was wonderful," Ari said.

"I'm sorry I couldn't last," Gage said. "It'll be better next time."

"That was a practice session," Roman said.

"We'll practice more later," Ari said. "Now I'm ready for breakfast."

AFTER BREAKFAST, they went downstairs to the gym. Even after all the physical therapy, Ari experienced moments of weakness in her arms and legs. Carlos, her physical therapist, had instructed her to use light weights for the next couple of months. After that, she could try increasing the weight in five-pound increments. Her PT didn't want her to over-exert her muscles.

Ari finished her reps on the leg press machine. She swung her legs around and stood. Her legs gave way underneath her.

"Roman!" she yelled.

He jumped off the machine he was on and grabbed for her before she hit the floor.

Gage sprinted across the gym from the free weight area. "Are you okay? What happened?"

Roman hung onto her.

"My legs got all shaky and wouldn't support me," she said.

"Did you increase the weight?" Roman asked. He eyeballed the machine. Three weights were on the stack.

Ari shrugged, guilty. "I only added five pounds."

"You probably think you look like a weakling, but your body has to recover," Gage said. "You can't manage fifteen pounds, as your legs proved to you."

"Do you want to work with Carlos again?" Roman asked. He was the physical therapist.

"I guess I'd better, so I don't end up worse than I already am," Ari said.

Roman pulled out his phone. Gage held up a hand.

"Why don't we take a break and go to the house in the woods? I'd really like to get out and fly in the mountains and over the forest," he said.

"I could go for that," Roman said.

He and Gage raised eyebrows in question at Ari.

"Yeah. That sounds good. I just want to sleep, read and make love," she said.

Roman and Gage got goofy looks on their faces as if they were teenage boys getting pussy for the first time.

"We shouldn't need many supplies," Ari said. "We stocked up and didn't stay that long last time."

"Let's go pack!" Gage said. They all headed to the elevator.

Ari pulled out her phone and called Jason. "Hi Jase. We're going to the house in the woods for a few days." She listened. "I don't need the wheelchair, but I'll bring my cane just in case."

She said this as Roman was holding her elbow because her legs were still shaky.

Roman squeezed her elbow, catching her telling the lie. She stuck her tongue out at him.

The elevator dropped them off at the penthouse and they all took different hallways to their rooms to get cleaned up and pack a bag.

An hour later, they were on the road.

THEY ARRIVED at the house a few minutes past three in the afternoon.

The guys were antsy to strip and be free. They dumped their bags in the bedroom and shed their clothes. They kissed her goodbye, went outside and shifted.

Ari watched them from the upstairs windows. She hung their clothes, unpacked their bags and set up toiletries in the bathroom. Then she perused the food in the freezer and refrigerator.

She removed a two-pound package of grass-fed ground beef from the freezer. Ari rooted around and took out a package of hamburger buns for tonight's supper and decided on a roast for tomorrow night. She also grabbed a family pack of chicken legs and wings. Ari planned to marinate and cook this tomorrow—Roman and Gage liked to snack on them when they needed protein.

ROMAN'S PANTHER ran like the wind through the forest. He climbed his favorite oak tree and sprawled on the branch that overlooked a stream. His eyes surveyed his domain. He projected his senses, inhaling deeply. Everything appeared to be in order. No strangers. No perceived threats.

Gage's wings took him over the forest to the mountains. He floated on the air currents, taking in everything on the ground with his sharp eyes. He saw squirrels and rabbits and other small game. Gage just wanted to fly; feel the wind ruffle his feathers.

Roman started on a perimeter run of the property. He wanted to make sure no hunters were about.

Notice anything unusual?

Gage soared over the property. Their two-thousand acres covered a little over three square miles.

Not finished yet, but nothing so far.

They didn't want any crazy hunters taking on action hero roles and screwing up their peaceful getaway.

ARI PULLED the cushions for the lounge chair on the patio out of the storage area in the garage. She adjusted the back of the chair flat so she could flip between her back and stomach. Ari settled in on her stomach, let out a sigh and drifted off.

A squawk from overhead woke her three hours later.

Ari shielded her eyes and watched Gage come in for a landing.

Roman's panther was sprawled out on the flagstones. He yawned. His enormous fangs glistened in the sunlight.

Ari reached out and ran her fingers over Roman's coat. "You should have woken me."

You were in a deep sleep.

Gage landed and folded his wings to his body.

I didn't see anyone on our land.

"That's good. Are you getting hungry?" Ari asked.

Roman made a purring sound. She took that as a yes.

Gage squawked. He was always hungry.

"Go get cleaned up. I'll check on the hamburger. It should be thawed." Ari got up.

The men shifted. They all entered the house.

THEY STAYED for four blissful days.

Roman ran through the forest while Gage floated on the wind.

Nighttime was Ari's, wrapped around her men. She couldn't get enough of them. The coma and recovery were long forgotten; her fears melted in their arms.

While they were driving back to the city, Sherm called. "Valk called. A trial date's set for Dominick McMahon. They're going to want Ari to testify, maybe you two as well. They've summoned Lonnie and me," Sherm said via FaceTime.

Fuck! This isn't good! Roman sent as he blocked Ari out.

Ari shrank into her seat. Waves of stress rolled off her.

Gage noticed Ari's withdrawal. *This can't be happening right now!*

"Why do I have to testify? I never saw that boy. I don't want to be made a spectacle of on national TV!"

Images of the slaughter room and Eddy's contorted face while he kicked and beat her ran through her head.

Homicidal rage rolled over Gage.

Roman's arms held her protectively as he prayed for control over his fury. He struggled to not shift in the SUV. He controlled his voice so he would sound as normal as possible. "I'll talk to the District Attorney's office and see what they want and how we need to proceed."

"It's too early to worry," Gage said. "Let Roman look into it."

"I should have killed him," Roman said.

"He didn't hurt me," Ari said. "From what you told me, it sounded like he was oblivious to what happened in that room."

"That's what he said, but I sensed a lie. I think he knew exactly what was going on in that room," Roman growled. He gripped his cat to keep from shifting. His panther roared in his head.

"Ari, our senses don't make mistakes," Gage said. "Our instincts are deeper and more dependable than human intuition or gut feelings."

"Sherm, has anyone mentioned if he will be accused of kidnapping all those other women, or just Ari?" Roman asked.

"Probably more than Ari," Sherm said. "Some of those bodies were down in that cellar for a decade. Others more recent. It will depend on when he was brought into the fold. I'm not sure if Valk knows—he'll probably bring in the mother to interview her. I imagine the kid got a court-appointed attorney. Depends on how much effort the attorney puts in to get his client a more lenient sentence."

"I don't care what anyone says," Gage raged. "That little prick was completely aware something bad was going on in that room. The problem is—proving he did. It's not like we can go to court and shift and then explain about our senses. There's no way he never heard anyone scream. I don't care what kind of fucking headphones he wore. I'll bet he jacked-off to psychotic daydreams."

"Thanks for calling, Sherm. We're on our way back to the city," Roman said.

Sherm signed off.

The inside of the SUV was quiet with everyone fully focused on the upcoming trial.

An hour later they parked in the building garage.

CHAPTER SEVENTEEN

ARI CAREFULLY DISENGAGED herself from Roman's arm, then climbed over Gage without waking him as she got out of the bed. She slipped into her robe and slippers and padded to the kitchen.

The clock on the stove read three a.m. Her mind was buzzing with bad memories and now the upcoming trial of that kid.

She walked over to the bar and grabbed the bottle of bourbon and a rocks glass, filled it with ice and poured the liquor. Ari checked the flue in the fireplace to be sure it was open, then turned on the gas starter.

Roman had three pecan logs stacked on the rack.

Ari sank into the sofa with her bourbon and stared at the fire. She felt bad about holding the men at arms-length tonight. Ari just couldn't get her head into the mood for sex with all these thoughts racing through her brain.

She was pretty sure they figured it would be a dry night after Sherm's call.

Ari took a slug of her drink and made a face as the bourbon slid down her throat.

Roman and Gage wandered into the room in their pajama pants, hair disheveled.

"You okay?" Gage asked. He eyed her drink. "What're you drinking?"

"Whiskey," Ari said.

"Couldn't sleep?" Roman asked.

"I wish Sherm hadn't called," Ari said. "Ruined our perfect getaway. Now I have all these images racing through my head and I can't shut them down."

Roman slid in back of her on the sofa and pulled them into the end of the sofa with their legs stretched out. He wrapped her in his arms and nuzzled her neck.

"Everything will work out," he said.

Gage crossed to the bar, grabbed the bottle of Blade and Bow 22-year Kentucky Straight Bourbon and brought it to the living room.

He took Ari's glass, filled it to the brim and took a slug, then passed it to Roman. They shared the glass between the three of them until it was empty.

Gage grabbed Ari's feet and massaged the bottom of one. "The trial is unavoidable. We need to sweep that out the door as soon as possible. Why don't you talk to Lorraine?"

"That's not a bad idea," Ari said. "I'll call her when we have more details." She appeared thoughtful. "You don't think he'll be exonerated, do you?"

Roman sensed her emotions spike.

"There's no way that little fucker is going to walk away from this. I don't care who his attorney is," Gage said.

After breakfast, Roman and Gage took the elevator to Sherm's office.

"WHAT'S UP?" Sherm asked as they entered his office. Gage pulled the door shut behind him.

Sherm raised his eyebrows.

Roman filled him in on Grandfather Silver Wolf and Gloria. "Gloria told us there were shifters all around us, but they were scared of us," Roman said. "We need to find them—force them out in the open so we can meet them. Maybe we can find someone to take care of this little problem—without Ari finding out."

"If I could figure out a way to kill him in the jail, I'd do it," Gage said. "Save the taxpayers a lot of money."

"We need a location where they'll consider it safe meeting with you," Sherm said. "We have that vacant warehouse space over on Fourth Street. It's out of the way, visible entry and exits and no one will feel trapped."

"Yeah, that would work," Gage said. He turned to Roman. "You're much more diplomatic than I am. You should be the one to call out to them."

Roman nodded. "Okay. Sherm, you and Lonnie get the space set up. I have no idea how many will want to meet with us. When you're ready, we can all go over there and I'll give it a try."

Two days later, Roman and Gage stood in the large parking area at the warehouse on Fourth Street.

Sherm and Lonnie, in business attire, stood on either side of the open doorway.

Roman broadcast a message loud and clear while blocking Ari.

We are aware you're out there and you can hear me. We want to meet your kind. We do not want to harm you. We are part of the same family, distant cousins, perhaps. Come to the warehouse on 1717 Fourth Street. Do not be afraid of us. Please come. Now.

Gage checked his iPhone for the time. Eleven-ten. "Some of them may be on their lunch break or getting ready for lunch," Gage said. He hoped someone would show up. Even one shifter would be a cause for celebration.

A car pulled around the corner, slowed, then stopped.

The lone occupant looked their way.

He made a decision. The car pulled into the parking lot and parked.

A fifty-year-old man in a suit got out and eyed them warily.

"Who are you? I heard your call. It was quite loud," he said.

"Sorry it was so loud, but we're glad you're here," Roman said.

Roman and Gage did not approach the man. They let him come to them. They introduced themselves.

The man eyed them—like he recognized them. He bowed.

His eyes darted to Sherm and Lonnie.

"They work for us," Gage said. "Yes, they're humans, but you have nothing to fear from them unless you do us harm. Then all bets are off."

Other people arrived on foot and in cars. A few people arrived via the bus.

"Let's go inside," Roman said. "If you haven't had lunch, we set up a buffet of sorts."

When they were all inside the warehouse and people were getting plates of food, Roman took the floor. He introduced himself.

"Gage and I are happy to meet you. We've been alone for a long, long time, and didn't know there were other shifters," he said. "We only recently discovered that we are not traditional shifters, but our kind are called Tothars."

"How could you not tell? We're all around you," a woman asked. She curtsied awkwardly.

"Because your kind never approached us. We thought we were the only two shifters on the planet," Gage said. "Like Roman said, we didn't realize we weren't regular shifters. No one told us what a Tothar was until just a few weeks ago."

"Who told you?" the first man asked after he bowed.

"Ben Hatahle—Grandfather Silver Wolf," Gloria announced as she entered the warehouse. She met Roman's eyes. "Next time, tone it down. I'm sure they heard you up in Alaska!"

"Oh, I had no idea," Roman said. He hugged Gloria. "It's good to see you, Gloria."

She kissed him on the cheek, then hugged Gage.

She turned to the group of around forty men and women. "You can trust Roman and Gage, and their human staff, Sherm and Lonnie."

"Why did you ask us here?" someone asked after he bowed.

Roman laid it all out. Ari's abduction. Eddy. Dom. The trial. What they wanted to happen.

"Why didn't you call out to us when your lady was kidnapped?" A man with a scruffy beard asked. "We would have helped with the search!"

Loud murmurs of agreement ran through the warehouse.

Gage shrugged. "We were trying to communicate directly with her. We didn't realize we should have done otherwise."

"If it hadn't been for Gloria, we never would have realized any of you existed," Roman said.

Gloria huffed. "Look, they didn't know anything until I showed them I was a shifter and there were others. Let's move on and let them explain why we're all here."

Nodding and murmurs swept through the group.

"Gage and I can't very well get into the jail as our animals," Roman said. He let his panther face and claws show.

A wiry man stepped forward. He bowed with a grand flourish. "I can."

He let his rather large wharf rat show through. "My pack and I can get in the jail and take care of this business."

Three men and one woman joined the rat-man. They all bowed.

"Are you sure? There are risks," Gage said.

"We're rats. Risks come with the territory. People try to poison or trap us every day," the woman said. "I've watched the interviews on the news. This guy doesn't even have an inch of regret or sorrow for all those women. He could have stopped that serial killer pal of his, but he chose to turn a blind eye. Or, in his case, a deaf ear."

"Is your mate okay?" a woman in the crowd asked after she curtsied. "They didn't give details on TV, but they showed that spiked tube thing. I'd like to take that and shove it up that guy's ass before he's killed!"

A rumble of angry sentiment spread through the shifters in the warehouse.

Roman rubbed his eyes. "I will never be able to erase the pictures in my head when we rescued her. I'm not even sure how she survived, but she did and she's okay."

He shared some images.

People gasped at the horror.

"Ari still has problems, but if that bastard goes to trial and they make her take the stand—that may crush her completely," Gage said.

"I was one of the nurses who attended Ari in her coma," Gloria said. "She literally hid in her mind. She was so afraid to wake up—afraid she was still in that hellhole."

Rat-man stepped forward and touched Roman's arm. "We'll take care of it."

THEY WERE JUST FINISHING breakfast when Roman's phone rang at seven-forty-five the next morning. He saw it was Sherm calling. He hoped nothing was wrong.

"Turn on the news," Sherm said.

Gage and Ari hurried to the living room.

"What's happened?" Ari asked.

"Not sure," Roman said with a touch of innocence.

Gage grabbed the remote and plugged in local news.

"... the two victims appeared to have been attacked by rats..." an announcer said.

Gage flipped to another channel. A picture of Dom filled the screen.

"Dominic McMahon had been incarcerated awaiting trial as an accomplice for the kidnapping and murders of fourteen women..."

Ari flinched.

Gage flipped back one channel.

"Loren Trevathan, accused of raping a twelve-year-old girl, was the second victim at the jail, killed by rats. The medical examiner said there were over fifty bites on Trevathan, but McMahon received the brunt of the attack with more than a hundred."

"The public is outraged, demanding a safer environment for incarcerated..."

The news showed a group of protesters outside the jail with placards.

Gage clicked the TV off. "No more trial to worry about."

"Rats?" Ari asked. She shuddered. "I hate rats and spiders. Add snakes to that mix."

Roman blocked Ari and blasted out a silent thank you. He received many acknowledgments.

"They must have attacked him at night while he was sleeping," Gage said. "I never heard about a problem with rats in the jail before."

"Rats are vicious," Roman said. "I imagine there will be more details on the news later."

"Roman, let's go see what else Sherm and Lonnie have come up with," Gage said. He kissed Ari on the cheek. "We'll be back in a little while."

Ari headed to the kitchen.

CHAPTER EIGHTEEN

ROMAN AND GAGE entered the elevator. Gage held his fingers in an X and pointed up to the penthouse. He silently communicated to Roman with Ari blocked out.

You'd better pray no one slips up, and she finds out about this, Gage said.

You want to level with her? Roman asked.

Yes. No secrets, remember? Gage said.

Roman worried for a few seconds, his face screwing up while he mulled it over. *Okay. When we go back upstairs, We'll tell her. You're right. No secrets.*

They arrived in Sherm's office and caught him stuffing half a cheese kolache in his mouth, so he couldn't talk.

Roman took a picture with his iPhone and sent it to Ari. "What a slob!"

Sherm garbled, "Sorry."

"We decided we need to confess to Ari about the rats," Gage said. "It wouldn't go over well if she caught us in a lie."

Sherm took a slug of coffee and swallowed the mess in his

mouth. "That's a good idea. She's going to meet the shifter community anyway, right?"

"Yes," Gage said. "Sooner rather than later."

"I'm glad none of the rat-people were hurt or killed," Roman said. "We need to meet with the community again and find out how they go about things. Like how they work with the humans, or even if any other humans have a clue about them."

"Yeah, we could be the only ones not on board," Gage said.

"I don't know about that," Sherm said. "I've never heard of a shifter community and never knew shifters existed, other than in novels until I met you two. And you know how long I've been running ops. Lonnie and I have our eyes and ears on things throughout the world with your businesses. We have *never* run across any shifters."

"They now realize we have a special relationship with you two, but they don't have any intel about our special ops team, you or Lonnie," Roman said. "We need to find out what kind of people these shifters are. If there's anyone in charge, or if they all do their own thing."

"It would be helpful if you brought Ari on board with this. She could organize the collection of information about this new community. That woman has a unique mind," Sherm said.

ROMAN AND GAGE stepped off the elevator and searched for Ari. They found her on the sofa in her library with one of the ancient books on her lap.

She looked up when they came into the room.

"What's up?" Ari studied their faces. "Did you do something wrong? You look guilty."

Their faces gave them away at that point. Roman huffed out an exasperated sigh.

"You know you can't hide things from me," Ari said. "Just spit it out. I know you had something to do with that young man's death. I can't figure out how you'd control a bunch of rats."

Gage grabbed the book out of her hands and set it on the coffee table. He plunked down on the edge of the sofa, facing her.

Roman took the other side.

"Okay, here's the deal," Gage began. "We found the shifter community."

Ari sat up straighter. She looked from one to the other, her face wide open with surprise. "How did that happen? Why didn't you tell me?"

"We wanted to protect you," Roman said. "The whole business with a trial could have pushed you back inside yourself, and we didn't want to take that chance.

"Remember Gloria telling us there was a shifter community? We were determined to connect with them."

They took turns explaining about the warehouse, the people who showed up, the plan and the rat-people carrying out the plan.

"The strange thing was, all the men bowed, and the women curtsied," Roman said. "I seem to recall the first time we met Gloria. She curtsied."

Gage tapped his finger in the air, pointing to Roman. "You're right. I forgot about that. We need to go see this Atsa person and sort this out so we understand all this shifter and Tothar business."

"I'm sure they have protocols they follow," Ari said. "We don't want to make any blunders—get anyone mad at us due to our ignorance."

"When do we want to go? Do we have to make arrangements with this Atsa ahead of time?" Gage asked. "Lonnie can get the jet ready. Should we have the team come with us just in case?"

"In case of what?" Roman asked. "You think we'd be attacked on the reservation?"

"I don't know what to expect, do you?" Gage asked. "I don't want to take any chances."

"Why don't you call Gloria?" Ari asked. "She probably has inside information on how to proceed."

Roman clicked on Gloria's picture in his contacts' list on his iPhone. When she answered, he put it on speaker.

"Hi Gloria. We hope you can help us out," Roman said.

Gage and Ari said, "hi."

They outlined their trip to see Atsa.

"If you bring your team, make sure they wear street clothes —you know, dressed down so they don't appear like military or government whatsoever. I don't see any problem with them going along. Ari needs protection," Gloria said. "Atsa doesn't travel much, so you're most likely safe to go anytime."

"Okay. We'll make arrangements on our end. Tell Grandfather Silver Wolf we're on it," Gage said.

Gage pulled out his phone and texted both Sherm and Lonnie to get everything in place to leave in the morning.

"We should bring the books," Ari said.

THE JET LANDED at Four Corners Regional Airport where two black SUVs awaited them.

After loading the luggage in the backs of the vehicles, Roman, Gage, Ari and Sherm claimed one while Lonnie and the team got in the other.

They headed out, Lonnie in the lead position following the directions to Shiprock, New Mexico. As they drove through small towns and rural areas, they noted pedestrians and people on their own property stare with distrusting eyes as the two SUVs passed by.

"They don't take to strangers here," Gage said.

Ari stewed as she looked through the windows. "You'd figure we were in a third-world country or something. I can't believe the poverty! Right here in the United States. The first, true Americans! Our government should be ashamed of itself."

"They probably assume we're government people in these SUVs," Sherm said.

He called Lonnie. "Be on the alert. People may think we're from Washington."

Lonnie slowed ahead of them. He turned his directional light on and turned left at a traffic light. The intersection sported a gift shop, leather goods store, a bakery and a one-pump gas station on the corners in weathered buildings.

They drove for another two miles, with dust billowing behind them.

Lonnie slowed, then stopped. He got out of the vehicle and walked back to theirs.

On the right side of the road, a couple of hundred feet back, stood a couple of hogans and some modular buildings.

Sherm lowered his window.

"It's one of these places," Lonnie said.

They all looked out the window and took in the lay of the land.

Nothing but hard dirt with scattered pinyon trees and cactus for as far as you could see.

A clothesline with a day's wash hung on the line with not even a breeze to sway the drying clothes.

"Well, let's pull into the driveway and find out where we can find this Atsa," Gage said.

A Native American man walked toward them from one of the modular buildings. He wore a long-sleeved faded blue shirt, jeans and tennis shoes. A cowboy hat perched on his head and his long black hair hung straight to the middle of his chest.

He walked to where Lonnie stood alongside the second SUV.

"Are you lost?" the man asked. His posture was stiff as if he waited for some type of action.

Gage and Roman got out of the vehicle. Ari leaned out the open door.

The man stared at them. A fleeting glimmer of surprise passed over his face.

Roman and Gage caught that and something else they couldn't identify.

"We're looking for Atsa," Roman said.

"What do you want with Atsa?" the man asked. He never took his eyes off Roman and Gage. "Grandfather Silver Wolf sent us," Roman said.

The man's posture softened. "That old wolf is still alive? He must be over a hundred!"

"One-hundred-two!" Gage said.

The man stuck out his hand. "I'm Yiska. Atsa's expecting you."

They all shook Yiska's hand.

"If you don't mind me asking, what does your name mean?" Ari asked.

"Night has passed," Yiska said. "I was born at dawn."

"Oh, that makes sense," Ari said. "It's a beautiful name."

Yiska gave a soft nod to Ari. He took in her beauty.

Roman felt Yiska's softness surround Ari with a hint of affection.

Gage laid a hand on Roman's arm, stopping him from an inappropriate possessive acting out.

"Pull up in front of that second modular building," Yiska said. He jogged back to the building.

"Did Gloria call him?" Ari asked.

"I guess so," Roman said.

They parked where Yiska indicated and they got out of the vehicles.

Sherm and Lonnie stayed with their team while Roman, Gage and Ari followed Yiska inside the building.

Despite the poverty on the outside, the interior of the modular building was attractive, with handmade Navajo rugs and artwork.

An artist had painted a mural of Indian life before reservation life. It depicted a life rich with tribal pride and traditions.

Several elderly Navajo men sat talking off to the side. They stopped speaking when they saw who followed Yiska.

Their eyes widened as they stared at the two white men and woman.

"Wait here and I'll go find Atsa," Yiska said.

Ari, Roman and Gage waited in an uncomfortable silence as the old men scrutinized them. Ari walked to the wall and studied the mural.

A tall, well-built man entered from an interior room, followed by Yiska.

"I'm Atsa," he announced. He studied the three before him.

His eyes flinched ever so slightly as he sensed their very large animals, but Roman caught the change.

"I'm Roman, and this is Gage and Ari," Roman introduced. "Did Gloria call you?"

"Who's Gloria?" Atsa asked.

"Silver Wolf's granddaughter," Roman said.

"No. No one called," Atsa said.

Why did Yiska say he was expecting us? Gage asked Roman and Ari.

"I heard you coming," Atsa said. "And the message you blasted out to your people. It was loud."

"Oh," Roman said. "I'm sorry. I didn't realize how far I could project. Gloria said they could probably hear me in Alaska."

"They did. I had people asking me who you were," Atsa said. "I told them we'd find out soon enough and now you're here. Come inside so we can talk."

He turned around and headed to the interior room with Roman, Gage, and Ari following.

Yiska joined them and closed the door behind him. Atsa invited them to make themselves comfortable. Gage positioned Ari between him and Roman on a sofa. Atsa sat opposite on a loveseat.

Yiska leaned against the wall, studying them. "Why are you here?" Atsa asked.

"Grandfather Silver Wolf said you could tell us about our kind and where we come from," Roman said. "He mentioned you had a document or a book..."

"You're Tothars, not normal shifters," Atsa said. "Tothars are royalty to our kind, but we thought the line was extinct."

"Grandfather Silver Wolf said it had been eighty years since he had seen a Tothar," Gage said. "What happened to them?"

"You need a history lesson," Atsa said. "Don't worry, I'll go easy on you—no test. First off, your animals are enormous compared to regular shifters."

He nodded to Gage. "Your eagle is twice the size of mine. Your wings must have a large span."

"They're about twenty-five feet across," Gage said. "Makes it difficult for take-offs in tight places."

Atsa nodded at that. He turned his focus to Roman. "*Panthera onca*, otherwise known as black jaguars in America. Your panther makes regular shifter cats, better known as ailuranthropy, or werecats, look like kittens in comparison. They like to swim—does your cat play in water?"

Roman smirked. "There's a stream on our land and my cat loves to get wet."

Atsa swung his gaze back to Gage. "I don't know the Greek term for eagle—I'll have to check with Google."

Yiska thumbed his phone. "I can't find a Greek word for an eagle or bird shifter, just aetós for eagle, and poulí for bird." Yiska spelled the Greek words.

Next, Atsa turned his gaze to Ari. "Your bloodline is so diluted I don't pick up any animal, but you are Tothar."

Ari pulled in a deep breath. "I'm a Tothar?" Her mind reeled. Her eyes met Roman and Gage's.

"Didn't anyone in your family ever speak of your heritage?" Atsa asked.

"No! The closest I ever came to shifters was in novels until I met Roman and Gage," Ari said.

"It is very unusual for three to bond," Atsa said. "But your bond is strong—for life. It has to do with the three of you being Tothars. Your family did you a disservice," Atsa said. "Is there anyone left on your mother's side? Any elders you can talk to?"

Ari considered for a moment. "I'm not sure if my aunt Aileen is still alive. I'll have to track her down. She would be over a hundred."

"Try to find her. She may be the only link to your heritage. Typically, shifters never have a problem with old age regarding dementia or Alzheimer's," Atsa said.

He turned to Yiska. "Go get the book."

Yiska left the room. He returned a few minutes later with an old, square, hand-tooled book in a rich brown leather cover. He handed it to Atsa.

Atsa stretched out on his side of the coffee table and opened the book. He flipped through the pages until he was about a quarter of the way into the book. He turned the book so they could see what he would explain.

"Therianthropy, sometimes referred to as zoanthropy, is Greek. Theríon means wild animal or beast, and Anthrōpos means human being. We're supposed to be these mythical humans that can metamorphose or shape-shift into animals. Almost every culture has stories of shapeshifters, and most cave drawings show humans changing into animals, or half human, half animal. Nothing mythological about us. We're here in the flesh in modern society," Atsa said.

"Cave drawings are pre-agriculture, around eight-thousand BC. Egypt's first dynasty began around thirty-one BC. According to this ancient text, Tothars came into existence before that time. We don't understand where, why or how shifters came after that, or why they are so different from Tothars. You have superior senses, strength and magical abilities than we do," Atsa said.

"Wait! Back up. Magical abilities?" Gage asked. "I don't have anything like that." He turned to Roman. "Do you?"

Roman shook his head. "Nothing like that. But we have extraordinary vision and sense of smell."

"Those abilities are there, just buried," Atsa said.

"Go get our books," Ari encouraged Gage.

He got up and left the room.

"Years ago, I bought this ancient Chinese set of eight books at an estate sale. There seems to be a lot of information about shifters. We've translated only part of a page, so we haven't discovered all the information that might be helpful. All we do is look at the pictures."

Atsa said something to Yiska in Navajo. Yiska left the room.

Gage returned with the box of books and set it on the floor. Ari opened the box and retrieved one of the books. She handed it to Atsa.

Atsa's eyes widened with surprise. He ran his hand over the cover. This old book predated his book. He opened the book and noted the neat Chinese characters. He turned the pages and studied drawings and sketches.

"This blows my mind," Atsa said. "Would you mind if I invited the elders to look at the books?"

"Go right ahead," Roman said. He pulled the rest of the books out of the box and displayed them on the coffee table.

Atsa got up, opened the door and spoke to the old men. They filed into the room.

The elders hovered around the coffee table, looking at the books spread out before them. One by one, they picked up a book. They sat and studied the pages, each with a profound expression on their faces.

Yiska and a woman came into the room with a tray of glasses. "Would you like some iced tea?"

"Thank you so much," Ari said. She reached out and took a glass and a napkin. She wrapped the napkin around the sweating glass.

The elders spoke among themselves in Navajo, each pointing to the book in their laps.

"This is quite remarkable," one of the elders said.

He spoke to his friends in Navajo, then in English. "We should apply for a grant to have the books translated."

"We thought about that," Ari said. "But we decided against it because we don't want this information to get out there— anywhere near government hands."

The elders and Atsa nodded.

"I'll hire someone to translate the books," Roman said. "I'd rather have someone under a non-disclosure agreement whose loyalty will be mine."

"Our company can afford to tackle this project, and we have great benefits," Gage said. "We could keep this person on the payroll. These books are pretty dense."

"Would you consider sharing the translations with us?" Atsa asked.

"You bet," Gage said.

There was a knock on the doorframe.

Atsa turned around and saw Sherm in the doorway.

Sherm met Roman's eyes. "I'm sorry to disturb you, but we have a little situation outside."

Atsa got to his feet and stormed out of the room followed by everyone.

They all piled out of the building. They saw Lonnie and the team across from some young warriors in their teens and twenties posturing aggressively toward them.

Navajo people had come out of their houses to observe the interplay between their young warriors and the strangers.

Ari heard the word *Tothars* as the people watched and talked among themselves.

"You would dishonor us by treating our guests badly?" Atsa asked.

"They bring their high and mighty superiority and look down on us," a young man spit out.

Atsa stared him down. "You're proving they are superior to you. You're acting like an ass instead of a welcome committee."

The guy snarled at Atsa. He shifted into his wolf form and growled menacingly. His drool spilled from his mouth as he threatened Lonnie and the team.

Atsa motioned to Roman and Gage. "Shift."

Roman and Gage stepped out of their shoes and shifted, along with Atsa.

Roman's panther growled at the wolf. His cat was twice the size of the wolf. He stalked over and positioned himself between the wolf and his security team. Roman hissed, showing gleaming, sharp fangs. His tail twitched, ready to engage.

Atsa and Gage took to the sky. Atsa's eagle was the size of a crow compared to Gage's large eagle.

The wolf snarled at Roman.

Just as Roman was going to retaliate, Gage swooped in and grabbed the wolf by the fur on its back. He hauled it into the air as if it were a mouse, shaking him.

The wolf shrieked in fright and pain as Gage's talons dug into the fur. Blood dripped down the wolf's sides.

Atsa swept in and pecked the wolf on its head. He screeched at the wolf.

The warriors and citizens outside gaped at the action unfolding.

Gage swooped toward the ground. He shook the wolf, then dropped him to the ground. Gage performed an aerial move gliding on his large wings, then landed. Atsa landed beside him.

The tension eased among the groups.

The young warriors did not go to the aid of their shifter brother.

Roman, Gage and Atsa shifted. No one seemed concerned about the three men standing naked among them.

"I'm sorry—," Sherm began.

Atsa held up his hand. "Not your place to apologize. My people are leery of anything and anyone who looks like the government. But that isn't any excuse for these young idiots to attempt to accost you or your people."

The young wolf shifted. He limped off as blood streaked down his naked back.

Soon, his pals followed.

"I'll deal with them later," Atsa said.

Roman and Gage opened the back of their SUV and dug into their bags and put clothes on.

Atsa returned inside.

The elders remained outside with Ari.

CHAPTER NINETEEN

"COME BACK INSIDE," an elder urged.

He motioned for Sherm and his group to come inside, as well. "It's too hot for you to stay out here. You don't have to worry about the cars or anything." They all went inside.

Atsa had put on clothes and was tying his tennis shoes. He beckoned Roman, Ari and Gage into the inner room. The elders followed.

Yiska played host to Sherm and the team. "Sit and be comfortable."

The woman entered the room with a tray of iced tea and passed them around to the team.

THE ELDERS RESEATED themselves and took up the books. Ari sat between two of them and they looked at pictures, carefully turning pages.

"Look at this," one elder pointed to a picture. "This must be about Tothars. See how much larger the animals are in this sketch compared to this one?"

"Even the cave dwellers could see the difference," another elder said.

"I wonder how many shifter animals there are?" Ari asked. "When I go back home, I'll make a list from every picture in these books, and our shifter community. I'll email Atsa the list. Study it and tell me if you are aware of any other animals."

"That is a good plan. I hope the translations begin soon," the elder said.

"Roman will find the right person and get the project underway. He's a man of action," she said.

The elders nodded.

ATSA, Roman and Gage sat huddled talking.

"It's important for you to understand the shifters in your community," Atsa said. "When you get back home, call a gathering. You need to know who they are, what their animals are, and how you can get in touch with them. Don't even worry about them getting upset. Shift and show them you're the boss. They recognized you as royalty from what you said about all that bowing and curtsying."

"Why will that make them want to tell us anything?" Roman asked.

"Try to understand. Tothars—you two—are the kings of all shifters. Even for us here on the rez, and Ari is your queen, even though she doesn't have an animal. You can make their lives easier by organizing them or make their lives hell. You'll have their scents so it's not like they can hide," Atsa said.

"It would be nice if someone among them would help you to understand their community. Do they meet? Are they in packs or clans in their own houses? Do they all live separately? You've got to understand how they've existed, and for how long —get as much information as you can. It will help you learn your place in their society."

Roman and Gage nodded in agreement. It sounded like a good plan.

"We can do that," Gage said. "Ari is a whiz at organizing."

"I will inform our people about you," Atsa said. "So, expect company."

"Are you sure there's no other Tothars in the United States?" Roman asked. "We don't want to step on anyone's toes."

"Believe me, you're it here in the US. I have heard no reports of Tothars from other countries or continents. If someone gets their hackles up, you can bet you'll find out," Atsa said.

"When we find our translator and get our books translated, I'd like to get your book scanned," Roman said. "I thought about finding a historian to help with the project. We're going to need someone who knows what equipment should be used to scan in all these ancient books. I read online that there's special equipment that can be used without damaging the pages or ink with the ultraviolet light.

"That may be expensive," Atsa said.

"Not for us," Gage said with a wide smile.

THEY ARRIVED BACK in the city with new goals and expectations. Roman and Gage met with Sandy to begin a search for a translator. They also spoke to her about a historian but decided to wait on that position for a while.

Ari was busy determining what information should be

collected about the shifters. She sat with Roman and Gage in Sherm's office.

Lonnie's fingers clacked on a keyboard. Sherm looked over Lonnie's shoulder.

"Information gathering will be easier once we have the basics," Lonnie said.

It was important to discover who was out there in their city, their professions, and what roles they played as shifters.

"Do you want to continue to have meetings in the warehouse, or do we want to use the event space on the first floor?" Ari asked.

Sherm screwed his face in thought. "I'm not too crazy about them being in the building. Think about those rats. They could easily get into the offices or the penthouse."

"Don't you think they could have done that at any time?" Roman asked. "They've known about us for a long time. We're the new kids on the block."

"When you put it that way," Sherm conceded. "This is more centrally located. And one problem will be partially solved. They'll need a badge to get in, so that helps with data gathering."

"We'll have to hire some contractors to make that area private," Lonnie said. "It's all glass, remember?"

Ari jotted notes on her notepad. "We need to help these shifters out a little. When you shift under emergency situations, it destroys your clothes. We should get an assortment of T-shirts, hoodies, sweat pants and shoes in an assortment of sizes for men and women. We could have a wall of cabinets for them with sizes noted on the edge of the shelf."

"You think of everything," Gage said.

"Comes with experience," Ari said. "I've seen you go through clothes that ended up as rags. Some of these people may not have the budget for more than second-hand shops."

"I want a camera focused on the door inside that area. Then cameras in each of the event rooms. Sherm, you can set up your facial recognition software," Roman said. "That way if someone decides they don't want to offer information, or be a part of our growing family, we can keep tabs on them."

"Wait a minute, Roman," Gage said. "Tothars are royalty. All the shifters in this city need to comply whether they like it or not. We don't want any hidden factions."

"For crying out loud, let's not turn this into a police state where you're squashing people under your thumbs," Ari said. "You'll never get anyone on your side. First of all, we need to get to know them. Find allies. Sniff out potential troublemakers. Key word—potential. Some may come across as nontrusting just because of their experience in the human world. Only time will tell.

"Now, this space downstairs—does it have a kitchen area? Are there round or square tables? A large screen and equipment to show overheads, presentations, Wi-Fi for laptops and phones?"

Roman stood. "I can't remember. Come on, let's go check it out."

They took the elevator down to the lobby. Alex, the doorman was at the front desk giving the receptionist a bathroom break. "Good morning, Mr. Roman, Mr. Gage and Ms. Ari," he said.

He tilted his hat to Sherm and Lonnie.

"Hi Alex," Ari said.

"We want to see the event area. Do you know if it's in use right now?" Gage asked.

The clack of heels brought the receptionist back to the reception area. "Good morning everyone."

"Is anyone in the event rooms?" Alex asked.

"It's open," the receptionist said.

Gage nodded to her and they walked around the desk to the door of the events area.

Ari noted the restrooms on either side of the area as she walked toward the event place.

"I don't like the idea of this room being open," Sherm said. "It should be secured at all times."

THE EVENT PLACE covered the ground floor and was divided into rooms with sliding walls to partition large venues into smaller meeting areas. It was a very dull location without any bells or whistles as far as the equipment was concerned. Ari opened a door in one of the rooms. It turned out to be a large storage area with old round and square tables and stacks of uncomfortable looking hard chairs.

Sherm opened another door and discovered the kitchen area. "Hey, Ari, I found the kitchen."

Ari left the storage room and joined the guys in the kitchen. She made a face.

"Uh oh. Looks like I need to increase the limits on your credit cards," Gage said.

"Not really. Any work will be through issued purchase orders. Is all of this event space available to other businesses in the building, or as an event place for anyone in the city?" Ari asked.

"It's an open venue for booking," Roman said, "but I don't know how often it's used. Let's ask the receptionist."

He and Ari left the room and returned to the reception desk. She was on a call. She raised her finger to them.

"Isn't there typically two people at the desk?" Ari asked. "Yeah, I wonder where the other woman is?" Roman looked at his watch. It wasn't lunchtime.

The woman finished giving directions to the caller and ended the call. "What could I do for you, Mr. Davenport?"

They asked about the event bookings.

The receptionist pulled out the booking binder and flipped it open. "There hasn't been a booking in a few months, and even then, there's not much interest in any of the rooms."

"Where's the other lady that works with you?" Ari asked.

"Oh, Susan's daughter has chicken pox," the woman said. "Makes me itchy just thinking about it."

The phone buzzed. The receptionist held up a finger while she grabbed the call.

"Call a temp agency and get someone else here until Susan gets back," Roman said.

The woman gave a thumbs-up while she directed the call.

Roman and Ari returned to the event rooms.

"The best thing to do is to hire one of those event planners to help get this place set up," Ari said. "Is this soundproof?"

"I'm not sure," Roman said. "We'll have to experiment."

Roman went inside and Ari stayed outside, listening. She heard Roman calling to her through the closed door.

FOR THE MOST PART, the meeting site was not that bad, the rooms were just desperate for a face lift. Ari worked with an event planner who worked with the contractor to revive the place.

They donated the old furniture.

While all this activity was going on, Sandy presented five resumes to Roman, Gage, and Ari for the translator position. There were four men and one woman, and their ages ranged from their mid-twenties to middle age. She starred one resume, but wisely placed it at the end of the PDF so the others would at least be glanced over.

They studied the resumes. All candidates had good qualities. They arranged interviews for the next two days.

The first candidate was a young man in his twenties with a master's degree in literature. He spoke three languages fluently. There was something about him they didn't like, so he received the 'we'll get back in touch'. Sandy would send the standard reject letter.

The woman was all business. She tried hard to impress the guys with her feminine wiles and flirted as if she were a contestant on a dating show.

Roman escorted her out before Ari had a chance to set eyes on her.

They spoke briefly with the third candidate and considered him with a promise to let him know their decision.

The last candidate was the starred resume. He came prepared with not only books he translated, but the original documents so he could explain his process. His name was An Da Tran, and he was middle-aged with thick black hair and had a scholarly quality about him. He wore a three-piece suit and a pocket watch that hung on a chain. They discovered he was a historian as well.

Roman, Gage, and Ari sat around a table with Mr. Tran. The man was easy to talk to. They looked over his show and tell and talked in generality on a number of subjects displayed on his resume.

"As you can see, when I translate a document, if there is any ambiguity, I bracket my thoughts as to what the difference could be. I also bracket things I researched to substantiate my notes.

Roman, Gage and Ari discovered that he lived a distance

away. They would have to relocate him if he wanted the job, which they hoped he would.

They took him out to lunch and learned that he was a widower with four grown children and three grandchildren.

"Would it be difficult for you to move away from your family?" Ari asked. As a mother, she was concerned about separation from family.

Mr. Tran waved a hand in front of him. "They're scattered. No two of them live in the same state anymore. They have their own lives and I'm an old man."

They headed back to the office. Roman brought out one of the ancient books and placed it on the table in front of Mr. Tran.

Mr. Tran ran his hand reverently over the cover as he looked up at his prospective employers.

"This is one of the books we would like translated," Roman said. "We have a set of eight and you may find the subject matter unusual, but I guarantee you will also find it interesting."

An Da opened the book. He studied the first page and flipped carefully through several pages. "If I'm not mistaken, this work is from the Shang Dynasty, which is 1200-1050 BC, but I will have to research this to make an accurate time-line." He lifted his eyes from the page and stared across the table with a radiated face. "This is the type of project I've waited my entire career for!"

"Mr. Tran, we think you're a great fit for this project," Roman said. "Would you like the job?"

An Da Tran nodded. "When can I begin?" He gazed at the big book with longing.

"I'll return you to Sandy downstairs. If you don't have time today, she can set up an appointment to go over the paperwork with you. We'll pay all your relocation expenses, even buying out your lease if you have one, or buying and selling your house. We have apartments in the building, and you can stay until you find your ideal home environment. Or, you can stay in the building apartment permanently. Once you get moved, you'll be able to learn the city and make that decision."

An Da bowed slightly. "Thank you for this opportunity. I look forward to working with you."

BESIDES THE UPDATE to the event space, Roman had the reception area updated to include two additional stations.

Sherm insisted that the front desk be occupied twenty-four seven because people lived in the building. Plus, different companies leased office space. He included two employees from the security business.

Ari was in charge of the grand reveal. She gathered her men, including Sherm and Lonnie and they entered the place.

Sherm and Lonnie had installed the double cardkey entry system. Not only was a special coded card required, but once it was inserted in the slot, a personal code had to be entered on the keypad. If a counterfeit cardkey was inserted, or the wrong code tried more than three times, the card would not be released. A silent alarm would alert security.

Ari walked them through the enormous, soundproofed area.

There were different sized rooms for specific types of venues. Meeting rooms, parties (one room had a dance floor), theater-type seating, and banquet seating. There was even a luxury kitchen for catering needs for wedding receptions or other festive occasions.

The shower room with lockers required a special entry code and would only be available to the shifters.

Ari showed them how the various rooms connected, and how they could be private and locked from accidental entry between rooms.

"This is first class. I'll bet once this venue is made available to corporate event planners, it will be booked up. We'd better book our Christmas party!" Roman said.

"You'll make your money back from the renovations," Ari said. "Event planners are going to love this space. You might want to think about the parking garage as well. Where should visitors park when there may be a couple of hundred people attending an event?"

"I'll study the garage and come up with a scheme," Lonnie said.

Roman texted Sandy about the Christmas party. "Looks like we're ready for our meeting," Gage said.

He turned to Sherm and Lonnie. "Have the cameras been tested?"

"Oh, yeah." Lonnie laughed. "We ran through dozens of tests with my entire crew. Even had some of the guys and gals play with wigs and makeup. This software rocks."

"You just need to tell me what type of venue this meeting will be," Ari said. "Do you want the theater seating, or comfortable seating? Will they be filling out information forms? If so, they need tables."

"For this first meeting we should go with comfortable," Roman said. "We can solicit their email addresses, have them drop business cards in a bowl, and email them a form to fill out. I don't want them to feel threatened."

"Remember, we'll be getting basic information from the facial recognition software and badge info," Sherm said. "There are multiple hidden cameras as well as exposed cameras. For your meeting the cameras and microphones will be set to document all conversations and who's having them."

"What should I say when I call out to them? Is this an invitation, a request—how do I word this so the majority show up?" Roman asked

"You don't want to make it an invitation," Ari said. "It's not like you want to give them an out with an RSVP. You want them here, so it's a request.

"We request your presence at a general meeting at our building. Give them the time, date, and address so they can make any arrangements they need."

"Can you write that down for me?" Roman asked. "I better tell them to bring an ID so they can get a badge."

"When would be the best time to do this? After typical work hours during the week or on the weekend?" Gage asked.

"Thursday at five thirty," Ari suggested. "Tell them to arrive no later than six, if at all possible with their work schedules. We can have finger foods—leave that to me. People will be hungry."

CHAPTER TWENTY

THE FIRST PERSON TO arrive at the meeting was Leander Stills. He was the gentleman who arrived first at the warehouse. Leander showed up at the building at five-twenty. He parked in the garage and wandered to the elevator and ventured up to the lobby. He approached the front desk, and a rather large human security officer greeted him.

"Good afternoon," the guard said. "How may I help you?"

"I'm here for a meeting," Leander said.

"Okay," the guard said. "Sign in here. Do you have an ID—a driver's license or something so I can create a badge?"

"Why do I need a badge?" Leander asked. He pulled his wallet out of the front pocket of his slacks.

"This is a secure building. To go anywhere, you need a badge for access," the guard said. "Even the restroom. We don't take chances on the security of our building residents."

Leander nodded, impressed. He slid his driver's license across the counter, then he filled in the information on the form.

The guard clacked on the keyboard, and within a few

minutes, a plastic badge was ready. "Would you prefer a lanyard or a clip?"

"Lanyard," Leander said.

Two people entered the building and approached the desk. The second guard greeted them.

The guard handed Leander his new badge on the lanyard plus a slip of paper and directed him to the events door. "You will need to enter this code at the door."

Leander followed the directions on the card over the security panel by the door. He noted the *three strikes you're out* plaque. He slid his card into the slot and entered his code on the keypad. The door made a noticeable clicking sound. He pulled it open and entered the room.

Ari greeted him. "Hello, I'm Ari. Thank you for coming. We'll be meeting in that room." She pointed to a door.

Leander bowed and took her outstretched hand. "My Queen."

Ari startled, but she recovered while his head was bent over her hand.

Leander entered the other room as the door opened behind him and the two people entered the room.

Plush white upholstered chairs, each with a fold-away tablet arm and cup holder, filled the room. There was a stage with three microphone stands and stools in the center and a large screen on the wall.

Leander noticed Roman and Gage at the other end of the room where tables of food and drinks awaited the shifters.

Upon seeing their first guest, Roman and Gage approached Leander.

"Hello," Roman said. "It's good to see you again."

Leander bowed. "My kings."

THE ROOM FILLED. People grabbed plates and loaded them with finger sandwiches and hors d'oeuvres, then settled into the comfortable chairs.

Leander chose a seat in front of the center of the stage.

Roman, Gage and Sherm huddled next to the stage.

"The software is working the way we planned," Sherm said. He tapped icons on his phone and showed them what the facial recognition software had gathered.

"That's amazing," Gage said.

"We'd better get started," Roman said. "Where's Ari?"

Gage left in search of Ari and found her in the other room.

"The guards will escort anyone who arrives late," Ari said.

She and Gage entered the meeting room and closed the door behind them. People stood and bowed as they passed. Ari nodded in acknowledgment as she and Gage approached the stage. This whole royalty concept was new to them. It would take a while to get used to all the bowing and curtsying.

They walked around to where Roman and Sherm stood. "Ready to begin?" Roman asked.

Ari took a deep breath. "Yes. Let's get started."

They climbed the three stairs to the stage.

"Welcome, everyone," Roman said into the microphone. "I met many of you at the warehouse, but for those who didn't make that gathering, my name is Roman Davenport. This is Gage Stryker and Ari Davis. We are Tothars."

The occupants of the room stood. They bowed and curtsied.

"My Kings; my Queen," Leander broadcast. The crowd followed his lead.

"Please be seated," Ari said.

"If you were at the warehouse meeting, you no doubt recall Gage and me telling you we were oblivious to your community. You hid from us to the point where we thought we were the only shifters in existence. Then we discovered we weren't traditional shifters, we were Tothars."

Roman sought the rat pack in the room. "We are grateful to our brave rats. They protected our queen by taking care of our little problem."

Ari motioned to the rats. "Please stand to be acknowledged."

The wiry little man and his pack stood, uncomfortable but honored. He bowed and waved to the room, then they sat back down with proud smiles on their faces.

A glaring alarm sounded. People were on their feet, searching the room with their eyes.

"Protect Ari!" Roman yelled. He and Gage gathered Ari and retreated to the back of the stage platform.

Sherm, Lonnie and the guards poured into the room through various doorways.

Leander leaped onto the stage and transformed in front of them, facing the audience. His monstrous King cobra, eighteen feet long with a wide girth, stood swaying on the stage. He hissed at the people on the floor. He turned to face Roman, Gage and Ari.

I will protect you!

Two guards leaped onto the stage, avoiding the cobra and flanked Roman, Gage and Ari with weapons drawn.

Sherm and his team apprehended a young man in his early twenties. He seemed to be working a program on his cellphone by the door everyone had entered through when they arrived.

The blaring alarm quieted.

"You were scanning the security system for coding?" Sherm asked.

"What are you talking about?" the guy asked. His face was a mask of innocence.

Lonnie yanked the phone out of the man's hands and

clicked a few times. He brought up the program that the guy was using. He handed the phone to Sherm.

"Did you create this program?" Sherm asked. Lonnie held his own phone out in front of Sherm.

"Travis Shelton, twenty-two." Sherm rattled off the guy's address, social security number, driver's license number, and stared at him. "Once again, did you create this program?"

"Yes," Travis said. He had a belligerent attitude.

"Lock him up," Sherm instructed. "I'll deal with him later."

Lonnie and the guards hauled Travis out of the room.

Sherm approached the stage. He was reluctant to get anywhere near the snake, but he went to the microphones.

"Ladies, gentlemen, if you'll take your seats, the program can continue," Sherm said. "The room is secure."

He turned back to see Roman, Gage, and Ari. She was shaken but seemed okay.

Gage nodded to him. Leander swayed on the stage.

Sherm made eye contact with the gigantic snake. "Come with me. We have a locker room with extra clothes for just this situation."

He grabbed Leander's clothing and his lanyard. Sherm walked across the stage and down the stairs to a door at the end of the room. The snake slithered behind him. People moved out of the way, fearful of the deadly cobra.

EIGHTY-FIVE TURNED out for the meeting. After everyone calmed down from the security breach, Roman, Gage, and Ari continued with their planned agenda, which was building a community.

Roman informed everyone they would receive emails or

text alerts of future meetings. He promised not to blast out anything else unless it was an emergency.

They invited Leander up to their apartment after the meeting.

Ari served drinks, Gage at her side helping.

Sherm had joined them. He brought two guards to stand alert by the elevator.

Roman invited Leander to sit in the living room while he lit the wood in the fireplace. After everyone settled, Sherm faced Leander.

"Don't think we didn't notice you were the only one to jump into action to protect the royals," Sherm said.

He shared a sofa with Leander.

"We are such a loose community," Leander said. "I don't know any of these people. We don't socialize at all, so I wasn't sure what to expect when that alarm sounded."

"It's obvious that someone needs to organize these people if we're to be useful to each other," Ari said. She shook her head at the situation they had experienced.

"We assumed you'd be like a big extended family," Gage said.

"We've got a lot of work to do," Roman said as he settled on the sofa next to Ari. "I'd like to make you our liaison, Leander."

Leander sat taller. "I am honored. Whatever you need me to do, I'll do my best."

"What type of work do you do?" Ari asked.

"I'm a shoe salesman," he said. "I own the shoe store on Main Street. It's a two-man shop and I'm the head salesman."

"Then you really understand people," Sherm said. "Certain types of salespeople are very valuable due to their interactions with customers. And it's not just the product you sell, it's your ability to read people."

"I've always been good at that," Leander said.

"And that's quite an animal you've got," Roman said. "I sure wouldn't want to cross you! Where are you from that your animal is a King cobra?"

Leander chuckled. "My father worked for a fortune five hundred company as an engineer, and he traveled the world. He ended up in India, where he met my mom. They fell in love and got married. That's where I was born. I've lived in so many places and attended so many schools that I never had the chance to make many friends. Do you know what Leander means?" he asked.

They all shook their heads.

"Lion man. My father's people were lion shifters. Guess what my mom was?"

"Ah, the cobra. How'd your father deal with your animal?" Ari asked. "I'll bet he wanted a lion cub!"

"My animal is so much bigger than my mom's. When I was a teenager, she and I had some tense standoffs—my father never got between us. I still find my parents' pairing strange. It took a long time for my dad to accept what I was."

"The turning point was when we were living in South Africa. I was being bullied by these three shifter boys—a pack of hyenas. It got to the point where my cobra and I had had enough," Leander said. "I took out two of them before they even knew what happened. You may have heard stories about how quick a cobra is—believe it. We strike fast. Our poison is among the deadliest in the world."

"We're glad you're on our side!" Gage chuckled.

"It was a touchy situation, but my father finally accepted me and was actually proud of me," Leander said. "Those boys didn't die, but they never bothered me again."

"Where should we begin?" Gage asked.

"To start, we should find out what types of shifters are in

the community," Ari said. "What are their animals? Are they in a pack or a clan or, are they on their own?"

"That's a reasonable line of questioning," Leander said.

They discussed matters further, then wound down the visit.

"What are you going to do with that young man?" Leander asked.

Roman and Gage deferred to Sherm.

"Not to worry—no water torture or anything like that," Sherm said. "We'll find out exactly who he is, what he does, and what he planned to do with the security coding. It can't be anything honorable when you're trying to hack into someone's security. We'll take it from there."

"Let's face it—that was fortuitous," Roman said. "Now everyone knows we aren't vulnerable. Not only do we have a security detail, but we have a King cobra on our side; they'd never cross."

SHERM JOINED Lonnie and part of the team who were guarding Travis Shelton in a cell. They didn't know what his animal was, and they weren't taking any chances. "What do we have?" Sherm asked.

"Not much," Lonnie said. "Only what we got through facial recognition and a quick background check. No warrants or arrests. Went to MIT."

An outer office door buzzed open and Roman and Gage entered the room.

Sherm acknowledged them and turned back to Travis in the cell. "What did you study at MIT?"

"Wouldn't you like to know?" Tavis snipped.

Lonnie clacked on the keyboard of a laptop. "What an immature ass."

"Masters in Math and just finished up his PhD in Computer Languages."

"Quite the little prodigy, aren't you?" Gage said. "Too bad you want to waste all that education and knowledge. You'll never get a job when we put the word out you're a hacker."

"Looks like you've been in college since you were fifteen. Impressive to get an undergrad, Masters and PhD by twenty-two," Roman said.

Travis squirmed but stayed tight-lipped.

"Was this just you screwing around, wanting to see how tight our security was, or did someone hire you?" Sherm asked.

Travis smirked. "Nobody put me up to anything. I don't take orders from anyone!"

"You might want to adjust that attitude if you plan to work anywhere, even as a solo contractor," Gage said.

Roman got close to the bars. He let his panther show. He growled into the cell. Two of the security team stepped back out of the way. They didn't want to take a chance of getting caught in a sudden shift. They respected Roman but were leery of the large cat. They had seen the damage those claws and teeth could do.

Travis scurried away from the bars. He tripped over the bunk and slammed the back of his head into the wall.

"Maybe we should settle this animal to animal?" Roman's voice was cold. "Shift!"

"There's no need for violence!" Travis showed his animal through his eyes: a large white dog.

"Open the cell," Roman growled.

Lonnie unlocked the cell and opened the door.

Roman grabbed Travis by the shirt collar and hauled him

out of the cell. He plunked him down into a chair. "You've got one minute before I shift and teach you some respect."

Travis stammered, incoherent. He gathered his wits and decided it was in his best interest to cooperate.

"Nobody put me up to anything. I swear! I figured with the guys at the front desk and the cardkey and keypad you had some hefty security going on," Travis blurted. "All I wanted to do was see if I could get through. That's all. I swear!"

Lonnie was playing with Travis' phone. "Pretty slick coding, Sherm."

"Is your father Dick Shelton?" Gage asked.

"Yes," Travis said.

"Are you going to work for his company?" Gage asked.

"No. My dad and I don't see eye-to-eye," he said. "I've got applications in with a bunch of companies. I'm a serious coder —not one of those gamers, so I'm most likely being picky and stupid about job offers."

"Have you applied with the military or any government branches?" Sherm asked.

"Yeah, the Department of Defense and a couple of other places," he said. "They take a while though."

"You could become a millionaire pretty fast if you developed a few great games," Lonnie said.

"My dad's a millionaire. I need a challenge," Travis said.

Roman, Gage and Sherm shared a knowing silent question and answer.

"We could use someone like you on our team," Sherm said.

Lonnie nodded.

Travis stared at them. "You're not going to have me arrested?"

ROMAN AND GAGE returned to the penthouse. Ari was reading on the sofa.

"What happened with that boy?" she asked.

"We hired him," Gage said. He flopped down beside her and rested his hand on her thigh.

"You sure that's a good idea?" Ari asked. "How can you trust him?"

"Sherm's going to put him to work trying to break into every system we have," Roman said. "If he can get around Sherm's coding he'll he tasked with developing code to make sure no one else can."

"He's pretty slick," Gage said.

Ari considered their plan. "That makes sense."

Roman cozied up to her and turned her head toward him. He kissed her, wanting in her mouth. He slid his tongue across her lips, and she invited him in. The kiss got hot. His hand slid under her sweater. He lifted her bra and rubbed her nipple. Her hand gripped his cock through his slacks.

Gage got involved. He pulled Ari's leggings and panties down and flung them over his shoulder. He buried his face between her legs while Roman sucked on her nipples.

Ari fumbled, determined to unzip Roman's slacks. "Help me, Roman," she said.

He disengaged from her nipples and undressed. He straddled her and pressed his hard shaft against her lips. She grabbed his cock and devoured him.

Focusing was a challenge for her as Gage circled her clit with his thumb and kept his mouth buried between her legs.

He sucked her little bud while his fingers sought her G-spot.

Moments later Roman's blow job ended as Ari screamed through her orgasm.

"Me first," Gage said.

"No fair," Roman said. "I started it."

"Okay, but don't take forever!" Gage yanked his clothes off.

"Floor," Roman said. He grabbed Ari around the waist and lifted her off the sofa. The three of them piled onto the floor, the coffee table shoved to the side. Roman positioned Ari on her hands and knees, and he slid into her from behind.

She moaned long and deep with his thrusts.

Roman pounded into her. She wedged against him. He reached around and latched onto her little jewel of a nub. She shrieked in orgasmic ecstasy as his fingers worked her into a frenzy.

Gage kneeled in front of her, his swollen cock hard and long. He slipped inside her mouth. His eyes closed as her tongue worked his shaft and her lips sucked him. His fingers held her hair out of her face as he mouth-fucked her.

Their orgasms hit within seconds of each other. They collapsed in a pile on the living room floor, panting, groaning, and moaning.

"I love you," Ari said.

Roman and Gage returned their declarations of love.

"I feel like we're still in the honeymoon phase," Roman said. "I wonder if all shifters have the same steady sex we do?"

"That's a little too personal to ask on a form," Ari said with a smirk.

"What about regular human marriage?" Gage asked. "You were married for a long time."

"Believe me, the honeymoon phase was over and done within two or three years. People fall into a pattern of comfort and companionship as I assume most married people or long-term relationships drift into. Once you have kids, a lot of things change."

"So, what we have is pretty good?" Roman asked.

"Oh, yeah," Ari said. "What do you think, Gage?"

"I wouldn't change what we have for the world," Gage said.

Ari was quiet for a moment. "I'm sorry we had such a rough patch."

Roman sat and stared down at her, his face stern. "Never apologize for that again, Ari. What you experienced was beyond horrifying."

"I realize that, but I knew you two suffered and there wasn't anything I could do about it. I wanted you two so badly, but I was frozen with fear." Ari sat up and wrapped her arms around her legs.

Gage moved her hair over her shoulder and massaged her shoulders. "We were scared you would leave us. We didn't know how to help you. I'm not sure if I can get through anything like that again. If I ever lost you…"

Roman stood. "Jesus Christ! We just had the best fucking sex of our lives—something we seem to experience repeatedly— so I believe it's safe to say no one is leaving!"

He gathered up his clothes and stomped off to his room and slammed the door.

Ari was about to spring to her feet when Gage rested his hand on her arm. "Let him go. He needs to work through some things. He hasn't let it go, even though he insists everything is okay."

"I need to wipe up," Ari said.

Gage slipped out of the room and returned with a damp washcloth.

Ari wiped her face, then held the washcloth between her legs as she stood. Gage grabbed their clothes, and they headed to Roman's bedroom. They joined him in the bed and settled into sleep.

CHAPTER TWENTY-ONE

ARI COMPILED a list of the animals in their shifter community with the help of Roman, Gage, and Leander. After the meeting, those who didn't have time to attend made themselves known.

There were one-hundred eighty-seven shifters in their city of three-hundred thousand people. Ari was curious as to how many humans were aware of the shifters. She guessed there were mixed marriages (shifter/human), but she wondered if the human extended family had knowledge of the secret community.

There were two packs of wolves. One with eight members and the other with ten. There were a couple of loose packs of dogs totaling twelve members, and six coyotes—the dogs and coyotes avoided each other.

Bears were mostly solitary, but in the shifter community they banded together in groups. Leander counted fourteen bears. The Kodiak stood over ten feet tall on its hind legs and no one argued with him or his mate. Even the grizzlies tiptoed around the big guy.

They counted only four big cats, but there were twenty-two domestic cats that lived either in colonies or feral. One calico lived with a human family and rarely shifted to her human form.

Thirty birds of all different types, including peacocks, were the largest group of shifters.

A dozen deer, four pigs, a stallion and four mares, and one goat. The remaining numbers comprised rabbits, mice, chickens, a nasty woodchuck, some chipmunks who were terrified of the rats, and a mole.

Leander was the only snake.

After she sorted the list, Ari emailed it to Atsa, telling him she hadn't gone through all the books yet and she'd update him in time. She was curious to see if he or the elders knew about any other animals, or if his community had shifters not on the list. She informed him they had hired Mr. Tran, and he would translate the books.

Sherm's group matched the animals on Ari's list with their human counterpart from the security photos. Roman wanted to make sure everyone was identifiable in either form for security purposes.

"We're such a small percentage of the population," Gage said. "Maybe we should dig deeper—find out about any hardships."

"I've been thinking about our land," Roman said. "We have two-thousand acres, but I'd like to buy some adjoining land. We could build some cabins and offer people a place to shift and spend some time in nature."

"That's a wonderful idea," Ari said.

"I'll bet there are enough contractors among the shifters to build the cabins," Gage said.

"That brings up another point. Sharing those resources. Whatever skills or occupations the shifters have should go into a shared database. We might as well call our own people for repairs, or whatever, instead of going to a complete stranger," Roman said.

EVERYONE ENJOYED the next general meeting. Ari talked to the community about the list she was compiling. She explained why it was important to document everyone's occupations and hobbies—so the community could benefit from shifter-related services and experience.

Roman talked to the room about the land.

"Everyone is welcome to use the land so you can shift. You can pick up a map at the back table near the door. There isn't a parking area, so you will have to park alongside the private road. I have strict rules. No one is to hunt anyone in this room as prey. Understood?"

His eyes wandered the room to make sure he saw nods. He didn't want bears, wolves, coyotes, large cats or anything else hunting their deer, pig or goat members or anyone else.

"There's plenty of wildlife on our land. You all have the ability to sense shifters. All of you will be able to determine whether to abort your hunt when you discover what you've been tracking is your neighbor from our community. We'll be there this weekend.

"And people, I won't tolerate litter. When we get to the point of building cabins or picnic areas, there will be litter barrels provided. In the meantime, you are responsible for your own trash."

"If there're any builders or contractors, electricians, plumbers, please get with Ari. I'm interested in pulling together a team to go over cabin designs and such."

Roman stepped back from the mic and joined Ari.

Gage strolled up to a microphone. "Since we are all newly acquainted and don't know how our different groups conduct business, I want to be very clear about one thing. We will not tolerate domestic violence or bullying.

"If you think you have to hurt your people to keep them in line, then we will have an issue with you. And trust me, you don't want us to have an issue with you," Gage said.

There was an uncomfortable silence for a moment, then conversations started again.

"I'm glad you brought that up," Ari said. "I won't tolerate that in any way, shape or form."

Roman nodded. "They'd better understand that going forward."

Sherm sauntered over. "Want us to bring anything this weekend?"

Ari did a mental inventory. "I think we have everything for the bar-b-cue, but if you guys want a specific beer or drink, stop and get some."

"I'm looking forward to some R&R," Sherm said.

ARI PADDED barefoot through the house in the woods. The sliding doors were open to let in the fresh air and the screens kept the bugs out. She heard car doors slam and determined Sherm and his group had arrived.

Jason wasn't due until two in the afternoon. She hoped Kevin was with Sherm's team, and that Leander wouldn't get lost since he was coming in his own car.

A tap on the door and it opened. Sherm and the guys piled in.

"Hi guys!" Ari said.

She hugged Sherm and pecked him on the cheek, then

Lonnie and the rest. They were part of her family, and she adored them.

"Hi, Mom!" Kevin announced.

"Hi, honey!" Ari said. She looked him over. "You're getting pretty bulked up, aren't you?"

He looked happy—the happiest she had ever seen him. "Where's Roman and Gage?" Kevin asked.

"Roman's panther is running and Gage's eagle is in the sky. They'll be back soon," she said.

Ari went to the kitchen and picked up a tray of hamburger she had already formed into patties.

"You going to start cooking?" Sherm asked.

"As soon as Roman and Gage get back. Gage will most likely tell Roman you're here. Want to eat in air conditioning or outside?" Ari asked.

"Let's eat outside. It's a beautiful day and we don't get outside enough. What do you want me to grab?" he asked.

Another car door shut, followed by a knock on the door. "Lonnie, that's probably Leander."

Lonnie opened the door. "Hey, Leander.

"Hi Lonnie."

Leander looked comfortable in shorts, a tank top and Birkenstock sandals.

"Everything on the island and counter goes outside," Ari said. "Hi Leander! You're just in time."

Ari brought the covered platter outside and put it on the stainless-steel shelf of the grill.

Sherm rounded up the guys and everyone grabbed something and brought it to the picnic table outside.

Some of the guys headed to the volleyball net while others drifted to the chairs to drink a beer and talk sports.

"I'm glad you didn't get lost," Ari told Leander.

"The map was very detailed and easy to follow," Leander said. "What can I do to help?"

"Grab a beer and enjoy the great outdoors. Or, there's wine inside and a well-stocked bar," Ari said.

"Beer's good," he said.

"Lonnie, show Leander where the beer is," Ari yelled.

Everyone was having a great time visiting and playing volleyball as they waited for Roman and Gage to get back from their wild exploits.

Ari walked across the grass toward the edge of the forest where a stretch of wildflowers bloomed.

A tawny mountain lion slunk out from the trees, growled and charged her.

Ari screamed and fell backwards as the cat lunged on top of her.

"What the fuck?" Sherm yelled.

Sherm's Glock was in his hand and he was halfway to Ari when Roman's panther rushed out of the forest, snarling and growling.

Leander shifted into his King cobra. It didn't take the eighteen-foot snake but a moment to get to the side of his queen.

"Mom!" Kevin hollered. He ran over to where Roman was attacking the cat.

Roman grabbed the cat's scruff and dragged it off Ari. He shook the cat while Ari scurried backwards.

Sherm and Kevin dragged Ari to her feet and away from the battling cats.

"Are you okay?" Kevin asked.

"Who the hell is that?" Sherm asked.

Kevin and Sherm looked Ari over. She had claw marks on her collarbone and one long scratch down her leg from when Roman dragged the cat off her.

Most of the guys were on their feet with guns drawn. The cobra swayed as he watched the fighting.

Roman had the mountain lion pinned to the ground. Gage shrieked from the sky and landed. He shifted. "Sherm, shoot that bastard," Gage demanded.

"Not so quick, they're too close." Sherm had his Glock trained on the battling cats.

Leander hissed at them. He was better than any gun. The cobra swayed, looking for an opening.

Roman shook the mountain lion by the scruff. He stepped back a few paces and shifted.

"Shift!" Roman roared. "I have your scent and you won't get far with this group."

The lion panted, then shifted into a naked woman with tawny hair and brown eyes. She appeared very nervous. She had her belly exposed, submissive, as she lay on the ground. There were claw marks down her body and Roman's fangs left puncture wounds around her neck.

Kevin grabbed the tablecloth off the picnic table and threw it at her. "Cover yourself, bitch."

Sherm took a picture of her face. He clicked and slid through screens. "Lisa Hamilton."

He showed the picture to Roman.

"Why were you stalking me through the forest?" Roman asked. He was almost blind with fury.

"I think it's a little obvious," Gage said. "Celeste all over again."

"What is the meaning of this attack on your queen?" Roman demanded.

He was having a difficult time staying in human form. His panther wanted to finish her off for attacking his mate.

"I thought you wanted me," Lisa stammered.

"Wanted you?" Roman said. Confusion crossed his face.

He turned to Gage with raised eyebrows, then turned back to the woman. "Who the fuck are you?"

Gage joined Roman. "Are you batshit crazy or something?"

Leander shifted.

Roman pointed to Ari. "Your queen is our mate—our wife. Do you not see how beautiful and desirable she is? I doubt if there's a man alive who would ever consider walking away from her for any reason.

"Why would you assume I *wanted* you? I've never seen you before in my life," Roman thundered.

Lisa blushed crimson. "I just thought you did, that's all."

Roman took a threatening step forward. "Don't move an inch." He turned to Leander. "Can you find out if she's in a group with a leader?"

Leander considered. "If I remember correctly, there are only four big cats in the community. I can try to find out who the alpha is and contact him. I've got all their numbers on my phone."

"Would you do that for me, please?" Roman asked.

Leander sifted through his shredded pants on the ground and pulled out his phone. He scrolled through his shifter contacts group and came across the cat group. There was a picture of a woman with such intensity he figured she was the leader.

Roman and Gage hovered over Ari, looking her over. "Are you sure you're okay?" Roman asked. He kissed her and held his forehead against hers.

"Just a little freaked out," Ari said.

Gage dusted the grass off her T-shirt and butt. "You sure you're not hurt? She slammed you to the ground."

"I'm fine," Ari said.

The kitchen door opened and closed. Jason stepped outside all smiles. When he saw Sherm's Glock, the tense stances of the guys with their guns drawn, he stopped in his tracks. When he saw Roman, Gage, and Leander naked, he ran over to his mother. "What happened?"

"This goddamn stalker woman in mountain lion form attacked your mom," Gage said. His rage hadn't settled.

"What?" Jason looked around. He saw her on the ground. "Why didn't you kill her?" His eyes pounded into Sherm with his gun in hand.

Leander joined them. He showed Roman the cat woman's picture.

"She looks like a leader," Roman said. "Get her on the phone and I'll speak with her."

"Because we can't kill everyone who makes us mad," Ari shrilled.

She grabbed Jason's arm and Roman's hand and dragged them over to the picnic table. "Let's all calm down."

"Maybe we should uninvite these people from our land," Gage said as he sat beside Ari.

"No, they need a safe place to shift and be wild. I'll get more land around us and we'll shift people over there," Roman said. "We need to figure out how to address this to the group."

Roman and Gage eyed the woman on the ground. Two men on Sherm's team stood over her.

Leander walked over and handed his phone to Roman. "Her name is Trisha Anderson."

"Trisha, I'm sorry to bother you on the weekend, but I'm sure Leander outlined the situation," Roman said. They talked for a few minutes. Then Roman handed the phone to Leander. "She wants to talk to Lisa."

Everyone watched as Lisa listened on the phone. She handed the phone back to Leander. He spoke to Trisha for a moment.

"Trisha wants Lisa to get back to town immediately," Leander said.

Roman nodded.

Lisa shifted and ran into the forest.

"Go get dressed. People are hungry," Ari said. "Get Leander some clothes."

Roman and Gage stomped into the house, followed by Kevin, Jason, Leander and Sherm.

Ari was sure that the conversation was far from over.

Lonnie and some of the guys hovered around her. They were still spooked.

"I'll get some alcohol for those scratches," Lonnie said.

The human ran into the house.

Kevin came back outside. He grabbed the tablecloth off the ground and went back inside. Kevin returned with another tablecloth, shook it out and settled it on the table.

The guys came back outside.

Lonnie wet a cotton ball with alcohol and dabbed it on the cuts and scratches.

Ari tensed.

"Sorry, I know that stings," Lonnie said.

Roman handed her a gin and tonic. "I figured you needed this," he said.

Ari accepted the rocks glass and took a slug. "Thanks." She kissed his cheek.

"I'll get this food cooking. I'm sure everyone's starving," Gage said.

He fired up the gas grill.

Ari sat at the table and nursed her drink. She wasn't as settled as she pretended to be and Roman picked up on it.

He sat beside her, his arm across her shoulders.

"Talk to me," Roman said. "Tell me how you're feeling right now and don't give me any bullshit by saying you're *fine*. I know you're not. Your emotions are roiling like a boiling cauldron."

She leaned into him and let out a deep breath. "It was scary. I'm still shook up. She wanted to hurt me—I sensed it—like it was an agenda."

Roman was about to jump up and go after the cat. Ari grabbed his arm.

"No! There has to be a better way to handle this," she said.

Leander sat opposite them at the table.

"The females, especially the cats, may react like Lisa toward our kings," Leander said. "And, the men—regardless of what animal—may act just as crazy to you, Ari."

"That's not going to work!" Roman said.

"Trisha will most likely have a meeting among the leaders," Leander said. "We'll come up with a solution." Sherm and Lonnie joined them.

Before long, everyone was at the table. They wanted the discussion to be out in the open.

"You can't go around killing everyone who—" Ari said.

"Why the hell not?" Roman thundered. "If their intent is to kill you or do bodily harm to you, then we have every right to use deadly force!"

Gage placed a plate piled with cooked burgers on the table. "Ari, listen, I understand you don't like what Roman, Leander and I would have done. But no one—and I mean no one—will ever walk away from a situation like today, alive. That's all there is to it."

CHAPTER TWENTY-TWO

GAGE AND SHERM walked the block between the manufacturing facility to the office building when Sherm's phone rang.

"Hey Lonnie, we're almost there. What's up?" Sherm listened. "Okay, this is something Travis and I can handle. You and Jack can run the back end here. Be there in a sec."

Gage looked over at Sherm. "What was that all about?"

"Wall Street client got an overload of spam, which their IT department took care of. But now it appears someone's attacking their security systems." Sherm grinned. "That kid will fix the problem and find out who's responsible."

"He's that good?" Gage asked.

"Oh, yeah," Sherm answered with glee.

He inserted his cardkey into the slot at the side door and they entered the lobby through a concealed door.

The greeters were busy on the phone or with visitors, but the guards eyeballed them and nodded as they walked to the elevator bank.

They rode the elevator to the twenty-eighth floor.

Sherm and Gage entered Lonnie's office.

"I've briefed Travis," Lonnie said. "The jet's ready when you are."

"Okay," Sherm said. "Let me pack up my gear and grab a change of clothes. Have Travis here in fifteen."

TRAVIS ENTERED Lonnie's office and set his computer bag and two other bags in a chair. He wore sloppy cargo pants that had seen better days, a T-shirt sponsoring a rap group, a backwards baseball cap and dirty high-topped tennis shoes.

Sherm groaned. "Don't you own a suit? We're going to Wall Street! Never mind." He turned to Lonnie. "Get him to Emilio's right now." He pulled up his contacts and made a call while Lonnie beat it out of there with Travis on his heels.

"Emilio? Sherman Foo. I've got an emergency. Lonnie's bringing a young man named Travis. He needs to look like Wall Street. Anything you have right now. We have to leave in an hour. I owe you, but I know you'll bill us."

He smiled at Gage. "You and Roman have built up so much respect with the people you do business with that we can ask for favors and they come through."

SHERM AND TRAVIS walked into a large Wall Street IT department escorted by the Wall Street security.

People ogled Travis—he looked like he owned the company, and because he was so young. They met with Roger Wilkinson who had brought them in to solve their problem that was only getting worse by the minute.

A bank of monitors on the wall showed scrolling code on

some screens and rapid line-by-line destruction on other screens. Whoever was hacking them was doing a thorough job.

Travis transformed into a savant before Sherm's eyes.

"I want to sit right here," he pointed to a place in the middle of a cube farm. It was positioned so that it was in the middle of the bank of monitors on the wall. "Give me complete access. Time's a-wasting."

Roger indicated to the guy whose cube Travis wanted, and his neighbor to his right, to clear out.

The IT guys scrambled to gather their laptops and things they'd need. "Where should we set up?"

"Use the conference room for now," Roger said.

A woman rushed to Travis and Sherm and handed each a sheet of paper with access codes.

Travis and Sherm pulled out their gear and settled in. They studied the monitors and conferred with each other while Roger frantically paced nearby.

Sherm and Travis agreed on a plan, and they attacked their keyboards.

People stopped what they were doing. They watched as the hacking code appeared to be eaten by the two specialists focused on the job.

Travis backtracked the pinging, jumping IP addresses. They bounced from place to place around the world in a quagmire of confusion and secrecy to keep the pirates hidden.

Travis located their base with his carefully coded program. "Bangkok. Give me a minute and I'll have their address."

Sherm got on the phone with Lonnie.

They already had a special ops team in the area and were on it. In less than two hours, the crisis was over, the firm was safe from further attacks, and the Bangkok hackers were being apprehended.

The room was quiet, with unbelieving eyes and mouths hanging open.

Sherm stood. "Finish up with backdoor traps."

Travis nodded as he clacked away on his keyboard, eyes focused on the large monitors on the wall.

"Where's your coffee bar?" Sherm asked.

SHERM AND TRAVIS were proud of a job well done.

Travis spent an hour doing clean up from the damage the hackers did to the Wall Street firm.

Sherm relaxed with a cup of coffee, chatting with various people in the IT department.

When Travis finished with the cleanup, he spent an hour with the IT team explaining what to monitor for through his coding and traps.

Sherm and Travis returned to the jet where Sherm billed the client.

He slapped Travis on the back.

"You earned your respect today, kid. That was fancy work you did. I saw the looks on the faces of those schmucks when we entered the room and they were not the same as when we left. I expect many requests for your services."

Travis's face colored. He kept his head held low. "It wasn't all me. You worked right alongside me."

"Accept your brilliance, Travis. Your career is secure as long as you walk a straight line."

Travis harrumphed. "You're never going to let me forget that, are you?"

Sherm drilled him with his eyes. "Have you ever thought about what would have happened if we had called the cops and pressed charges? You'd never even be able to get a job as a dog walker. Your father might be able to buy your exoneration due to his deep pockets, but I don't think that's on the top of his list these days.

"Furthermore, you don't know Roman and Gage all that well. While they're the kindest, most generous people of anyone I have ever known, the flip side is a deadly ruthlessness you will never come up against—or survive."

When the jet landed, the SUV returned them to their home base. As they entered the twenty-eighth floor, Sherm headed over to Lonnie.

"Be on the lookout for attacks from Bangkok."

"Already have everyone on alert, including the external teams," Lonnie said. "Bad bunch of fuckers, those Bangkok pirates. Our guys rounded up all but one who got away. I hope they rot in the prison system. We'll find that little weasel so he can keep his pals' company."

ROMAN, Gage, Ari, and Gloria arrived at Singleton's Assisted Living Center south of downtown. Gage retrieved Ari's special wheelchair from the back of the large SUV. Gloria led the way inside to Grandfather Silver Wolf's room.

"Hello, Grandfather," Gloria said. "Are you ready for your exciting excursion?"

The old man was lit with smiles as his eyes landed on the wheelchair. "Where are we going?"

"To our house in the forest," Roman said. He leaned in and whispered, "So we can shift."

Grandfather cackled.

Roman gently lifted Silver Wolf out of the bed while Gage grabbed the bed pillows and placed them in the chair. Roman settled the old man in the wheelchair and everyone inspected him.

A nurse entered the room. "All set?"

Gloria and the nurse conferred for a minute. "Looks like you've got a weekend pass, Grandfather. Let's get going."

There were more pillows in the middle row of seating in the SUV along with soft blankets to keep the old man warm. Roman and Gage got him settled in with Gloria on one side of him and Ari on the other.

Roman drove.

Silver Wolf napped off and on through the two-and-a-half-hour drive. He woke when they were on the private road that led to the house. Gloria lowered her window and Silver Wolf breathed in deeply.

"Ah, trees! There's nothing like the smell of the forest to make you think you're in heaven," he said.

Roman parked the car. Gage hopped out, unlocked the front door, and left it open.

Ari and Gloria got out.

Roman retrieved the wheelchair but thought better of it. He carried Silver Wolf into the house, followed by Gloria and Ari hauling the pillows and blankets.

They propped him on the sofa with a view of the outdoors through the sliding glass doors. Gloria handed him a bottle of water.

"Keep hydrated, Grandfather."

Gage and Roman brought in all the bags. When everyone was settled, Roman brought the wheelchair outside.

They settled Grandfather Silver Wolf in the chair.

Gage became serious. He stooped beside the chair and balanced on his toes. He stared into Silver Wolf's eyes.

"Roman and I are going to shift. I don't know if you have

the energy, but do you think you can shift? You could go into the forest with Roman," he offered.

Grandfather Silver Wolf's eyes lit with excitement. "I haven't shifted in twenty years. I'm not sure if I can."

"Give it a try. We won't shift until you do, then Roman can walk with you and I'll take to the sky," Gage said.

"Help me take off my clothes," Grandfather demanded. "Can't go back to the center in rags."

Gage removed the old man's shoes, socks and pants. Roman helped him with his shirt.

"Stand me up! I can't shift in a wheelchair," Grandfather claimed.

Roman and Gage stood Grandfather Silver Wolf and held on to him. He teetered.

"Be careful!" Gloria said.

She stood in front of him with her hands spread in front of her, ready to catch her grandfather if he tumbled.

"You ready?" Gage asked.

"I've got nothing to lose," Grandfather Silver Wolf said.

The first time he tried to shift, his nose muzzled out and fur sprouted on his arms and head. He popped back into human form.

"Good first try," Gage said.

"Focus more tightly," Roman encouraged.

The old man stared through Gloria, eyes soft. He shifted completely.

His wolf had shrunk with age. He stood on four wobbly legs.

"Look at you! You did it!" Ari grabbed her cellphone out of her pocket and snapped pictures.

Roman steadied the old wolf. "We'll go into the forest. When you feel you're getting tired, we'll come back to the house."

Roman and Gage stripped down and shifted.

"Maybe I'd better shift?" Gloria asked Ari.

"It's up to you. He's having better luck with four legs than he has with two," Ari noticed.

Gage took flight.

Silver Wolf watched the huge eagle soar overhead. He gave a little half bark half howl. Then he coughed.

"Don't overdo it," Gloria chided. "You're not some young pup."

Roman nudged Silver Wolf with his muzzle. The old man tottered beside the huge panther and they stepped into the forest.

Ari turned to Gloria. "You need a drink."

CHAPTER TWENTY-THREE

THE OLD WOLF trotted beside the panther. He stopped and sniffed the ground, trees and ground cover along the way.

Silver Wolf smelled other animals.

They continued on for another half hour when Roman noticed the old wolf stumbling.

Roman shifted.

"I'm going to carry you back to the house so you can rest," Roman said. He picked up the old wolf and walked back to the house.

Ari and Gloria sat in lounge chairs on the grass. When Roman stepped out of the forest with Silver Wolf in his arms, Gloria jumped to her feet.

"Grandfather!" Gloria was alarmed.

"He's okay, just tired. Figured I'd better get him back so he could rest up before dinner."

He settled the ancient wolf on the ground.

"Better shift before you fall asleep in your wolf form," Roman said.

The old man shifted back to his shrunken old body. He cackled up a storm.

"That was marvelous! I'm so glad you brought me here, and I had this last chance to honor my wolf."

"Let's get you dressed, hydrated, and down for a nap," Gloria said. She guided her grandfather into the house.

Ari hugged Roman. "I'm so glad you did this for Silver Wolf."

"I'm going for a run," Roman said.

He swept her into his arms and kissed her. His hands roamed her body and his mouth devoured hers. He scented her juices, pooling. He grabbed her ass and hitched her up against his hard-on.

Ari pushed back from him. "Don't make a spectacle out of us. I'm pretty sure Gloria thinks you're going to mount me any second now."

Roman smirked. "Oops. Can't help myself sometimes. I'll go for my run, but you'd better want a nap later."

He winked at her, grabbed her for another quick kiss, then stepped back and shifted.

His panther nudged her.

She ran her hand over his head and down his sleek sides. "Love you."

The panther took off into the woods.

GAGE LANDED on the grass and transformed. He sauntered to the house and grabbed his clothes from one of the lawn chairs. He dressed and headed inside.

Ari was sacked out on one of the sofas.

Gage sensed Gloria and her grandfather in the downstairs bedroom, napping. He kneeled beside Ari and brushed her hair out of her face. He loved watching her sleep. She was so beautiful. He loved her so much.

She stirred.

Ari's eyes fluttered open. She smiled up at Gage and held her arms out to him.

He eased onto the sofa, half covering her with his body. His lips swooped in for an all-encompassing, smoldering kiss.

"Did you have a good flight?" Ari ran her fingers through his sandy colored hair.

"I wish you could fly with me," Gage said. "It's the most incredible experience you could ever have. The wind through my feathers, soaring over the land, seeing beyond what human eyes could ever hope to see... it's exhilarating." Gage looked around the room. "Roman's not back yet?"

"No, he should be back soon. Grandfather had a wonderful romp in the forest, but he wore himself out."

"I'm so glad we could do this for him," Gage said. He snuggled down, and they dozed off.

ARI WOKE and untangled herself from Gage. He grunted and eased his eyes open.

"What time is it?" he mumbled.

Ari lifted her head and read the digital clock on the stove across the room.

"Six. I'm surprised Roman didn't join us. He was a little amorous before he shifted for his run."

"Oh yeah? Leave it to him to start something when I'm not there." Gage snickered.

He kissed Ari.

She batted at him playfully. They sat.

Gage's sensitive hearing detected Gloria tending to Grandfather Silver Wolf in the other room.

He got up and walked to the bedroom, Ari on his heels. "All rested up?" Gage asked the old man.

"I'm ready to go again," Silver Wolf said.

"Ha!" Gloria said. "I think once is enough, don't you?"

"You're such a spoilsport," the old man said.

"Have you seen Roman?" Ari asked.

"No, he hasn't been back here. We just woke up about ten minutes ago," Gloria said.

"Huh. This isn't like him," Ari said. "He's usually back around the time Gage lands."

"Why don't we start supper," Gage said. "He'll most likely be here in a few minutes. I'm starving."

"What else is new?" Ari poked him in the ribs.

She and Gage headed to the kitchen and pulled food out of the refrigerator to start cooking. She decided on soft foods for Silver Wolf, so she and Gage prepared a meatloaf and mashed potatoes.

Ari approached the sliding glass doors and looked outside. Her eyes scanned as far as she could see.

Roman? Supper's almost ready. Come get cleaned up.

There was no response.

"Gage, call Roman. He's not responding," Ari said. There was more than a hint of unease rolling off her.

ROMAN! Where the hell are you? Gage mentally yelled from the kitchen.

Nothing. Gage relaxed and let his senses open up.

He didn't feel Roman's presence like he typically did. He put down the spoon and headed to the sliding doors, and stepped outside.

Gage stood on the grass and pulled in a deep breath. He didn't detect Roman. He walked to the edge of the forest.

"ROMAN!" He called out in his human voice. Then again, in his silent voice. *ROMAN!*

He walked determinedly inside, grabbed his phone and called Sherm. He explained the situation, disconnected the call.

Leander called. "Is something wrong? I heard you call for Roman."

Gage explained the problem.

"Can you get a hold of everyone in the community? We need to cover as much of the acreage as possible. It's going to be dark soon. I'm not sure if he came across a hunter, another animal, or what."

Ari placed food on the table.

Gloria rolled the wheelchair up to the table.

"Meatloaf, my favorite!" Grandfather said. "Roman better get back here pretty quick or he's not getting any."

Ari grabbed the salad bowl and dressing bottles. She, Gage and Gloria sat. Ari picked at her food.

Gage ate for five people, it seemed. Grandfather Silver Wolf enjoyed the meal.

In the distance, Ari could hear the helicopter approach and land.

Gage got up and took off through the front door to meet Sherm and the team. Ari followed.

Sherm one-arm hugged Ari.

"This is so not like him," she said. "He's very attentive toward guests. He should have returned hours ago."

Gloria rolled Silver Wolf outside and joined them.

"As weak as I am, I've always been able to sense these boys," Silver Wolf said. "I got nothing. It's as if Roman has disappeared out of my range."

"We don't sense him either," Gage said. "Leander's gathering the troops. They'll be able to cover a lot of territory in their animal forms, even in the dark, but it will take them another hour to get here."

"Okay, we'll spread out and search while we still have light," Sherm said.

Gage stripped his clothes off. "I'll take to the sky." Ari grabbed him. "Be careful."

He captured her face in his hands and kissed her. "It's going to be okay. We'll find him."

Gage shifted. His giant eagle took to the sky. He let out a screech and circled the forest, eyes alert.

Silver Wolf stared up at the eagle. "That's the most spectacular vision I've ever seen!"

An hour later, an army of cars, trucks and SUVs arrived. The shifter community, led by Leander, stood outside the house while Leander got Ari.

She came outside, followed by Gloria pushing the wheelchair.

They bowed and curtsied to Ari.

"Thank you for coming. Sherm and his team are in the forest searching. Their human sight won't be any good when it gets dark unless they have night vision goggles," she said.

"We'll find King Roman, my Queen!" Leander said. The shifters voiced agreement.

"Let's shift and get in there." Leander turned to Ari. "Can you tell Sherm to expect a lot of different animals? No one will harm the humans, but we need to be sure they won't get trigger-happy if they see a bear coming around."

Ari pulled out her cellphone and called Sherm. "Our shifter family is here. Just make sure your team doesn't hurt these animals!" She hit the speaker button.

"My team knows you're here and no one's going to start shooting. We look forward to working beside these people in their animal forms."

The shifters shifted. Birds took to the air.

Bears, wolves, coyotes and the rest of them dashed into the trees.

Silver Wolf rallied them on lifting a weak arm to over his head.

Leander patted Ari on the shoulder.

"We'll find him, my Queen. Why don't you wait inside?" In an instant, the man undressed and shifted. The huge King cobra slithered into the forest and disappeared.

Silver Wolf had to shut his mouth from his jaw dropping in surprise. "Was that a King cobra?"

"Yes, that's Leander," Gloria said. "He's unbelievable, isn't he?"

Ari circled her arms around her gut. "What if he's dead? What if someone killed him for a trophy?"

Gloria reached out and drew Ari to her. "Stop thinking like that. Maybe he had an accident—fell—he may be injured, unconscious. That may be why no one can sense him. They'll find him. Those animals will cover the entire forest."

They headed back inside.

Ari lit a fire in the fireplace and they waited.

A LONG WHILE LATER, Ari and Gloria heard an animal call out in mind-talk.

There's blood on the ground. Looks like a battle.

Ari called out. *What is your animal, so I can phone our human team? Where are you?*

"Wolf," Grandfather said.

I'm a grey and white wolf due north of the house—about three miles ahead in this little clearing.

I'll be there in a minute, Gage said.

Leander and other shifters acknowledged the silent call.

Ari called Sherm and gave him the location. She fretted. Ari paced in the house, then outside. She returned to the house.

"I hate not being able to be in there! Why is my bloodline so damn weak that I'm useless?"

"Stop it, Ari," Gloria said. "You're far from useless. While you may not have an animal, you have special skills—even if you don't know what they are yet."

"A lot of good it does me when Roman is missing." Ari shook her head, angry at her missing heritage.

Leander was in her head. *Ari, it looks like humans attacked Roman. There's boot prints—more than one set. Your team is just arriving and Gage just landed.*

Sherm called. Ari put the call on speaker so Gloria and Grandfather could listen.

"He's not dead. Someone shot him with a tranquilizer dart. We're spreading out, going further north to search for more clues. Let's hope they left fingerprints on the dart. When we get back to the city, we can check for prints and run them through the system."

Ari covered her eyes with her hand. "Okay. Keep me informed."

Gage was on the phone. "Honey, don't worry. We'll find him and whoever did this. We will exact revenge. They'll wish they never crossed our path."

"Please just be careful," Ari said.

ARI WAITED PATIENTLY. No one called or communicated silently. She got a bad vibe from the silence. Ari determined Gage called for total silence. That meant bad news.

She practically passed out when Gage landed in the backyard.

Sherm, his team, and the shifters emerged from the forest.

Ari started crying, hard. She ran to Gage. "What? What aren't you telling me?"

Gage wrapped his arms around her.

She felt his stress wafting out. She sobbed uncontrollably, waiting for the news.

"Someone loaded him into a chopper," Sherm said. "I've got everyone searching the satellites. We need to identify the chopper to be able to track him down and find out what direction they took."

"He's still alive?" Ari asked, through sobs.

Sherm produced the dart in a plastic bag. "They wanted him alive."

Gage's rage boiled to the surface. "They don't know who they're fucking with. Whoever did this will never know what hit them!"

"ROMAN!" Ari screeched. *ROMAN! ROMAN!*

Gage grabbed her shoulders. "Stop! He won't be able to hear you, and you're just getting yourself worked up."

Gage's cellphone rang. He hurried to his pile of clothes and pulled it out of his pants pocket. He checked caller ID.

"Atsa?" Gage listened. "Someone's got Roman."

To be continued

ABOUT THE AUTHOR

Dawn Greenfield Ireland is also known as D.E. Greenfield, DG Ireland. Dawn is an award-winning author of 22 novels, which include 5 series (cozy mystery, sci fi/fantasy, billionaire shapeshifters, and dystopian), and a stand-alone sci-fi romantic adventure.

Most of her 7 nonfiction books have won awards. Dawn has adapted a few of her screenplays into book format, and several of her books into TV series format. She also created over 50 themed notebooks.

She had two screenplays optioned, and she worked on a screenwriter-for-hire project. Dawn has a certificate from the Professional Program in Screenwriting from UCLA (2002), and a certificate from ScreenwritingU (2023).

Dawn writes full-time. She lives among dreams and fantasies with two cats and moving boxes. Her head is filled with stories. She doesn't suffer from writer's block.

Her business, Artistic Origins, has been around since 1995. Besides writing, she coaches writers, edits, formats, and publishes clients' books.

Dawn's former day job as an award-winning technical writer played a major role in her fiction writing. She is detail-oriented, the organizational queen of the known universe, and never misses a deadline.

If you buy her books and products, she'll love you forever.

Visit the website. Sign up for the newsletter. http://www.
degreenfield.com

Please leave a review on the retailer's website where you
bought/downloaded the book!

facebook.com/dawn.ireland.18
x.com/dawnireland
instagram.com/dawngreenfieldIreland
goodreads.com/dawnireland
linkedin.com/dawnireland

Tothars

Roman is gone. Shot with a tranquilizer dart. Abducted to an unknown location by way of a helicopter. Panther Industries Security Division watches all airports within a 300-mile radius.

They discover the helicopter landed at an airport in Massachusetts. Due to terrorism, flight information is highly guarded, but Lonnie knows Travis can hack into anything to get what they need.

Travis discovers the pilot's name, and the destination is Italy. Someone must have paid off people because not only is no city destination listed, but there are no exotic animal documents for Roman's panther.

Gage, Jason, and Kevin help Ari cope. She's barely over her own horrific experience and now, with Roman's kidnapping, she's fragile.

The Navajos come to Gage's aid. Ari has a dream-like experience—remote viewing—where she sees through Roman's panther eyes. She tells them Roman is drugged in a cell. It looks like a rounded room made of stone—maybe a tower—in a very old building. She thought she saw a banner flapping in the wind through the bars of a small, high window.

Gage asks her if there are any words on the banner. She says 'Something, something Palazzo'.

They gather the bear shifters—they have the strongest sense of smell of all terrestrial animals. The bears fly to Italy. They are each assigned a quadrant of the country to search.

Sherm dings Gage in the middle of the night. Someone contacted them via the website contact form. They didn't leave a name, phone number or email address, but they told him who held Roman captive: Giuseppe Genovesi.

Travis finds Genovesi through a massive online search.

The rescue is on.

Be prepared for unexpected surprises.

www.ingramcontent.com/pod-product-compliance
Lightning Source LLC
Chambersburg PA
CBHW021005260626
47169CB00006B/1959